LAND OF NO REGRETS

A Novel

SADI MUKTADIR

HANOVER
SQUARE
PRESS

HANOVER
SQUARE
PRESS™

ISBN-13: 978-1-335-45376-1

Land of No Regrets

First published in 2024 by HarperCollins Publishers Ltd. This edition published in 2024.

Hanover Square Press
22 Adelaide St. West, 41st Floor
Toronto, Ontario M5H 4E3, Canada
HanoverSqPress.com
BookClubbish.com

Printed in U.S.A.

Dedicated to no one, or everyone

... وَلَا تَنسَ نَصِيبَكَ مِنَ ٱلدُّنْيَا

No one recognized the song on the radio.

Not because we'd been at Al Haque for so long and couldn't recognize what our peers were listening to these days, but because the song was in another language. We'd been silent, taking advantage of the serene February morning. I reached my hand out to change the dial to a station we'd understand, but Farid stopped me.

"Wait," he said. "Listen. Pay attention."

From the passenger seat, I raised an eyebrow at Nawaaz, our driver. That look, oft-shared between Maaz, Nawaaz and me, that said, "What the hell is Farid up to?"

I leaned back while the woman on the radio sang. Her voice had a notable weight to it that pressed the four of us down in the car. I leaned so far back in my seat that I could only see the crisp blue sky and long-dead branches spreading in every direction on either side of us. I didn't want to see the road anyway. I didn't want to see what was ahead or behind. Truth be told, I didn't want to see Maaz, Nawaaz or Farid either. I wanted to see nothing, and failing that, I wanted to see a weird made-up universe of blue and black, skies and branches bleeding together into something only I'd know as I floated up through the atmosphere.

Heavy synth, heavy bass. Nawaaz reached forward without taking his eyes off the road and turned up the volume. Now we felt the beat in our bones. It shook us. We understood that one of the prevailing theories for why music was unlawful was that it could be so powerful. It could hold you and command you and challenge *something*. But we'd always believed that you needed to at least understand the words in order for music to sway you.

The song conjured images of faraway places as we drove and dreamed in equal measure. As the cabin reverberated, the shitty, fraying grey interior melted away on Taunton Road, our eyes now privy to other worlds, roads not taken and the expanse of eternity.

I turned in my seat to look back at Farid and Maaz, and they were swaying back and forth to the beat. Farid reached over to roll down his window, but it stopped halfway, stuck. It didn't matter. Being wiry and diminutive, he squeezed his body through the small opening and started dancing, putting on a performance for the dead trees and melting snow that lined our corner of the world.

I rolled my window down too and stuck my hand out to feel the cold. It bit, but I felt the breeze caress my fingers, sliding all the way up my forearm to my elbow. No one wanted to talk and ruin the moment. Sometimes, you just know you'll never find a specific song on the radio again. You're grateful for whatever error blessed you with the experience, understanding that there was no way in hell that that language, artist or instrument was known to someone in Northumberland County. But moments pass.

"Guys, I think I'm stuck!" shouted Farid.

"What's wrong with this idiot, sticking himself out the window?" I said. "He should have known that was gonna happen. Beat him."

I heard the unmistakable sound of slaps and turned around, surprised to see that Maaz was actually hitting him. Thankfully it was just playful, enough to make Farid squirm and us laugh.

"Pull his ass in before he gets hit by something!" Nawaaz yelled over the dying moments of the song.

Maaz yanked Farid in by his ass, and they fell into a heap on the back seat. Seeing them there, I understood how people could be so happy with only a few square metres. I needed even less, after all. I only needed a car. Could we make it happen?

Here there were no banyan trees, no bats going extinct. The soil was covered in pine needles and dying dreams, and yet, the troubles were the same. Where do you fit in, and how do you fit happiness into that? This was how you passed the time in any era, travelling between dead trees or living trees, on your way to a trading post, a market, a school, a church. You spoke of worldly things while seasons came and went and bark faded and frayed around you. Snows, rains and winds saw their cycles repeat. You stuck your head out of the car window from time to time to look up at the sky; before that, a man stuck his head out of the trading caravan. Before that, a person looked up from the back of a horse. Before that, someone looked out through an opening in the tent or the rocks. Clouds and stars. Cosmos and the great horizon. They all wondered, "When will it get better?"

None of them gave any serious thought to when they would die.

CHAPTER I

The White Umbrella

It was middle school, June, the zenith of my life, right before things ended. A triumphant tempest of a year that culminated in the district baseball championship. I was due to pitch on the final day of the two-day tournament and was both nervous and filled with vigour at the prospect. I arrived at the field at eight that morning, squished hot dogs in my knapsack, ready to pitch. I was sweating by ten, my T-shirt stuck to my back as the sun beat down on us all and the cicadas hummed their dirge in the distance. The dust from the pitcher's mound only served to obstruct my vision, but I was ready to throw my heart out. Halfway through the day, just as the final game was starting, I noticed Alana and her friends in the bleachers—they'd come to be our unofficial cheerleaders. With Alana watching, there was no way I'd let myself perform poorly. I threw the ball harder than I'd ever thrown it my whole life, and when the final batter hurled his bat to the ground in frustration, I was elated. And not just because the game was over. We'd actually won.

I looked around in disbelief, shocked that something this jubilant could happen. My teammates were all celebrating around me, and Alana and her friends were jumping up and down in the bleachers. Even in the handshake line, exchanging dirt and sweat with the kids on the losing team, I still couldn't believe it. Not just that we'd won but that something so unfiltered in its goodness could happen in the midday sun, in the afternoon heat, to me. I was accustomed to cutting things off, going home early, leaving TV shows and movies unfinished. There was always a prayer that couldn't be missed or a sermon that needed attending. There was always something more important than a baseball game. And yet here we were, three games in, one day later, celebrating success. My face was red and purple on the long walk home, and I began to feel the breeze of the cooling day as I meandered back. I didn't know it then, but that was one of the best days of my life. That tired ache as one step led to another was a welcome pain, the kind I cursed at the time, yet secretly loved because it meant I'd done something. I heard a muffled shout behind me and turned to see Alana running to catch up. I wasn't expecting her. It seemed almost too good to be true.

It was no secret to our friends that Alana and I had a thing for each other. We'd first met two years earlier, when we sat next to each other at an assembly on the first day of school on a hot September morning. Before classes began all the incoming students had to sit in the gym and listen to the principal deliver a lecture. I tried to remain interested in his inane speech about a new school year full of promise, but I didn't really care about what he had to say. I cared more about finding a first-edition holographic Charizard than making sure I smelled nice.

When Alana and I were assigned to the same homeroom, we exchanged scrutinizing glances to size each other up. I guess that's when I first started caring about smelling nice. Once school began, we stuck to our own cliques, of course, but continued to examine each other from across the room. She was always with the girls who were popular and smart. They were never messed with—not by teachers, not by bullies. They never had any trouble ponying up cash for field trips or extracurricular activities. They were on the right side of life. And then there were me and my friends. A real kaleidoscope of a group—some smart, some dumb, some rich, some poor. None white. It took some time, but eventually our two worlds collided.

We were in gym class when it finally happened. We were the last two kids standing in the beep test, a satanic ritual masquerading as a fitness assessment that forced kids to run faster and faster between loud beeps. Alana and I wouldn't give an inch to each other. When I finally lost to her, I was angry. Here was a chance, in my mind, to announce to everyone that I wasn't just smart—I was athletic too. The dumbest things are so important to us at that age. It especially bothered me that I'd lost to Alana, though, because I thought for sure she'd remember the guy who beat her, but not another one of the countless guys who'd lost to her. Alana convinced me otherwise after class that day.

"Wow, you made me sweat in there. I can't remember the last time someone hung in that long against me!"

"You're lucky I was taking it easy on you."

"Oh really?" She laughed. "Well, I'm sure you'll get your rematch one day. We'll see then, won't we?"

I didn't know what else to say; I was just happy that she'd

laughed. At that age, the smallest connections render us speechless. That exchange was the start of our awkward flirt-dance, which persisted for the rest of middle school. We lived sort of near each other, so I'd occasionally see her walking home from school with her friends while I walked home with mine. Neither group would make any motion to say hello or interact with the other, even though we all shared classes. I do wonder if the girls even saw us, or if we were just background colour to their starring roles. I know I wasn't background colour to Alana though.

Sometimes on my walk to school in the morning, I'd see her up ahead of me. Even when she was by herself, I never moved to catch up, but would just keep pace with her some yards away. On rainy days, when the sky was a grey haze and the pavement was black and wet, I would spot her ahead of me, holding her white umbrella, trudging through the storm. My own umbrella was nowhere to be seen, and the rain would fall on my hair and face without mercy, clouding my vision and sometimes the path ahead. But even through the sheets of rain, and the fragrance of wet grass, I would notice her white umbrella. It wasn't a beacon for me so much as it was a fire. Warming my walk as I kept sight of her on the horizon. I wanted to keep her ahead of me always. I never wanted to catch up to her, or to walk to school with her. I'd ruin the whole thing. I was just happy seeing her ahead of me in the rain, walking to school the way I was walking to school. Like we were part of the same world, treading the same dirt and concrete. Her feet, then my feet.

But she dared a bit harder than I did. At that age, she wasn't content for us to remain that far apart. Her legacy was the Disney legacy, where furtive looks led to furtive kisses. And my legacy too was some weird morphed one, where I bought and believed that good things could happen, just like in the movies. Remember Aladdin saying, "Do you trust me?" So in those classrooms—indoors, away from parents and prying aunties—I'd let a look linger longer than it had to.

We began stealing shy smiles from each other across classrooms, eating near each other in the cafeteria, then sharing class assignments and supplies, and finally partnering on projects and class duties—all of it adding up. And none of this was missed by anyone, though we'd deny it if asked. If a classmate so much as giggled in our direction while we studied together at the library, we'd shoot them a chastising death glare for their immaturity. But if it got too quiet between us, we'd have trouble looking the other in the eye for too long.

Finally, in that early June heat, city championship secured, there was a meeting, a moment, engineered by friends who'd tipped her off to my route home. I applauded their effort, however futile. There were already forces larger than them at work, preparing to rip me away from everything I loved.

But since when have middle schoolers cared about that? I watched Alana running up the sidewalk. Her brown hair bounced up and down, and some of it stuck to her brow in the heat as she caught up to me, out of breath. She bent over, hands on her knees, breathing deeply, and when she stood up, she wiped the hair out of her eyes and tucked it behind her ear. Finally, when it was unavoidable, we looked at each other. She examined me with uncharacteristic shyness. This was a girl who was normally anything *but* shy. The sight of her reaching out for something in my eyes was enough for me. I looked back, unsure of what to give.

"Hey, that was crazy today," she said. "You guys were amazing!"

"Really?"

She laughed, knowing the game I was playing, fishing for more compliments. She raved about our performance while I walked silently beside her. After a while, we turned off the sidewalk and into a nearby ravine along a creek. Here in the city, where idyllic tranquillity was supposed to be impossible to find, lush branches hung above us as gigantic trees grew unencumbered, thick trunks reaching towards the sky. We walked from grass to pavement and back, with only the odd runner or biker breaking our privacy. Here, no one could find us. There was no fear in this place—my parents never ventured out this way, though the ravine was close to our home. I would wonder sometimes how they could not feel what I felt there. After the midday sun began to wane, when the cooling day took over, how could they not feel the quotidian magic of this place? I couldn't remember them ever going on a walk just to appreciate the weather or scenery. The closest they ever got to pleasure was saying, "This sun is good for the garden." Or, "The crops will benefit well from this."

Alana and I reached a fork in the ravine. One path led back to my street and the other led deeper into the forest.

"Well, I guess I'll see you at school on Monday," I said.

"Yeah, for sure. Hey! Um . . . how come you never asked me out this year? Or, like, tried to hang out with me ever?"

The direct question knocked me back, but it shouldn't have. It had been a long year of clandestine glances and switching seats just to be next to each other. She'd reached the limits of her patience. I had no idea what to tell her, and because of that, I accidentally told her the truth.

"Alana, if I'm being one hundred percent real with you, I really, *really* wanted to. There was nothing I would've liked more. The whole year, I really wanted to figure out a way to, like, talk to you and hang out on the weekend or something."

"So . . . did you figure out a way?"

"No . . . I mean, I'm still thinking. It's just . . . my parents—my family—they're just a bit old-fashioned."

"I know. I've seen them. At the honour roll assembly and stuff. I wondered if that was part of it. You get really stiff around them. It's kind of cute." She laughed, and I slow blinked in surprise. I had no idea it was that obvious.

But even then, she didn't understand how deep my parents' fear ran. In her mind, they were a long conversation away from permitting their son to date. In my mind, three generations of change had to happen before that conversation could even occur.

"I do want to see you outside of school," I said. "I think we'd have a lot of fun together."

"Yeah! Like this summer, we should hang out. Do you want to try to meet up?"

"For sure. I hope I can figure out a story that works for my parents," I said, muttering to myself.

"Maybe this will help you find a way." She leaned in and kissed my cheek.

I went purple as she turned and walked away. I had no time to react and could only walk up the path and onto my street. I couldn't believe she'd kissed me. I was soaring for half a moment before the feeling sank and drowned. I looked around to see if anyone had witnessed our moment together, and then I touched my face again and again in the spot where she'd kissed me. I was worried she'd left a mark, so I started to rub my cheek, wiping away phantom lip prints that, I feared, were forever stamped there. I was paranoid. If the kiss was visible, then I was in for a reckoning. I couldn't let my parents see. To my touch, the kissed cheek felt warmer than the other—probably because of my incessant rubbing, and yet I couldn't stop touching it. I was in a near panic by the time I reached my house. I climbed the steps at a snail's pace, my petrified legs refusing to move. I slowly creaked open the screen door and stepped inside, hoping my mother was busy and I could inspect my cheek in the mirror before she saw me. I was greeted by sounds of playing children, the smell of fried onions, a pot sizzling in the background, and my mother, standing right in front of me.

The grey hair at her temples had arrived too soon, on account of the constant worrying over me and my four siblings. Her eyes were sharp, missing nothing, searching expressions for anything out of place. I could only hope she wouldn't find remnants of Alana's touch inside me as she searched me top to bottom with a single look.

"Where were you?"

"I told you I had a baseball tournament today. You knew I would be late."

"School ends at three! You should leave right after, baseball or not baseball."

"It doesn't matter—it's over. We won."

I walked past her, making my way to the bathroom to wash up.

"You can't play baseball anymore!"

This was a frequent command I frequently ignored.

"Okay."

"You have to come home on time. How do I know something bad hasn't happened? You can't be this late!"

I looked up from washing my face to check the clock in the hallway. It was barely four thirty. And yet, I wasn't surprised my mother was behaving like this. This was life. Paranoia was given legs and called love. My mother had endured cold weather, cold people and both the quiet and loud discriminatory jeers of the friendly and open Canadian. Freshly married at nineteen and without much English, she had climbed onto a plane alone to immigrate to Toronto, protective sutras and mantras pronounced all over her person by family members, imbuing courage and fear in equal measure. And this wasn't a you-at-nineteen type of marriage—this was her, excited to start a family, happy to see her parents so proud and pleased with her. When was the last time you made anyone but you happy? Still, of course she was afraid. It's important for a country to make a good first impression on someone. So on her second night in the country, together with my father in a decrepit basement apartment, she experienced a violent armed robbery by two masked men who broke in while they were sleeping, cursing and shouting and taking absolutely nothing. Disappointed to find absolutely nothing. Afterwards, the police had humiliated them, thundering all over their two hundred square feet in muddy shoes, turning things over with batons and rolling their eyes while my father tried to make himself understood. Where was the better life?

My face was still red and hot even after I'd washed and dried it off. Alana's kiss had left me exhilarated, but also more twisted and torn up than before. Here was another problem with a window fast closing on a solution. Deep down, I suspected that her feelings would only survive as long as I kept feeding them. And I could not feed them if I could not see her. Our middle school romance was built with middle school materials and would not survive time or distance.

—

Later, the school year ended amid the pageantry of graduation, and I noticed a few bad omens portending to summer vacation and the life to come. At the graduation ceremony, the principal mispronounced my name pretty badly. Normally this meant nothing, but he'd known me for three years and shouldn't have made that kind of mistake. And afterwards, when we were all mingling, a female classmate hugged me to say goodbye. This was witnessed by my parents, who were in the crowd with the other parents, but I felt their omnipresent gaze. Every insignificant error or stumble convinced me that there was some nefarious force at play, and that every joyous moment would be marred by two disappointing ones. I was not wrong, as I discovered on the car ride home.

"You have to tell them stop. Say, 'Don't disturb me!' You can't let them touch you. It's indecent and wrong!"

Their parenting was timeless. Wrong was wrong, even a millennia ago. If it was wrong a thousand years ago for a man to lay with another man, then it was wrong today. If it was wrong a thousand years ago to abandon your children at eighteen, or twenty-two, or twenty-six, then it was wrong today. If it was wrong a thousand years ago for a person to choose their own partner, then it was wrong today. If it was wrong to ask your children to pay you rent a thousand years ago, then it was wrong today. These precepts were adhered to with special vehemence in times and places where you were unsure what the rules were. Hence the most nineties decree ever, "Mushroom cuts are haram," was a thing, just as driving adult children back to university every Sunday evening laden with home-cooked meals for the week was a thing. Things *can* change. Slowly. But change has to come from on high. From whatever you worshipped. Whether that was Chandler Bing or Allah depended on who you were and what you were afraid of.

My father began to talk about sending me away to a madrasa so he could see at least one of his children become a scholar. I didn't think much of it at the time. I figured that he'd forget about it in a few weeks, as he always did, and I'd see my friends again in September. I was afraid of losing what was already lost. That summer, in between memorizing pages of the Quran, I would run out in the early evening sun to play basketball or swap Pokémon cards. I don't know how I did it. Memorizing pages and base stats. From where the game's secret Rare Candies could be found to how Surah Bakarah ended. One because I wanted to, and the other because I had to. I needed every card, every Pokémon. But my time was already spoken for. It was only when the evening redness of the sky revealed itself that was I able to indulge my dying tradition, stuffing hours of obsession into a few minutes, forcing kids on the courts and those standing nearby into horrible trades and giveaways.

Was I aware I was headed to a madrasa? No, not really. Even when we finally began touring religious seminaries across Ontario and Quebec, I didn't take it seriously. I found a reason to dislike each and every one and thought that would be enough to dissuade my parents. The beds were too hard. The food tasted horrible. I'd seen cockroaches. There was one teacher for every forty students. It was too far from home.

My father, bless his soul, drove through the summer heat and rain without complaint, believing I would eventually pick the school I liked. His grand plan was coming to fruition. Five kids, three girls and two boys. One a doctor, one an engineer, one a religious scholar, one in government and the last one to be doted on, to live a relaxing life. We were still kids, all of us, but this didn't stop my parents from promoting their plan often and at length. As if all it took was dedication and perseverance to turn a child into an imam and make him forget that Golbat evolves into Crobat when its happiness reaches a certain level.

I was hoping that if I said no to enough madrasas, my parents would take the hint and relent, and I'd be able to go back to school. I was wrong, of course. They eventually decided that I would go to Al Haque Islamic Academy, a place that was neither too far nor too near, and could be reached by car, if necessary.

Like a prisoner on death row, I counted down my meals to the day I would move into Al Haque. I cherished every dish my mother served and swore to remember each one. Purple hyacinth beans. Ash gourd chicken curry. Squash and bitter melon stir-fry. Stewed jackfruit and fish. Shutki satni. Shatkora beef. Each serving was heaping, as my mother tried to fatten me up and send me off in her own loving, non-verbal way. Or maybe she knew I was miserable. Was this just her way of saying, "Sorry, there's nothing I can do about it. But here, have some more chicken"? I doubted it. I knew my mother would miss me, but she'd raised me for this. As a child, I'd memorized surahs under her tutelage, learned rudimentary prayers under her watchful gaze as she prepared me for more serious study. She knew she'd be letting me go one day. There was no protesting on my part either. There was no choice available to me beyond sulking. I'd been sentenced.

CHAPTER 2

The Château d'If

We left for Al Haque in late August, my father playing a sermon on the car stereo louder than it had to be played. He was taking time off from the construction site to drive me, and I was slumped in the back seat, dispirited and absent, my eyes saying goodbye to every landmark I'd taken for granted in the past. My silence meant nothing to my father. Even at that age, I knew I couldn't speak to him. There were too many years and lands between us—he leaned on faith, while I leaned on Marle's love for Crono, which crossed the years and lands between them. It would be years before I'd remember how full of fear my father was, justified though it might have been. After all, how could I have known? When was the last time an immigrant parent told their child what they'd *really* been through? In that moment, in a beat-up jalopy crossing Durham County into Northumberland, all I remembered was Alana. And I knew then that I'd never see her again.

—

We turned down road after road, each one narrower than the last, until we finally rumbled onto a dirt path that ended at the top of a hill, at the bottom of which lay an enormous brown stone building. It was three storeys tall, reaching into the sky, and had an ancient appearance with the rough edges and pocked bricks that made up its exterior. I was so shaken up that I had to turn away. The building looked as if it had been there forever, like it had grown with the trees and been planted in Northumberland County centuries before. In reality, it was constructed in the 1920s as an all-girls school for a strong French-speaking Catholic community that became a weaker one over time. The intention had been to foster and grow the Catholic presence in Ontario, but by the 1970s, times had changed and education and religion had evolved, and a declining enrolment led to the school's bankruptcy and the property became derelict. Meanwhile, a growing new community began looking for a place to foster and nurture the *ummah*.

The abandoned school was prime real estate for entrepreneurial spirits looking to save souls. These men were in the business of building new lives in a new country and would not be able to do so without their immemorial institutions. If they could not hear the *adhaan* from the minarets, they would at least make sure there was a minaret to remind them of their responsibilities.

And so, a number of prominent Gujaratis went about pooling their money and purchasing vacant properties in an attempt to capture some of the glory that places named Al Haque held in Hyderabad and Karachi. After heavy renovations, they had a madrasa where bearded men could sit and smile fondly and recall the way things should be done, with whips and sticks to serve as inspiration for younger generations with beards still yet to grow.

As part of the renovations, the property was literally hosed from floor to ceiling before anything else was allowed to happen. No expense was spared in cleaning and preparing the building for its new students. Lye, salt, charcoal, industrial soap and, of course, prayer. Prayer after prayer and blessings by the thousand were recited under every door frame and window, over every stairwell and in every bathroom stall. A hundred *kalimahs*, a thousand different *du'as* and *zikrs*. They scrubbed the place clean of its previous tenants, every trace of what it once was. They were cleansing the building of its blemishes, purifying it to make it unrecognizable as a bastion of Christianity. But it's impossible to completely erase the facade of a building once it's built, or to purge what happened inside it. The facade was revivalism at its finest, evoking the sculptors and architects of the Italian Renaissance, while inside students practised Arabic hymns and lessons and sat cross-legged on a carpet, learning of the famous negotiation between the Prophet Muhammad (SAW) and Allah, which decreased the number of daily prayers from fifty to five. A scarce twenty years earlier, the same room had played host to a brimstone sermon about the differences between cardinal and venial sins.

Unlike my public school, the madrasa had no first-day assembly. No principal's address. There were only eight classes. Two for the very young kids, from eight to twelve. Another two for the thirteen- to fifteen-year-olds. Then two more for the kids above sixteen. And finally, a couple of small classes for the young men about to graduate, who worked with the scholars on a more intimate basis. Those classes functioned more like tutorials on specific subjects. Jurisprudence to exorcism. Whether the role of the *ummah* was practice or proselytization. Even though my understanding of *fiqh* was limited, I was placed in the second-level class for thirteen-to fifteen-year-olds. The hope was that I would be able to fast-track my studies by working hard with students my own age, most of whom had already been at Al Haque for a few years.

Madrasa life seemed simple. The mornings would consist of reciting and memorizing the Quran under one teacher (in my case, Maulana Hasan—greybeard), while the afternoons would be dedicated to learning about the Prophet's life and example, through the four main tomes of hadith and Seerah, under a second teacher (Maulana Ibrar—blackbeard). Some afternoons, we would learn various supplications and the proper ways to perform and teach worship. We had one day off a week, on Sundays, as well as summers and the two Eids. But even on Sundays, we were expected to spend at least a small amount of time on recitation in the morning. It was also the responsibility of the students to take care of the madrasa. Everything from cleaning and laundry to cooking and maintenance was shared by us, under the watchful eye of Sharmil Bhai, the full-time live-in caretaker.

The first few days and weeks of this new routine were unbearable to me. The whole situation was a stark lifestyle change, and I was completely isolated, partly by design. I didn't want anything to do with the other kids because I didn't see myself as similar to them at all. I insisted on my differences. In public school, I'd successfully fit in. I wasn't some odd, out-of-place freshie sporting colourful clothes and a bad accent. There's nothing wrong with that, of course, not that a thirteen-year-old brown kid would know.

And yet there I was, in the main prayer hall every morning, sitting on the plush red-velvet carpet mixed in with the rest of them. I was full of salty resentment and brushed off any friendliness the other students showed me. The sun beamed in through the high windows around us as we hummed and recited and filled the room with *Qirat*, both classes in our year sharing the large space, while the morning slowly turned to afternoon. I buried my face in the pages and tried to memorize the bare minimum needed to get by. I was given leeway at first because I was a new student, and the *ustads* understood that I was joining them straight out of public school, so my knowledge wasn't there yet. But every once in a while, I'd see another kid catch a beating for not knowing their lesson, or talking too much out of turn, or being caught with contraband, or taking too long in the bathroom, etc. My father would have loved it.

Racked with melancholy and resentment, I was obsessed with grieving my previous life, mourning dead baseball exploits and friends I'd never see again. But you couldn't survive at Al Haque stuck in permanent mourning. No one gave a shit what you were missing, not the teachers and not your classmates. Lessons needed learning, towels needed folding and vegetables needed chopping. The kids who were loners were suspect, or so devout they didn't need anybody. If I was going to survive, I'd need a group around me.

In my second week, chores were divvied up by Sharmil Bhai. I would grow more acquainted with him as the months wore on—learning more than I should have—but for now, he simply served as taskmaster. Old and crooked, with a hunched back and white hair sprouting from his ears, he was actually much stronger than his appearance suggested. We'd seen him lift objects heavier than we were and discipline kids without hesitation or perspiration. Each week, we were on a rotating schedule, and my first chore was to pick up clean laundry and distribute it to the student dorms on the third floor. That's how I met Maaz and Nawaaz.

Maaz was the shorter of the two, stockier in build, and he always seemed to walk slowly to wherever he was headed, even if he was late. It was like he had no speed other than slow. His face was round, his eyes sharp and full of clarity. His hair was the palest shade of black, almost reddish, and in some lights, you may have been fooled. Nawaaz, on the other hand, was huge. No one believed he was fourteen because of his height and sizable frame. He had a long face and long black hair slicked back under his cap. He seldom smiled, but when he did, it was just the corners of his thin lips, and his laugh was more of a bark. Both were intimidating—Nawaaz because of his size, and Maaz because of his eyes.

I was going door to door with my laundry cart, heart still in my stomach due to my new fate, placing linens and towels on each bed, when I saw something I shouldn't have. In my defence, I knocked on each door before entering—just as I had with this one. I'd knocked, waited and then pushed the door open with my back since my arms were full of sheets and towels. When I turned into the room, I witnessed the two of them doing something they shouldn't have been. I didn't know what to say or how to react. I didn't even know people did that stuff in real life.

"Oh! Sorry. My bad." I turned and exited, forgetting to leave the linens and towels, hoping I wasn't in any trouble and they wouldn't follow me. I wanted nothing more to do with the incident or the people involved, and secretly prayed it was behind me. But walking into that room was only the beginning.

That evening at dinner, as we all sat around on the carpet, huddled over the eating mats, I saw the two boys in another row, muttering to each other and looking over at me. Then I started seeing them everywhere. During prayer, they'd supplicate next to me. They'd often volunteer to take out the trash with me. They'd even come out of the bathroom stall beside mine. Finally, one night as I was heading upstairs for bed, they cornered me in the empty green stairwell, one covering my ascent and the other, taller one covering my descent. This was how I officially met Maaz and Nawaaz.

"Listen fam, you gotta knock before you come in. You can't just go into man's room like that," Nawaaz said from behind me. Even without seeing him, I could sense his intimidating size, a men's size jubba on his large frame.

"Yeah, for sure. My bad," I replied, ignoring the fact that I had knocked.

"It's all good. What did you see?" Maaz asked. His amber eyes were focused, piercing me, and I noticed the beginnings of a beard, soft wispy hairs on his round cheeks and chin.

"Nothing," I replied. I wasn't an idiot.

"Good." He reached out a fist and I bumped it. They let me go on my way, and I thought that was the end of it.

It wasn't.

I continued seeing Maaz and Nawaaz everywhere. After every chore, every meal and every prayer, they lurked nearby, a little too close. I wasn't stupid. It wasn't just fear on their part. It was a threat. They were watching me, making sure I told no one. They needn't have bothered. I was no snitch, and wholly uninterested in the affairs of boys I insisted I had nothing in common with.

After a few days, though, my testy jailers and I became friends. We had to. There was no other choice. All we had was each other.

As hard as I'd tried to remain separate from everyone, the loneliness was killing me.

It was impossible for Maaz to help me with the dishes without telling me he'd sold his drawing of Mats Sundin for five hundred dollars. He'd found out I was a Leafs fan and explained how easy it was to defraud people on eBay for their fandom if you could forge autographs. He told me he used to draw all sorts of stuff—Patrick Roy, Goku, Vince Carter, Spawn, whoever. He'd frame the drawings and sell them at flea markets with forged signatures until his parents grew devout and didn't want him drawing anymore. The money no longer outweighed the sin for them. Nawaaz opened up too. He was less talkative and more protective of Maaz, but once he realized I had no intention of speaking to anyone about what I'd seen, he eased up. Most of the students were afraid of Nawaaz. He clenched his jaw even while he rested, said little and wouldn't hesitate to twist any arm that blocked his path. I found out he'd come to Al Haque the year before, after getting suspended from public school. He'd got into too many fights with kids who'd learned English at home, not at school.

Maaz and Nawaaz told me which maulanas to stay away from, which kids were noted thieves and would steal the snacks our mothers sent us and which hallways belonged to which groups. (You'd be courting violence if you crossed these lines.) If I was ever late to lunch or dinner, they would get extra daal and roti and save it for me. I, in turn, would do the same for them. Through it all, I pretended I hadn't seen what I saw the day I first stumbled upon them in their room.

Our time together would send us hurtling down a path we'd refuse to regret. Shared crimes and passions, with each of us holding

25

a smoking gun, would tie us together as our list of transgressions grew. And if one of us suddenly decided to be a goody two-shoes, he would become a liability, with fewer crimes to answer for than the other two, who would continue their campaign of sin. So we threw ourselves into a performative friendship that became less and less performative over time. Sneaking into the fridge after hours. Hiding whips and books of hadith. Warning me when I was flirting with a beating by breaking roti with my left hand, or when I was courting extra chores by being late to morning prayer.

Eventually, I told Maaz and Nawaaz about my baseball exploits, and then about Alana. Nothing was sacred in that sacred place. At night, suffocating beneath the weight of my exile, I would wonder what Alana was up to. I'd never even said goodbye to her. I'd had her number, but how could I call from home? I'd wanted so badly to reach out, but the fear of being caught by my parents scared the shit out of me, and so weeks turned into months, and eventually I disappeared from the neighbourhood forever.

Sometimes at night, surrounded by three empty beds in my dorm room (I was yet to be bunked with anybody), I was possessed by some spirit that urged me to go, then and there, to visit Alana. To run, to act. To get away, to return to my old life. These fits passed unnoticed for some time.

Some nights, Maaz and Nawaaz would sneak out of their room to hang out in mine. I didn't really want them there, but they came all the same, my desires be damned. In a fit of abandon one particular night, when I couldn't shake Alana from my head, I revealed my desire to escape and visit her.

"I'm thinking about going to see her," I said, much quieter than normal. I didn't want to believe what I was saying.

"How the fuck you gonna do that?" Nawaaz asked.

"I don't know. Just leave with a bag and order a cab?" I answered, not really serious.

"Wait, you know where she lives?" Maaz asked.

"Yeah, she lives near my parents."

"Yo . . . you gotta chop that shit. If you have the chance, do it," he said, excited.

"Yeah, 'cept I don't have the chance. I'm here."

"I'll call you a cab. Reach, bro," Nawaaz said with a dark laugh. "We'll wait here and make sure you don't get caught."

Maaz shot him a furrowed look of disagreement.

"I have a better plan," he said. "We can all go. Together. Me and Nawaaz know how to sneak out."

"What? No, wait. I wasn't serious!" I protested.

"Yeah, that seems like a dumb thing to sneak out for," Nawaaz said, now that he'd been volunteered to join.

"Well, I'm serious! What do you have to lose? You may as well find out so you can move on. Plus, we know how to sneak out," Maaz repeated, trying to sell the crime instead of the outcome.

"We'll get caught." I had no idea how we'd even leave the madrasa. It was locked from the outside every night.

Maaz and Nawaaz both laughed.

"We won't get caught, bro," Nawaaz said. "We've reached Pickering Town Centre for bare movies and shit. Chill."

"What? How?" I was in disbelief.

"We'll show you," Maaz said. "Just be ready for tomorrow night."

The next day passed in fretful fashion. I held my breath through every class and meal. Every cursory glance from the imams felt like an accusation. I was afraid that Maaz and Nawaaz were pulling some cruel prank, and that I was sure to receive a heavy beating when I tried escaping. I'd seen it happen to other students for much less.

I waited in my room that night, sweating harder than I had on the pitcher's mound in June. I'd put on the only normal outfit I had: old blue jeans and a T-shirt showing off the city skyline. It had been only a few weeks since I'd last worn that stuff and already the clothes felt awkward on my body. I knew it wouldn't do. No one who was anyone wore a Toronto T-shirt.

When Maaz and Nawaaz joined me, my heart sank a little further when I saw how they were dressed. Maaz was wearing almost the same outfit as me—blue jeans and a faded T-shirt—but Nawaaz was in a full kurta, not one shit given. Both had caps on their heads. I was in no position to negotiate. I felt that if I'd tried to back out, they would've strong-armed me into going anyway. I remember wondering if they were really helping me or just looking for an excuse to sneak out. But I wasn't innocent either. These were not friends by choice.

"All right, I've called a cab I know that will drive us at a flat rate," Maaz said. "It should be waiting for us out there."

"How much is this going to cost?" I whisper-shouted back, suddenly alarmed.

"Oh, don't worry—I'm good for it. I have the money, just nothing to spend it on."

Nawaaz held a finger to his lips and stuck his head into the black hallway. He opened the door wider and motioned for us to follow him. We crept quietly past the sleeping students towards a staircase leading down to the main foyer and then the lobby inside the front door. I still had no idea how we were going to get out.

When we reached the door, Nawaaz motioned for Maaz to keep a lookout at the lobby entrance while he investigated a high window. Peering up, I could see him fumbling with some clasps, and then I heard a soft click before I saw the window slide open. How Nawaaz was going to fit through the opening was beyond me. It looked way too small for any human form, let alone Nawaaz. He grabbed the window ledge and hoisted himself up. He somehow managed to contort his muscular frame, angling himself diagonally to fit through the small opening. I had no idea what the fuck to do. I didn't get it. The window was too small and Nawaaz had no right getting through it. It looked like the frame had stretched and grown to let his body through. Not enough, though. He appeared to be stuck at the hips, his legs pushed together by the frame, squeezing him while he squirmed in discomfort.

I heard the muffled shuffle and wiggle of Nawaaz's body while he tried to inch himself through. Finally—mostly because I didn't want to get caught—I stepped forward and pushed his heels, propelling him easily into the night. There was a gentle crunch on the other side as his body hit the gravel.

Then I heard the clang of the lock, and the door groaned loudly as Nawaaz pushed it open a crack. I felt Maaz touch my back and gently nudge me forward. I stepped out into the night, my heart pounding with the exhilaration of our crime. I understood this. Our escape made me feel alive, the same way I felt on the pitcher's mound. I looked up at the night sky while the door thudded faintly behind us. I wasn't used to seeing stars.

I followed Nawaaz and Maaz up the gravel hill to the main road. It had rained recently. The pebbles were wet, and the air had that unmistakable scent of soaked greenery. We walked in silence on the shoulder of the road, listening to the odd car zoom by us in the dark. Every breath of cool autumn air was a welcome, stolen one, and it was hard for me to remember the purpose of our excursion until I spotted the cab. Nawaaz hurried ahead of us to open the back door, and we got inside. My friends turned to me when the cabbie prompted us for an address. I cleared my throat and gave Alana's address. Our escape was now real.

The driver took off slowly, glancing at us in the rear-view mirror. "Is everything okay?" he asked in an unfamiliar accent. Soft reggae played on the radio.

There was no hiding our flustered appearance, as I don't think any of us had ever taken a cab before. Luckily, between the money our parents sent us and Maaz's reserve funds, we'd have enough to pay for the ride. But we must have been a curious sight: three teenagers crammed into the back of a cab in the middle of the night. I felt compelled to say the *du'a* for taking a vehicle, whispering it while Maaz raised an eyebrow and Nawaaz ignored me altogether. My fear was palpable.

"Yeah, we're fine," Maaz said quickly. "We're just going to see a sick friend." It sounded like he'd had the response prepared.

The cabbie shrugged his shoulders. A fare was a fare, especially at the distance we were travelling.

Over an hour later, when we finally arrived and got out of the cab, I looked around to get my bearings. In the middle of the night, from my new vantage point as an interloper, my old neighbourhood was unrecognizable. Things that had been familiar now looked like the strange sights of a new land. Brown and green facades became mushy greys and blues under the night sky. There was no sound, no movement, no moon. Streetlights shone their orange pallor on the sidewalk, revealing the wet pavement and glowing puddles. We moved silently towards Alana's house.

Even in that warped light amid my disorientation, I recognized her house immediately. It was painted white, but at night, it took on an odd glow. I never thought we would make it this far and had no idea what our next step should be.

"Well, I can't just knock on her front door now, can I?" I said, hoping this was the end of our foolish excursion.

"Fam, this would be so much easier if you knew her number," Nawaaz said, kissing his teeth.

"It's fine. We'll just throw a rock at her window," Maaz said with confidence. He bent over and searched the pavement for a stray pebble. I couldn't believe that Maaz of all people was suggesting something out a John Hughes movie.

"Yeah, but which window is hers?" asked Nawaaz, sounding increasingly frustrated.

I took off my shoe, looking for the pebble I'd felt earlier on the walk up the gravel hill from the school. I didn't bother answering Nawaaz—I knew which window was hers. Pulling out the holy pebble, I stepped onto her well-kept lawn underneath the starless sky. I chucked it and missed. I half hoped that would be the end of it. I was starting to panic. What if her parents woke up and called the cops? What would she think of me for doing this? What the hell would I even say to her?

I stepped off the lawn, secretly happy, but my relief was premature. Maaz strode forward with a fistful of stones and handed me a few before turning his own attention to the window. Watching him hurl stone after stone and miss was too much. I took an extra second to aim one at her window, and this time I hit it. Behind some curtains, a soft light clicked on. The window slid open and a head popped out. It was Alana, her brown hair tied back with something white. It had grown a little longer since I last saw her.

I waved up at her. Maaz and Nawaaz looked stunned, mouths agape and staring up at her. I don't think they'd expected us to get this far either.

"Hey, it's me, Nabil!" I whisper-shouted. I had no idea what else I was supposed to say.

"Nabil?!" She put a hand above her eyes to see better in the dark, though I'm not sure it did anything to help.

"Yeah! It's me! Uh . . . do you want to come out and talk?"

"Why?" She was straining her eyes.

"You know, I just . . . haven't seen you in a while." I was searching for words to describe a feeling that had no words.

"Hold on," she whispered. She retreated, closing the window behind her.

I heard Nawaaz snicker. A short while later, we heard another click. The front door opened, and Alana stepped into the night. She was wearing a hoodie and pink pajamas with white rabbits on them. In her hand was the white umbrella, reminding us of the recent rain. White canopy, white handle, white cord. My heart skipped a beat.

"What are you doing here?" she asked. She was too young to feel fear or to tell us to get lost. She was compelled by the story she'd be able to tell her friends at school the next day. Just as we were compelled by something else, too young to stay away. We were all still at that magical age when irrational actions were committed to, in the off chance that love was supernatural, and that the night would be something beautiful and not ugly. Would you take a bus two hours to go meet someone for the first time in this day and age, in your day and age?

"Yeah, I just . . . I go to a new school now, and we never got the chance to talk over the summer." I was fumbling for logic where there was none.

"But why are you here in the middle of the night? And who are those guys?" She was bewildered at the sight of Maaz and Nawaaz.

"They helped me sneak out," I said, hoping the word "sneak" would intrigue her. It worked.

I motioned for Maaz and Nawaaz to give us some privacy, and they walked away. Nawaaz had a smirk on his face, and Maaz's eyes were wide with concern. They walked out into the middle of the empty road, muttering quietly, the amber glow of the street-lights shining down on their backs.

I took a seat on the curb under one of the lights. Alana sat down beside me to share the last few precious, final minutes of a make-do September night together.

"I'm sorry I never called or anything. I was busy all summer, and I thought that once September came around, I would see you at school. And talk to you then."

"What's on your head?" she asked, chuckling.

I yanked off the cap. I'd forgotten about it. I'd been wearing it for so long that it had become a part of me. A practice that would bring me endless blessings in the afterlife, but none here.

"Sorry, it's my new school. Yeah . . . um, I go to a new school now." I had no idea how to explain.

"Where is it?"

"It's a religious school. In . . . uh, Ajax . . . ish." I didn't want to say the name of a more distant place.

"Oh. So why did you come here?" She was playing with the cord on her umbrella handle, twisting it into shapes.

"To see you."

She smiled the same smile as Nawaaz, and I could tell I'd lost. Lips curled with an ugliness unbecoming of a smile.

"When will you be back?" she asked.

"I don't know. Maybe next semester." I tried to make it sound confident.

"You didn't have to come all the way here to see me, you know." She was looking at Maaz and Nawaaz, who'd begun wrestling under a streetlight. Nawaaz's cap fell off his head, and his kurta flapped in the night.

"Yeah I did," I said quickly. I was staring into nothing.

"Well, I'm really busy these days, so I don't know how I'm going to keep in touch," Alana said just as quickly.

"Well, what's your number? I could call you."

"Uh . . . I'm in between phones right now. But I'll see you when you're back, right?" Her response seemed ready.

"Yeah, for sure." I wasn't stupid. I understood what she meant.

"You guys are so weird," she said with a soft laugh.

I had no idea who she was referring to. She had avoided looking me in the eye on that sidewalk curb, using my companions as surrogates instead. They continued their wrestling, foreheads slick with shining sweat as one of them cussed loudly in Gujarati.

"Listen, I have to go back inside," she said, inching backwards towards her front door, the white umbrella clutched in both hands. "You guys should leave before someone calls the cops."

She waited for a response, some twist that would captivate her again and bring that umbrella a tiny bit closer to my world. But there, in the middle of the silent night, I had nothing. No words. And I couldn't pitch a nine-inning no-hit shutout in that moment to remind her of who I was. Gone was the adulation from her eyes.

Before her now instead lay the strange vision of two wrestlers cussing in a foreign tongue while someone else tried to plead over the noise. I smiled weakly.

"For sure. I'll holler at you when I'm back."

"Okay. Stafe!" she whispered.

Stafe. Stay safe. It was our inside joke. One of us had said it by accident once, and it made us laugh till we cried, so it stuck. That was the last time I would ever hear it.

Alana crept back into her house and closed the door. I heard the lock turn. I walked out into the middle of the empty road, where Maaz and Nawaaz were still play-fighting.

"Let's go," I said.

Maaz escaped Nawaaz's headlock and turned to face me.

"How did it go?" he asked, out of breath.

"Not so good, I think. I don't know. Let's go back before we get caught."

I was done with this night.

"Fuck that fam. Let's reach Tim's!" Nawaaz said.

"Yeah, they're open late. Come on, it'll cheer you up," Maaz piled on.

"All that *masthi* talking to girls must work up an appetite." Nawaaz jokingly poked my shoulder.

"How are you still hungry after all that daal? You could barely fit through the window sneaking out," I shot back.

Maaz and Nawaaz laughed, and I wondered why I felt closer to them. The night was early. The prospect of coffee enticed me.

But something else enticed me more now. I was no longer ready for the night to end. The darkness was nothing but light to them, and now to me as well. Squeezing through windows, writhing and squirming like desperate creatures clinging to life, and the chance at clutching a white umbrella.

CHAPTER 3

Lions to the Slaughter

There were really only three kinds of kids at Al Haque—or any madrasa, for that matter. Three groups.

First were the religious kids: kids who had always been very pious, very respectful and very quiet. They were predisposed to and predestined for a spiritual life. They were meditative in public school and uncomfortable around practices they didn't understand, like school dances and Christmas plays. These kids were mature beyond their years and understood their parents' sacrifice—or at the very least, their parents and community had impressed upon them the importance of the afterlife. The other life. The one that began when you died and lasted forever. The one that was eternal. The one that wasn't a test. These kids were compliant and pliable, and felt the grace of Allah easily and were looking forward to tasting the honey of the hereafter. They didn't need much pushing. They did well in school, but even better in their after-school religious instruction. They were curious, but not truly. One answer was enough for them. They were content with the first answer they were given. "What happens if you don't pray five times a day?" "Allah will punish you." And that was enough. No "Isn't that kinda mean?" They understood something the other kids didn't. That most of the world didn't. Maybe they already had an answer for "Isn't that kinda mean?" so they didn't need to ask. They were the target audience. They were the ones the madrasas were made for. And they were the minority.

The second group of kids were the troublemakers. The ones who didn't fit in at public school because they were always wildin'. They misbehaved and had struck out too many times. Their parents were tired, and like parents who threatened their kids with military school, these parents would threaten theirs with madrasa. Which wasn't fair, and was a gross misuse of both institutions. These kids were born ruffians, or raised ruffians, without comfort or control in a new land and only anger to act out with. Sure, no kid at a madrasa had ever fit in at public school, but we all reacted differently to not fitting in. Standing out as a South Asian, a Middle Eastern, or an African kid had its drawbacks. Every flaw and fault was a characteristic of our people. In protest, these kids would torment teachers, brawl and get poor grades. They became the after-school adage you heard from your parents. "Look how violent those people are! They don't know how to act. I mean just look at what they do to their women." These kids approached life like it was a playground, nothing was sacred. Not even the mosque. And later, when their weak and tired parents were at their wits' end, they would send them away to the madrasa, incorrectly treating it like a correctional facility. These kids were not curious. They were also not *not* curious. They just didn't care for your answers. Having no place to belong, they wanted to see something break, something smash. They wanted to shove a heavy thing, even half an inch, to prove that they were alive and could make a difference. Every beating they received in response was a success. They'd gotten you to reveal your true nature.

The third group of kids, a minority similar in size to the first group, were the ones caught in the middle. They were intelligent and respectful, but also social, gregarious and inquisitive about more than *just* religious things. They got good grades, which their parents mistook as a sign they would do well at a madrasa. They caught on to the Quran and hadith quickly. They learned stories and lessons as fast as the religious-good kids and were often mistaken for them. Their aptitude was misunderstood as an actual expression of faith, and they were pushed towards an ascetic life of worship, regardless of their own interest or say in the matter. But in their old schools, they hadn't been shy around Christmas plays or school dances. They enjoyed life, participated in everything and never stopped asking questions. They usually had passions here or there, however, that fell into the grey areas of Islam. Nothing outright haram, like singing (don't look at me, this is according to Surah Luqmaan and *Tafseer al-Tabari* and *as-Sa'di*), but maybe something that was seen as frivolous, unnecessary, distracting or unimportant. Something like reading or drawing. Arguments were often made for and against these pursuits in Islam. "It's okay if you're doing it to glorify Allah," some would say. "But otherwise you're doing it to challenge the Almighty's creation by creating something of your own." These kids asked too many questions, including "Isn't that kinda mean?"

"We are slaves of Allah, and to disobey our Master's commands, his gift of Salaat to us, is a major sin."

"Yeah, but why is disobedience a major sin?"

Later, at a madrasa, the curious kids would pick a crowd and fall in with them, either the troublemakers or the religious-good kids. They wouldn't really fit in with either, but you couldn't survive there alone. You needed *somebody*.

In the end, upon graduating, there was only one kind of kid— or rather adult—left. Only one kind of person came out of the madrasa. A religious, respectful maulana who was ready to serve his community and spread the *deen*. All of the kids would eventually learn and grow and become good, studious young men in the service of their faith. *All* of them. Every single one, without fail—whether or not the madrasa was for them—would accept their fate. The passage of time erodes away at us all, until we find a way to live with ourselves.

Either you gain so much knowledge and zeal that your allegiance to your previous life dies. Or, left with no choice and nowhere to go, you break under the weight of an institution stronger than you and come to terms with your new life. Or, you forget about a different future, a different dream and all the strange stories from other parts of the world that have never even heard of you, and your old life is no longer even a memory. Or, the literal hand of God comes down to kill you because you don't quit.

Al Haque, and institutions like it, had a 100 percent success rate in graduating guiding beacons of *noor* to lead us all into the hereafter. Not a single soul would be lost or left behind.

—

I thought I would be the last new kid at Al Haque that year. By the time I arrived, the other kids had already been there for a few years, entrenched in their lives and relationships. And then I'd shown up out of the blue one September day and thought, Great, *I'm* the new kid. This is my life now. And with Maaz and Nawaaz as company, I thought we'd endlessly entertain each other like that, stealing weed from the older kids to flip, locking kids in the bathrooms and brawling over whose spot was whose on the eating mat. But these were all ordinary sins. The extraordinary sins came with the extraordinary spark, and he showed up well after we'd thought people could still come to Al Haque that year.

The administration was not prepared for Farid—and for that matter, neither were we. Most of us had learned to stay mute and value silence, but Farid knew only one volume: MAX.

We'd been at peace with no view to entertain us, the large window in the cavernous classroom revealing nothing but the swaying grey branches of a dying maple tree in the fall. But suddenly, there was a view. Amid the white kurtas and white caps, a kid shows up one day in a mustard-yellow kurta and a plastic gold-beaded rainbow cap. You could tell it was his first day.

We were in the middle of reviewing the last *sabaq*. The other students looked on snidely while the maulana pretended not to see the approaching kid in yellow led by the caretaker, Sharmil Bhai.

Farid had his head down, customary modesty worn upon his face, his diminutive frame appearing even smaller than it already was. Maulana Hasan had a few words with Sharmil Bhai before dismissing him. He then surveyed the class, looking for an empty spot on the carpet. I watched through the corner of my eye, pretending to be absorbed in my review. Finally, Maulana Hasan gestured to the spot next to me. Farid approached and squeezed in next to me on the carpet behind the long desk. Great, I thought. A FOB. That meant he couldn't be trusted. We spoke two different languages, belonged to two different cultures. His allegiance was different.

As the hymns and intonations resumed, I felt a nudge in my ribs and turned to see the new kid looking at me.

"Hey man, I'm Farid."

"*As'Salam'u'alaikum.* I'm Nabil," I replied, gaining the upper hand by falling back on faith but noting that he didn't have an accent.

"How long do you guys do review here for?" he asked. There was no danger of being overheard because we were many rows back.

"Two hours every morning," I said.

His reaction was not what I expected.

"Pffftt, Jee-zus! Two freaking hours? I could review all of my pubes in that time!"

I had to bite down on my lip to keep from laughing. This was no FOB.

Later at lunch, with Maaz nowhere in sight, I was eating on a mat directly across from Nawaaz when he saw the new kid a few spots down from us, sitting by himself. Nawaaz looked up at me with a mouthful of daal from our shared plate and jerked his head towards the kid as if to ask what the deal was.

"New kid. He's not a FOB though," I said.

"What do you mean?" Nawaaz asked through a full mouth. We had only twenty minutes for lunch, and he made the most of it.

"Well, look at him. He's dressed like a FOB, right? But he's not," I clarified.

Like everyone else in the room, Nawaaz and I were in white jubbas and white caps. From overhead, all you would've seen were white-robed bodies huddled over plates of food in neat parallel rows, two to a plate, and then one mustard-and-rainbow mess eating alone.

"Yo!" Nawaaz barked down the line.

Farid and a few others turned.

"Why do you look like that?" Nawaaz asked.

I coughed and nearly choked on my roti.

"What do you mean?" Farid replied, looking down at himself.

"Your kurta and hat are fresh, eh?" Nawaaz asked. It was an easy test. If Farid was a FOB, he'd be deaf to sarcasm, unsure if Nawaaz was being friendly or making fun of him.

"Fresh as fuck! If I look like this, all the muftis and maulanas leave me alone, treat me right. No one gives me shit cuz they think I'm a FOB. And when was the last time you thought a FOB was up to some *masthi*?" Farid shot back.

"What about when you speak to them and you have no accent?" Nawaaz asked. I could tell he was amused.

"You ever heard any of them speak to us beyond *'Par ni!'* and 'Stand up!' and 'Sit!'?"

It was true. Whenever a maulana spoke, it was always in one- or two-word phrases. Farid was playing it all up, engineering an image of modesty through flamboyant clothes, unconcerned with fitting in. He seemed like an average student, but I began to suspect that this, too, was engineered. The teachers suspected nothing. But the ruse didn't last long.

—

One day in the middle of review, underneath the blinding fluorescent lights of the main classroom on the second floor, Farid revealed another shade of his character.

"Yo, do you know how to sneak out of here?" he asked me.

"No," I replied, slightly annoyed, and quickly returned to my review. I was not the right person to ask as I'd never be forthcoming with someone I'd just met.

"Listen, I know someone's probably figured out how to get out of here at night. I'll give you a straight-up bill if you tell me who."

I looked at him for a second. He was an idiot, behaving like an immortal in a place where bones cracked and teeth were lost for questions sillier than this. He had no idea how lucky he was that he hadn't asked Nawaaz, who would've taken him for two hundred dollars and then set him up to be caught. Nawaaz was a Flema kid, and that was enough to make him a master enterpriser.

"No man. I don't know. *Par ni?*" I told him.

Farid shook his head.

"Yo, man, why you gotta study so hard? You know your shit."

"I'm here to study and learn, aren't I? What else am I going to do?"

"Really? You don't have to study *that* hard. Think about it. Your parents are paying a massive tuition, right? No one's gonna fail you here as long as you do okay. They need your money. Plus, if you study a bit less, slack off, it will bring the class average down, and the rest of the slackers will look better. We'll all be held to a lower standard."

"Why would I do that? There's gonna be beatings all the way down for me!"

"So what? You afraid of a beating?"

He had a smile on his face, and his earthy eyes narrowed, waiting for an answer. I studied him again. He had a mousy face and a long nose, with a few hairs on his chin that he could do nothing about even if he wanted to.

"You don't care about beatings?" I asked.

"Why would I give a shit? It's just a beating! Watch this. Just watch what happens when I go up."

Farid went back to his Quran. I had trouble focusing, wondering what he was going to do. When his name was called, I peeked over my pages while Farid walked up and sat down in front of Maulana Hasan. I heard the mumble of his voice, and everything was fine for the first few minutes while he recited his chapter. I was on edge.

Suddenly, the maulana's hand came down and delivered a quick slap to the back of Farid's neck. Farid rocked back and forth, continuing his recitation.

The maulana's eyes widened until I could see the white bulging around his brown pupils. He delivered another slap to the back of Farid's neck.

"*Par ni!*" he commanded.

Farid had his head down, silent. Maulana Hasan grabbed the collar of his mustard-yellow kurta, then brought down his other hand again and again in a flurry of blows raining discipline on Farid's neck and back. The gold-beaded rainbow cap flew off, and Maulana Hasan banished him with a gesture, whispering insults through gritted teeth and flying saliva.

Farid picked up his cap and walked back to his seat beside me. When I turned to look at him, he adjusted the rainbow cap and flashed me an unambiguous wink. The back of his neck had gone from brown to red, but he'd survived. I realized it was possible that we'd built up the beatings in our minds into mythic trials. I was in disbelief. This kid caught a beating from Maulana Hasan on purpose. What the fuck?

I was dumbfounded with what I would later learn was respect. And then, I was dumbfounded again when I realized that Farid had begun to quietly sing the lyrics to a Fall Out Boy song. Over the hymn of Arabic recitation, I could make out the sad lines of some sorry boy pining for a girl. Farid was rocking back and forth like it was a religious chant, and when he caught me staring, he closed his eyes and shook his head, singing a little louder. As brazen as Maaz, Nawaaz and I had become, we had our limits. Farid couldn't care less about living within them.

Sitting on the mat together at lunch, Maaz and Nawaaz brought up the beating. Beatings during review rarely caught any-one off guard, but they were normally reserved for Bilal and Jara, who were poor students.

"What's up with your boy?" Maaz asked. The soft hairs on his chin belied the sharp acuity reflected in his focused eyes.

"What do you mean?" I responded, slurping the daal from my fingertips, glad for conversation to distract from the tasteless food. The meals never got much better.

"Why'd he get beat?" Nawaaz asked. They could tell some-thing was off. Farid seemed to know his stuff.

"Yo, that guy's fucked up, bro," I said. "Stay away from him." I shook my head too, knowing they'd press me for more details.

"Why—what happened? What did he do?" Maaz's amber eyes lit up at the prospect of an interesting story.

"He got beat to prove a point," I said, shrugging. "I told him

46

I'd get beat if I didn't study hard and know my shit, and he wanted to show me that beatings weren't a big deal."

"Wait, he caught a beating on purpose? From Maulana Hasan?" Nawaaz's eyes narrowed.

"Yeah. He took the beating just to prove the point. And then, get this—afterwards, this motherfucker was singing punk rock and shaking his head and shit."

Maaz laughed out loud and clapped his hands together once, quietly. Clapping more than once would attract attention and a reprimand. Nawaaz was silent, his brow furrowed. Maaz and I understood Farid's actions. Nawaaz did not. He subscribed to a world where blood and violence motivated, and weren't courted for subversion. In Nawaaz's world, right and wrong hadn't changed for thousands of years, but Farid, Maaz and I weren't so sure.

—

That night after classes, we all gathered for the evening prayer with the *adhaan*. As was customary, Maulana Hasan performed his ablution right before the prayer started. The prayer hall on the main floor stretched twenty feet behind where we were standing and ended at a single door, which led to the main foyer and a flight of stairs down to the bathrooms, another classroom and the kitchen. In that bathroom, Maulana Hasan was finishing up his Wudhu and would soon join us. My eyes were focused on the beautiful navy arches stitched into the lush red carpet at my feet in an intricate design that looped in front of every student supplicating himself before the Almighty. Before Hafiz Abdullah could say the first *takbir* to lead prayer, my ears picked up the sound of someone rushing to the door. Everyone but Hafiz Abdullah turned to look at who was walking *away* from prayer.

"*Allah-u-Akbar!*" Hafiz Abdullah convened the prayer.

None of us turned back to face him, or Him. All eyes were on Farid. He went up to the door and turned the lock. Even across the hall, we could hear the soft clack of the deadbolt. Farid sprinted back. The rest of us smirked in understanding and turned back around, saying a soft *takbir* and joining Hafiz Abdullah in his recitation and Farid in his prank.

Soon after, we heard it. The twisting of the knob, the pulling of the door. I suppressed a smile. I sensed the others doing the same. We heard banging on the door, and then the laughter began. Some of us couldn't hold it in. Maulana Hasan was not known for his cool head. He'd probably expected someone to break their prayer and come to unlock the door for him. Instead, we faked devotion and followed the devout Hafiz into prostration, the thick door muffling the sound of our mirth so Maulana Hasan couldn't hear us. He could only bear witness through a small window to our submissive backs imitating prayer. Our faces remained hidden while the heavy door shook and thundered. Each ham-fist against it doubled our laughter. We were caught in a frenzy the way Maulana Hasan was caught in a frenzy. If he'd simply given up and stopped banging in futility, we could have stopped laughing. But he would not relent. No one would unlock the door for him, but he believed that if he could only hit it hard enough, loud enough, fear of him would motivate some poor soul to break their prayer and let him in.

We were not allowed to break prayer for fear of him, though. We were in a trance and could take from the bountiful and limitless treasures of God, plucking immaterial rewards from immaterial trees, oblivious to the temporal world, our senses deaf-mute-blind-dumb-numb through communion.

Maulana Hasan continued to hammer on the door furiously. We smiled through closed eyes, the final prostration and the *salam* to each recording angel on our shoulders. Nothing would be missed by them. And we would be punished anyway, of course. Twice, actually. Once after the prayer by the maulana, who wouldn't believe our piety, and then again in the grave after we died. The maulana would be punished once, by us.

I looked across the line of students, searching for the cause of the mayhem. I spotted Farid being discreetly prodded and cajoled, other students eager to share in the prank while he grinned, revelling in the pleasure, drinking in their adoration, eyes alight with life. He caught me looking and flashed me two mocking middle fingers, mouth open and shoulders swaying in a dance move. I rolled my eyes, but my heart sang, eager to see what else he would do. I knew some people would hate him, and some people would love him. For some people, it would be something in between. Whatever it was, they'd remember him forever.

CHAPTER 4

Quadruple Bypass

With Farid in our midst, the atmosphere changed. We didn't know it yet, but the seeds had been planted for something far more permanent. Escape wasn't even on my mind in those days, however; freedom was too heavy an abstract I couldn't afford, so I didn't even entertain it. What would I do? Where would I go? Who would have us? My parents wouldn't accept me if I left Al Haque. No matter how miserable we were, we all knew this was it. There was nowhere to go and nothing to do, so we threw ourselves into that nowhere-nothing in search of foretold ambrosia. Bodies supplicant in search of somewhere-something. But for some people, that wasn't enough.

"Has anyone seen my keys?"

It was a Friday evening in mid-October, that time of year when the night sky creeps up on the sun too early, snuffing out its descent. Maulana Ibrar's car keys had gone missing. He lived an hour away, in Peterborough, and as class neared its end, he was growing fidgety. If he couldn't find them, he would have to bum a ride home with Heart Attack Three. He rushed through the final lesson of the day, an exegesis on the order of the chapters in the Quran, absent-mindedly checking his pockets and fumbling around for keys that weren't there. He turned his spectacled gaze on the class.

"I know I had them with me."

He looked at the class over the top of his frameless glasses, condemning the room from right to left. We stared back with ignorance, busy in memorization.

We heard his tongue click, and the maulana shook his head, his long black beard moving with him.

"If anyone steps forward with information, that will be the end of it. No one will be punished. No harm, no foul."

He looked at the class one last time. The snitch wouldn't have the strength to step forward in front of everybody. To be honest, the snitch probably didn't even know he would end up snitching at that point.

"Okay. I'll deal with this on Monday then." Maulana Ibrar gathered his black bubble jacket and left, his tall frame making no noise as he exited the room. Even his long white jubba neglected to swoosh behind him as he went.

Most of us had no idea what had happened to his keys and didn't really care. Farid, however, knew exactly where they were. As soon as the coast was clear, he flashed them to the room, spinning them in his hand and offering his trademark grin. I should've known it was him.

"Fam. Why?" I stretched my palm towards him in the Gujarati style of our teachers. We all knew Farid was crazy, but we also knew he didn't do anything without a reason, even if it was a dumb one.

"Maulana Ibrar called my dad last month. Told him shit about how he caught me on Derry Road after Isha. My dad flipped. Came here just to beat my ass in the principal's office after Zuhr and then left."

We hadn't seen anyone unfamiliar at the madrasa, so it really must have been a drive-by beating.

Everyone around us cracked up. Farid lived his life in between beatings and we bore witness with mirth, and something else. Farid was indifferent to our laughter.

"Why some maulanas gotta act all mighty and shit? Can't deal with madrasa issues *inside* the madrasa?"

Farid had a point. The maulanas usually didn't alert the parents unless it was absolutely necessary. They liked maintaining the illusion of control over the student body, as if nothing was ever wrong. Unless a transgression was especially egregious, they preferred to deal with things themselves. Maulana Ibrar had broken protocol by contacting Farid's parents directly.

We also had no idea how Farid was managing to sneak out, as Maaz, Nawaaz and I had not shared our window trick with him. No one was in the mood for sharing anything in the madrasa. Knowledge was power, and power meant freedom.

"Why would Maulana Ibrar call your parents right away? Have you been caught before?" Maaz asked. We were all draped around the red-and-navy carpet after the evening prayer. Most of us were unsupervised until Isha. There was only one window, and the pitch-black night projected nothing into the room as Farid narrowed his brown eyes towards us. The fluorescent bulbs above us provided the only light.

"*Wallahi*, on my life I haven't been caught yet. That's why I don't understand why he called my dad. And get this—now they think I'm a troublemaker!" Farid said.

We laughed again at his incredulousness, unsure if he seriously thought he could sell the piety act. The maulanas themselves had bought it for only a few weeks. Too many people had been caught laughing around Farid. He hadn't been careful enough with his language, and there was no accent to sell the pious FOB charade either. It's like he didn't care about keeping it up. I could tell he was growing bored of the role. He relished a new one.

"Now what am I supposed to do with car keys?" Farid said, twirling the shiny silver bundle in his hands. Half the kids were watching us, and the other half were engrossed in their own conversations. "If only there was a car for them. Hmmm. If only the principal and the maulanas weren't here tomorrow night. Hmmm. If only they were going to a huge *bhaiyan* in Toronto. If only it was just Sharmil Bhai left here to watch us. Hmmm. HMMMMM!"

"You're crazy, bro," I said as I shook my head. The heist he was proposing was on another level. We had no idea how Sharmil Bhai could get so distracted that he wouldn't notice a missing car. I wanted no part of it. But Farid, idiot that he was, was harder to dissuade. There was forever a strange light in his eyes that never dimmed. It helped him convince us of anything, but it also helped the maulanas find him.

"Pickering Town. Tomorrow night. Bare shordies at the movies. Who's reaching?"

He leaned over a bench to stare at me, Maaz and Nawaaz. He knew who would be most likely to join him. Of the students in our year, none were older than fourteen, and most hadn't spoken to a girl in years, or possibly ever. It was a bad mix. We were fitted

53

with holiness young, the garb too long and large for our grow-ing frames, but we didn't care about our appearance without girls around to impress. Now, though, there was the prospect of girls. For some, it was an easy decision.

"Fuck that. I don't wanna die," I replied. As a newer arrival, I was not as starved as the others. I tried to ignore the whisper in my head. For others, it was impossible to ignore.

"Lemme talk to you after Isha, still," Maaz said with a glib smile. He was smart. It was wiser to hold these kinds of talks in private. Conspirators only. He didn't need to say why.

Unspoken facts are unspoken for a reason. Nobody had to tell the first men and women not to snitch. You don't snitch. You just don't rat. That law never had to be articulated until rats showed up. Scions of the early Quraysh, they couldn't handle the pain of hunger and quickly turned to any hand that would feed them, sell-ing out Companions under a crescent moon like pelts in exchange for full bellies. But if you were weak and couldn't handle pain, you couldn't be trusted and we'd have to adjust our behaviour around you. You were just another cop, another teacher. Even the good kids—Hafiz Abdullah, Syed, Jara and the others—knew better. You could be studious without snitching. Don't ask, don't tell. Feign ignorance. Even if the maulanas started whupping us to find out who'd snuck out of the school, or who had stolen cash from the principal's office, or who had hidden Heart Attack One's belt, the good kids knew to stay tight-lipped and take the beating. You'd retain respect that way, even gain some. But more importantly, you'd remain unharmed.

While other maulanas might be more lenient if they caught you in the middle of mischief, there were three who were notorious for their brutality. The Three Heart Attacks were aptly named because of their propensity to instill exactly that upon sight. Seeing one meant an instant heart attack, out of fear for what you were about to endure. But what the Three Heart Attacks did behind closed doors was nothing compared to what we could do. And I was just as guilty—I participated. But only part of me feels remorse. Violence motivated, and we would much rather be villains than victims. Villains survived longer.

If it had been up to us, we would have added a few extra questions to the Al Haque admission interview, to screen out the weak and hungry. "Have you ever been accused of being a snitch?" Or, "Describe the toughest beating you ever caught, and what was your crime?" As it was, we couldn't determine with certainty who was strong and loyal and who was weak and spineless. We thought Bilal was strong and loyal.

—

On Saturday night, when Sharmil Bhai was busy supervising the students on kitchen duty after dinner, we got ready to sneak out. No one besides Farid had had much of an appetite, so we cut out early, dragging him with us to the shoe foyer. We slid our shoes off the racks and silently slipped them on, slinking away into the evening. The plan went off without a hitch. When we got to the parking lot, Farid walked over to the only remaining car, a nondescript black vehicle that defied attention, and unlocked it. Then he took his place in the driver's seat. Maaz, Nawaaz and I filled the other seats, unsurprised that Farid somehow knew how to drive.

By the time we got to the mall, it was almost closed. There was barely an hour left. The sky above us was purple and red and fading fast. A breeze cut through the near empty parking lot and reminded us it was October. We welcomed the bite, as the chill was something we seldom felt now, living our lives indoors, underneath cheap chandeliers and white ceilings. It had been some time since we'd borne non-windowed witness to a bleeding sky and a whistling wind. Being closer to it all changed things. Red turned to purple on our brown skin as more cars emptied the lot, heading one way while we headed the other.

We entered the mall and walked the sparse halls, wandering from quiet storefront to quiet storefront. It didn't bother us that we weren't there during peak hours. There was no way we could have been. Sean John jeans, Rocawear shirts. Caps and the beginnings of beards. The beginnings of piety for some of us; the beginnings of the end of piety for others. We trod on marble tiles and pretended to be engrossed in all that we saw, trying to make our truancy worth it. There were girls around, but none of us dared speak to them. Just the idea of them—the *sight* of them—was enough. We just needed a reminder that night. That they were out there. We drank in freedom and walked like drunkards. Paused at the knockoff retailer. Loitered too long at Starbucks and stole straws and napkins like desperate men. Postured under awnings of light. Stood on benches and chairs like Renaissance statues. Rode escalator rails like broncobusters of yore. Pitched together enough coins for a shared Iced Capp.

We walked along the black tiles, evading the eyes of security guards, and eventually followed the herded crowd out. Chrome pillars on either side of us shepherded us into the night. Everything looked shiny and clean in that industrial consumer purgatory. Our feet dragged us along, each step aging us as we grew all fucky and pledged our campaign of pain in favour of all that was beautiful but temporary.

Our hearts reached for pleasure as we walked away from it all. Farid, Maaz, Nawaaz and I were caught in the dream of our brief escape. The dangerous satiation of desire in temporal things led only to addiction, and then a fall from grace, but there was nothing else we wanted more. And we wanted more. The drive back to the madrasa was made more difficult as a result. I remember looking down every side street and intersection thinking about what would happen if we just . . . kept driving? I twisted in my seat a few times to face my companions and give voice to this desire. But no words came out. Just Maaz and Nawaaz with lifted brows, wondering what was on my mind. Did they feel the same way? How could they not?

We made it back safely that night, and everything seemed like it would be fine. But on Monday, during our regular lesson review, I saw Sharmil Bhai fetch our classmate Samir. They disappeared quietly and returned sometime later. Sharmil Bhai then took Alif with him. That's when I realized that something was up. We all did. They were trying to be discreet about the one-on-ones, but as I hummed *ayat* after *ayat*, I exchanged glances with Maaz and Nawaaz to make sure they were seeing the same thing I was. I nudged Farid beside me.

"I know," he said. He then began to bellow out his review louder than anyone else, drowning out the others. Maulana Hasan didn't even look up at the noise. Passion was good.

I watched Alif come back. He seemed a little shaken and set-tled himself uncomfortably on his knees before continuing his recitation. Something was up. I knew it couldn't involve Saturday's excursion as we'd pulled that heist off successfully. We'd made it back for the last bit of the Isha, and nothing seemed amiss. I wondered if it could be about the missing car keys (which we'd discreetly returned to Maulana-sab's cubby in the main prayer hall), but Maulana Ibrar wasn't there and his class wasn't until later that day.

Soon, Sharmil Bhai motioned for me to follow him to Principal Abbas's office. I swallowed my fear and did as directed.

As I entered the office, I was surprised to see Maulana Ibrar leaning against a windowsill in one corner. Light framed his darkened form, but I could still clearly make out his long white jubba, white cap and white eyes behind the rimless glasses. In those eyes, I immediately saw why the maulana had broken protocol and gone straight to Farid's parents. I knew now that Maulana Ibrar had no sympathy for worldly desires. He'd been in the country for thirty years, since he was a kid, and yet remained unchanged in all that time. He seemed to have more in common with the earliest Companions of the Prophet than anyone else alive. His was one of the first families to come in the 1970s, as part of the first wave of immigrants from India and Pakistan to settle in Toronto. I'd heard that his father was a prominent maulana in his Gujarat village, and that he had quickly enrolled his son in an Islamic school in England out of fear that he would lose his faith in the new land. That expensive but necessary education across the pond soon created a dour, no-nonsense man who decried anything he had not learned indoors. He had a serious disposition and was attracted solely to study, *ibaadat*, teaching and devotion. He rarely cracked a smile, meeting each joke with a cliff, and took pleasure in being steadfast. As a matter of fact, the only time I remember him smiling is when another maulana complimented him for something. The corners of his lips raised slightly before he checked them and politely and modestly declined the compliment. I knew he'd been commended many times on how well his class behaved, so he'd be greatly troubled if a student's misbehaviour challenged the pleasing paradigm he'd established. Maulana Ibrar believed his class behaved because they respected him. Farid was there to remind him.

The principal was seated behind his desk. White kurta in the subcontinental style, white beard in the natural one. The smell of oud from the agar tree permeated the room. He looked at me through his glasses. Maulana Ibrar didn't look at me at all, instead adopting the posture of someone who was there by accident. As if he just happened to be passing through. He would not dignify the crime by speaking. He let the principal speak in his stead.

"A very serious crime was committed on Friday," he began. "Do you know what it could be?" Principal Abbas was rarely the arbiter of crimes at Al Haque. His inexperience showed.

"No," I said quietly.

"Maulana Ibrar's car keys went missing. This is a very serious issue. Do you know who took them?"

"No. Not at all."

"Maulana Ibrar is your respected *ustad*. He's come from Dewsbury just to teach here. He didn't come here for this nonsense. I know you spend time with those troublemakers Farid, Maaz and Nawaaz. Did they do this? Tell me now because we're going to find out anyway."

The principal was a portly, aging man with a loud but warm

voice. Anger didn't suit him. He was more accustomed to shaking hands, waddling, winking, smiling and finger-wagging.

"No sir. I don't know anything."

"Place your hands on the table and spread your legs. Look down at the ground." This was Sharmil Bhai's hard voice.

I did as he asked, putting my hands on the principal's desk and looking down. The air whistled softly, and then there was a crack. My knuckles screamed in pain.

"Tell us who might know something!" Sharmil Bhai demanded.

His voice was in its customary place above me. I knew he had his yardstick in hand. He was frustrated with the principal's bumbling interrogation. Because he was around us every day, Sharmil Bhai had a deeper understanding of the most effective techniques to elicit information from us. Sharmil Bhai, who'd been duped out of a good job, a good salary and a good life by his lack of education and gumption. He'd heard that Allah preferred the modest and poor man with nothing, and so he found solace in being modest and poor and having nothing. The school needed him more than anyone would ever care to admit, as he was the only full-time live-in caretaker. I'd heard that he'd been in Canada for many years, but bouncing around from odd job to odd job took its toll. He'd been sponsored by some distant family member, but without an education, his prospects were limited. New lands, languages and people had made him uncomfortable, so the familiar hymn of the *adhaan* brought comfort inside a mosque, and there he found a job where days turned into years, and dull routine brought purpose, and dull pain was whisked away at every sermon praising a shitty life's rewards still to come.

"Do you think it was him?" The principal's voice was turned

towards Maulana Ibrar. A moment passed that felt like an eternity. I stared at the faded teal carpet that hid any signs of dirt and dust.

"No." The maulana's voice was barely audible.

"Swear you know nothing." Sharmil Bhai poked my ribs with the stick at this demand.

I was about to swear when I heard a shuffle in front of me and felt a hard blow land on the back of my neck. It wasn't from Sharmil Bhai, who was standing to my right. The principal had stood up to relieve his anger, proving that he was weak and imperfect and undeserving of something.

"I swear," I said quietly, biting my lip to keep from yelping in pain.

"Not every student is as tight-lipped as you," the principal spat. "If we find out later that you were involved, you're going to be expelled. This is absolutely unacceptable." His threat was as empty as the unused dorm rooms on the third floor, and we all knew it. He needed our tuition. I was summarily dismissed and quietly returned to class.

Most of the students had been called in at that point. The too-red carpets moved me up and down stairs, and I continued to memorize tracts and passages, swallowing dull pains like daily vitamins until the agony was default and thought normal. Sometime around sunset, I finally noticed that Farid was missing. I didn't think too much of it until he failed to appear at dinner as well. No one missed a meal. He also missed the night's final prayer, and that's when I knew for certain that something had happened.

After the prayer, I alerted Maaz and Nawaaz to Farid's disappearance. We went up to his room to look for him. The door was ajar. Maaz pushed it open, and it gave way with a soft creak.

The room didn't have much in it. One window on the far wall in each room overlooked unused fields of green and yellow. Land that had been purchased with the ambition of raising a second building, one for girls, was left empty for now. We all saw the same thing looking out onto the land.

We found Farid in bed, lying on top of the covers. His eyes were bloodshot, and he was staring up at the ceiling. He didn't seem to notice that we'd entered.

"Yo, where the fuck you been bro?" I said loudly, trying to rouse him.

He didn't even look alive. He just stared at us blankly. We were afraid. Farid was never quiet.

"Did you . . . did you guys eat daal again tonight?" he finally whispered, his bloodshot eyes fixed on our white jubbas.

"Actually, no. It was aloo gosht tonight. And carrots," Maaz answered, his eyebrows raised.

"FUCK!" Farid shouted. He bicycle-kicked his legs at nothing and thrashed his right arm around in frustration. I noticed he held his left arm unmoving against his chest.

"The one day it's not daal for dinner—"

I cut him off. "What's wrong with your left hand?"

He wouldn't answer.

"Let me see." I moved forward. "Nawaaz, hold him."

Nawaaz moved to the top of the bed and grabbed Farid's right hand, pinning it above his head. Farid squirmed but could do nothing. I tried to lift his left arm, but he yelped and I stopped. Looking closer at his forearm, I noticed it was red and swollen beyond belief between the wrist and elbow.

"What happened?" I asked. I'd never seen anything like it.

62

"Maulana Ibrar found out it was me. I don't know how. Anyway, it's just a beating," he replied sheepishly. He tried to shoo us away, which was difficult with his only functioning arm pinned above him. Instead, his chin jerked up and down.

"What do you mean just a beating?" I asked. "He fucked your arm. Maulana Ibrar did this?" I had trouble believing it. That someone so serious and concerned with worship and supplication could betray themselves like that.

Farid only nodded.

"This is bad," Maaz said, shaking his head. "Someone musta snitched. If we don't find out who, we're fucked."

"You're right," Nawaaz said. "This is bigger than just Farid. We can't do anything until we figure out who's snitching."

He and Maaz were both right. The rat could compromise every future excursion if we weren't careful.

"I think I know who it was," I said quietly. That morning, after my trial, I'd watched to see if Maaz and Nawaaz would have similar experiences. But their turns never came. Instead, the interrogations stopped abruptly after Bilal was called to the office a few spots after me. I wondered why, and now I knew.

"It was Bilal," I said, looking at the group.

"How do you know?" Farid asked.

I explained what I'd seen.

Farid was skeptical. "Yeah, but are you certain it wasn't someone before him and they were just looking for corroboration?"

Maaz, Nawaaz and I looked at each other.

"I'll bet my life on it fam." My voice dripped with venom. We all knew Bilal. He was quiet and studious, and he never took part in our pranks. All of which was fine. But he also knew Maulana

Ibrar from outside of Al Haque. They were distant relatives or something; their fathers knew each other.

"I just . . . I don't want him to get hurt or anything on my behalf," Farid said.

"It's not on your behalf," Nawaaz replied firmly. "We just gotta keep this place under control." He would be impossible to stop now and could not avoid violent recourse. He understood what we only understood sometimes—that reason was a luxury where men and boys were base animals absent their gentler nature. Breaking things led to more broken things.

We snuck into Bilal's room that night while he was asleep. And not just me, Maaz and Nawaaz either. Six of us snuck in, including Jalil and Maruf, two asshole older kids we usually tried to stay away from. Those two were regularly seen jerking the younger kids around and making them do their bidding. When we spread the word that Bilal was the snitch, they joined our campaign to send a message. None of us could survive with a rat among us. That would be no life, some holy unnatural order where spirits were crushed instead of labouring onwards. Bilal's roommate, Samir, unlocked the door for us and helped to tie each of Bilal's limbs to a bedpost. It was dark, but we could make each other out in the blue light of the moon. The window gave us only the ugly that we needed.

Bilal needed to know that there was a worse pain out there than anything he could feel at the hands of Sharmil Bhai or Maulana Ibrar or the principal. We covered his face with a pillow so he couldn't scream or identify us later. Samir held the pillow steady. Bilal tried to sit up through a muffled pleading, but his tied limbs held him back. Maaz stepped forward first and punched him hard in the stomach twice. We heard a scream through the pillow. Bilal tried to curl up his knees, but the long white kurtas that we'd tied around his ankles wouldn't let him. One by one, we stepped forward, taking our orderly turns, waiting politely in a silent queue, socking him hard and then slipping out of the room without a word. He could feel in the varied strength of the blows who felt guilty, who was dispassionate, who didn't want to be there, who was cruel and relished his role. When it was my turn, I punched him hard in the stomach, then heard him cough and weep through the pillow while he squirmed on the bed. Only part of me feels remorse.

Maaz and I watched from the doorway as Nawaaz gestured for Samir to step aside and go back to bed. Nawaaz untied Bilal's hands and took the pillow away from his face. Samir was in bed, pretending to sleep now. The weird pale light from the window shone down on Bilal's tear-stained face while he stared at the ceiling with a blank expression. He was breathing heavily, and his brown skin was illuminated in places where rivulets of tears had formed. Hellfire would never be permitted to touch his skin in those hallowed tracks.

Nawaaz leaned into Bilal's face so they could eye each other with barely an inch separating them. "The others," he whispered. "You can't snitch on them cuz you didn't see them. Your face was covered. You don't know who was here tonight and who wasn't. Except for me. You know *I* was here and *I* did this. You can see my face. Now I *dare* you to snitch on me. I'll throw you off the roof of this fucking building."

Nawaaz turned around and walked out. His role was universal, eternal. In every year and in every moment in between, in some

65

corner of the world, he was propelling things one way. When men had convinced themselves they could afford the luxury of morals in places where they were being simultaneously built and broken, Nawaaz was there to remind them.

We took no joy or solace from that night. Simply put, a catastrophe would've resulted from our inaction through the multiplication of rats. And we'd much rather stay some halfway beast-humans. Maybe Bilal thought that he could afford something he really couldn't, or that we could all be good students like him, devoid of our troublemaking nature. That he could help us rise and live like Companions of the Prophet. But we weren't interested in living, and one eternal, rising life didn't sound better to us than one that sank and died. That's what Al Haque's victims did: rose and lived eternal. But we weren't victims. We were interested in living a life of the dying, clinging to middle school passions as they were beat out of us one by one at the slowest pace known to humanity. Until we were villains.

Farid

Heart Attack Four (the newly dubbed Maulana Ibrar after he orchestrated the interrogation and beatings over his missing keys) has just assigned us all a student sermon to perform on any topic of our choosing, and I'm in business. These guys have no idea what they're in for. Oh man, oh man, dis gun' be good. But first I gotta test my sermon out on the homies. Nabil, Maaz and Nawaaz have no idea. I dunno. I mean, I think my topic is fine, but, like, mans are wack. As soon as they hear anything new, it's an innovation. And just 'cause someone with a white beard hasn't said it before, it's appalling and shit. Aite. I see that. But just for a second, think about it.

Frodo Baggins loved knowledge and learning, right? Remember when he solved that riddle? You know who else had a thirst for knowledge? Imam Mahdi the saviour. For us, Jesus is known as Eesa the Messiah, right? In Arabic that would be Maseeh, right? Do you know one of the other definitions for Maseeh in Arabic? Strider. That's right. Aragorn. Another fun fact: our holy garb, the preferred clothing of the Prophet, was a crisp white jubba, long, flowy and clean. Something that projects purity. How's that not what Gandalf the White looks like?! Not all Western media is ever truly Western. Not all harmful media is ever truly harmful. These aren't, like, coincidental things. There are too many things for it to be coincidental. That's all I'm saying. I've thought about this for a while.

I remember the first time Nabil walked into our dorm and saw me posted up on the windowsill just looking out and thinking about all this. They'd just moved me into his room, and he raised his eyebrows and twisted a few fingers to ask what I was doing in that fobby style. I didn't say anything. I couldn't say anything. He's a good guy. I like him. But how could he know? They laugh and I know it's just a defence mechanism of being here or whatever, but I'm not laughing. It's not funny. There are too many coincidences. Saruman was like the fake Messiah, the deceiver who tries to build an army of his own. Doesn't that sound like Dajjal? Tolkien was probably a closet Muslim. Hear me out. He spoke Arabic and borrowed from the story of Mahdi because, let's face it, we have the sickest stories. Is Al Haque ready for it though? Are the imams and muftis ready? Man, if this window ever opened and the snow was ever deep enough, I could just . . .

I can see the trees from here. Shit, I don't even know what kind. All the leaves are gone, and they look like spindly old-man fingers now, but there's so many of them that I think there are still enough to hide me if I was ever among them. I could disappear and find out for myself. Shit, if it wasn't so cold out, I might actually do it. Gah, I'm probably screwed. They're not ready. The world moves way too slow for shit like this. I know Heart Attack Four is probably gonna beat my ass for this one too, but fuck it.

It's a fun assignment and worth the whupping. Even years later, when he can't beat me anymore, I'll be pulling out this sermon. The people need to know.

Probably not what Abbu had in mind—third madrasa in two years. What do you want though? What do you want me to say? *Wallahi* the first one was like a fucking prison, no lie. We weren't allowed to do shit. But it made sense because we were all crooks, lying and stealing and shit. After I locked out all the teachers that one night and played "P.I.M.P." on the speakers, I can *kinda* see why they had to expel me. Kinda. Yo, it was so easy! When we found out that Hafiz Shiraz wasn't showing up until Isha and we'd be unsupervised for a few hours, we put all the benches and chairs under the doorknobs and locked what we could. Shit was lit for a few hours.

Second madrasa, it probably wasn't a good idea to bring in a girl, but what was I gonna do? Mans didn't believe me when I said I chopped a shordie. What was I supposed to do? Not bring her? Oh man, the looks on their faces though when she walked in. What do you want me to say now? That I learned from my mistakes? This shit just goes on and on, and if it wasn't me, some other rando would've gotten expelled. I know exactly what they were doing before Jumma on Friday. There was a room of four boys who always snuck off and we all knew it. Who was helping *them* with their urges? But eh, the fuck you gonna do? This is Abbu's will, so may as well have fun with it right? As long as no one calls home, I should be okay. But I dunno if I can survive another expulsion. My ass is still sore from Pops the other day, smelling like nasty-ass car grease from the body shop. Mix that with the fresh fucking I got for stealing Heart Attack Four's car keys and you got someone with bruises on his bruises.

Nabil's back in our room, and I can see the droplets of water falling off his elbows. He picks up a pen and throws it at me, landing it square on my face. Jesus, how does he throw so well? It stings.

"Isha time, *bewakoof!*" His eyes bulge in mock insult.

I fucking love this dude. He's new, so he still has that impressionable mojo about him. I dunno how to describe it, but he's not jaded like Maaz or Nawaaz. They never should've moved me into the same room as him, haha.

We make it in time for Isha, but just barely. And you already know what's happening during Isha. Your boy's back in the forest, slaying orcs, riding on the shoulders of ents and being a general pain in the ass for Saruman. Honestly, destroying the One Ring would've been so much easier with me as the tenth member of the fellowship. Or as no member. I wouldn't do anything stupid like touch the *palantír* or put on the ring. I'd form an alliance with the good orcs. I'd find them, wherever they are. You can't tell me they're not out there. The fellowship didn't even bother trying. It's no wonder they fucked up the quest so bad and it took them forever to destroy the ring. Did they bother to ask for help from anyone named Grishnákh or Uglúk or Bokbok? Nah, they fucked up bad. My alliance of orcs would've had that shit destroyed. We would've saved Rohan without any issue, tamed the Nazgûl, all that shit. But nah, you see someone dark and with a difficult-to-pronounce name and it's automatic, on sight, that they're evil, eh? All good. I'm in my forest, doing my thing, raising an army to save y'all asses anyway. Stay vilifying us and shit. God, I can't remember what part of the prayer we're on anymore. Is this the third or fourth *rak'a*? Fuck, looks like the fourth.

I'd feel bad. Normally. I know I'm supposed to. This is supposed to be unvirtuous, harmful, eroding typa shit. Letting my mind wander like this. I know. But the same way Abbu's making a killing at the auto body shop, I was making a killing online. Sure, school was shit—you can't expect other kids to listen when you tell them *The Lord of the Rings* was all copied from Islam. But damn, online? I was killing it. I was almost at 3K on ladder, and my stories on MuggleNet were popping off. People say this shit isn't that serious, but it was to me. That was my living. So when Abbu sent me here, it was all over. So fuck it then. Imma behave like it's over. Remembering every last fucking thing until they beat it out of me. Some way or another, I'm going to become an *aalim*, right? No reason to feel bad about this stuff then. It's all a part of life. Nothing can distract or make me forget Allah. It's all a part of life. I turn my head to the right, hearing the first *salam*, and I see one of the older kids on my right, eyes closed, fixed on prayer. I turn my head left for the other *salam* and catch Nabil's eye before he quickly turns his head. Had his heart and mind been wandering as well? If they had, he was probably torturing himself with guilt like those weird Catholics with whips and shit for daring to allow his mind to wander during prayer. Poor Nabil. *It's all a part of life man.*

I said that shit like I had it all figured out. Like I knew what I was going to do the next day, or the next year, or the next ten years. The hopelessness, the listlessness, that zero-energy shit was still there and eased only a bit by being around Nabil, Maaz and Nawaaz. And to be honest, I probably *could* graduate. I probably *could* be anything they wanted me to be as long as they let me make my boys laugh every once in a while and remind them that Venom was weak to fire and sound, and that the Leafs had made a push by getting Joe Nieuwendyk. Those dumbasses needed to know.

When Nabil and I got back to our room after Isha, we waited for Maaz and Nawaaz to show up. They came most nights now after everyone went to bed, just to chill and chop shit for a bit.

When they hopped onto my bed, I got into it almost immediately. I'd been so close to making Nawaaz throw a plate of food at me at dinner, I knew I had him on the verge of a meltdown.

"Okay," I said, "I still think it's ridiculous that you guys think Nawaaz can beat the shit out of the older students when most of them don't even fight. They're huge!"

"Well that's exactly why I know I could run them," he replied. "They don't even fight!"

"Well, what about Heart Attack One then?" I asked.

"I could take him," Nawaaz said without hesitation.

We burst into laughter, applauding Nawaaz's ego. Now that Maaz and Nabil had joined in, though, it was only a matter of time before Nawaaz came flying at me.

"Fam, are you dumb? C'mon. Heart Attack One isn't even human. Have you ever even looked him in the eyes?" Maaz asked.

"I could take him. I swear," Nawaaz said, ignoring the question. "I've been looking for a reason to anyway. Always wanted to humble that asshole. Been itchin' to take him on for years."

"Uh-huh. Sure buddy," I said, trying to bait him.

"I understand kids and people close in age to us, but how you gonna talk about beating grown men in fights?" Nabil added on.

"Yeah you gotta chill fam. Mans acting like a big man all of a sudden. No one to kick his ass here. Could you even take the three of *us* at the same time?" I asked.

Nawaaz's answer was to come flying at me while Maaz and Nabil hoot-whispered and held him back while I danced on top of the bed, goading the barking giant. I loved him, but mans were so entertaining while he was this sensitive.

Very quickly though, I grew bored of the silent wrestling and dragged them down the dark hallway to the secret landing at the end. We'd found the seldom-used spot one night after dinner, and our sneaky creepy-crawlies now often led us there. The door to the landing was normally locked on the dorm side—the teachers and Sharmil Bhai probably did this on purpose, to prevent loitering—but once we figured out that the door was left unlocked on the stairwell side, we kept it slightly ajar so we could come and go as we pleased. All the other kids respected that this was where Maaz, Nawaaz, Nabil and I hung out and steered clear of the area for the most part.

This was where I told them about how one of the signs of Qiyamat was the future robot uprising, and how aliens were actually djinns in disguise, hiding on other planets and soon to arrive. Oh, I also made sure they knew that Alexander the Great was actually Muslim, and his true name was Zul-Qar-Nayn, and he was so much better than the white people version. I'm not sure if we met there to discuss those things, or if we discussed those things because we met there. Either way, I figured that was it. I'd entertain them like that, to infinity and beyond, 'til one day, we'd grow up. Beyond meant adulthood. Tears would exact their cost, and love would beget love. The end. 'Cept not. *Every* love must have its due.

CHAPTER 5

Dear Diary

The discovery of the stairwell landing was a godsend. The walls were thick enough there that we could yell about whether Orc truly *was* OP in *Frozen Throne* or go into minute detail about the size of Chun-Li's thighs or if we could truly flip an ounce for three bills. That's also where we made the acquaintance of Cynthia Lewis.

There was a second door on the landing—a smaller one that was kept permanently locked. We were told by the older students that this door led to a storeroom. We tried to open the door multiple times out of sheer boredom but always failed. Eventually, we just ignored it, until one evening when Farid overheard something.

We were on the darkened landing with the dorm's hallway light shining through the window when Farid spoke up.

"After Isha, I heard Maulana Ibrar tell Sharmil Bhai to check one of the generators on the roof. He said there were a few lights and power outlets that weren't working in the basement."

"And so?" Maaz asked. He was lounging on a pillow, like we

all were. We'd pulled them from unused rooms and beds to soften the landing.

"Well how's he going to get to the roof?" Farid asked.

"I don't know. How?"

Farid stretched his foot out and tapped the nondescript locked door a few times.

"You're an idiot." Maaz turned on his back to face away from Farid, in mock dismissal of his suggestion.

"No, wait. I'm serious, guys," Farid implored. "C'mon, think about it. What else do you want to do up here?"

"Shit, I don't know man, but that's the dumbest idea I've ever heard," I said in response, rolling my eyes. I didn't believe there could be roof beyond that door. Farid was always coming up with hare-brained schemes, and this one made no sense either.

"Have you seen any other locked door up here? Where else is there a locked door?" Farid asked.

"What does that even mean? So what if this door is locked?" Maaz said without turning back to face him.

"Think about it. How is Sharmil Bhai supposed to get up to the roof? And before you say, 'I don't care,' my answer is there's no way up there. We know every door in this building. The only way is through this one right here. At the very least, we oughta break into the damn room. It's bothering the hell outta me," Farid finished.

We were quiet. I was mulling over whether there truly was access to the roof at the top of the stairs, and what that would mean for me if there was. There was no real reason for us to venture up there, even if the view was nice. Nawaaz, no doubt, was thinking about what he could use the roof for, how it would give him power over the other students, provide him with leverage in his disputes. The knowledge of how to access the roof could be bartered or used as a threat if someone got in his way. Maaz would've been thinking about having another secret, and wondering whether the view up there could make him feel something. For me, it was simply a new challenge, an escape from boredom. I broke the silence first.

"Okay, how do we get past the door though? We've already tried literally everything."

"Not everything, my fine numbnutty friend. We haven't tried lockpicking," said Farid.

"What the fuck?" I started laughing, thinking it was something only done in movies.

"It's possible," Nawaaz said quietly. "But we'd have to do some research. We'd have to find, like, paper clips and needles and shit."

Maaz and I moved towards the door to check the lock. It was hard to see in the dark, but there was definitely a keyhole.

"Okay, so let's say we get some paper clips somehow. We try this door and then what?" Maaz was on his knees, trying to peer through the keyhole.

"Shit. Man, it's the middle of the night and I'm bored out my damn mind!" Farid replied. "You think I've thought that far ahead? I'm just tryna get through this door for now."

The next day, we realized we could get some safety pins or paper clips from Sharmil Bhai by claiming that we were low on clothespins and needed something to hang up our laundry or fix some clothes. That night we gathered again on the third-floor landing, with the rest of the student body none the wiser.

"Okay lemme try this shit." Nawaaz unbent the paper clips and approached the door on his knees. None of us had any idea what we were doing. He fiddled around for some time, jamming two of them inside, trying to wiggle them around. Nothing happened, of course.

Maaz shoved him aside. "Here, lemme try. You possess none of the grace of Musab ibn Umayr and all the pride of Abraha."

But after fiddling for some time, Maaz too came up empty. Farid took the paper clips from him and tried as well, but to no avail. It was finally my turn, although I had no clue what to do. My idea of lock picking came from video games, where you simply move the mouse around until you hear a click.

I held the lock up with one paper clip and gently wiggled the other around the keyhole. Maaz and Nawaaz were leaning against their pillows, resigned to failure.

Farid, too, was finally being realistic. "I should've known it wouldn't work," he said. "My bad, man. We've never picked locks before. Just being here sometimes makes me go crazy. I just . . . had to try something to get away, even if it was just to a place in my head where there was a roof beyond this—"

"Shhh, I gotta focus," I said.

The keyhole made sense. It was a problem we could solve. It was an obstacle with a solution. We couldn't go anywhere or do what we pleased, but I felt that if I wiggled the second paper clip around long enough, with enough precision, with enough bated movement, I could do this one thing.

"The door won't open man," Maaz said. "Just give it up."

He, Nawaaz and now even Farid were prepared to live with beaten spirits. I was not quite ready. Just then, I felt the lock's pins disengage, and I pushed the door handle down with my chin. The handle went down the entire way. My hands were too busy holding the pins up, and I was too afraid to move them and accidentally lock the door again. I held the handle down with my chin, my nose pressed up against the door, and with a muffled voice, I shouted to Farid.

"Oy *sala*, grab the handle and pull."

Farid approached quickly and pulled on the handle, swinging the door fully open. It gave way in silence, and Maaz and Nawaaz leapt to their feet. I was elated. It was the middle of the night, but I didn't care about hiding my excitement.

"Holy shit, I can't believe it. I fucking did it!" For the first time in a very long time, I was proud of myself. It didn't matter that I was committing a crime.

"Yeah you did!" Farid said, pushing me forward. Behind the door was a narrow dusty staircase leading up. The staircase was a faded reddish brown, and as we began to climb, it whined and groaned with each quiet footfall. At the top, we were submerged in darkness and scared shitless. When our eyes adjusted, I noticed a string in front of me and pulled it. A light bulb clicked on and blinded us. When we opened our eyes again, we looked around and realized we were in a storeroom, true to the rumour. But that didn't matter. What mattered is that we'd successfully done something we weren't supposed to.

We walked quietly around the room, sifting through brooms and mop buckets, looking for anything interesting. We found cleaning supplies and lockers with stacks of old towels and dishrags. We found unused lumber and tarps and even a few baseball bats and tennis rackets. We were rummaging through boxes when we heard Farid's voice ahead of us.

"Holy shit it's true. It's true! Guys, look!"

He was getting louder and louder, turning to shout over his shoulder at us. Maaz was rummaging through a cardboard box, and Nawaaz and I were against the walls going through hockey sticks when we turned and saw Farid silhouetted in a doorway by the wintry night sky.

"Holy shit, I can't believe it," I whispered.

We followed Farid through the door and onto the rooftop, cold gravel underneath our toes, biting into the soles of our feet. It hadn't begun to snow yet, but we felt the cold all the same. Up that high, the wind whistled, buffeting our bodies as we walked across the rooftop, trying to make it to the edge. We could tell we were moving towards the back of the building, away from the light that shone from the front facade. The crunch of our steps finally reached the edge of the roof, which came only up to our waists. As we looked out over the building, we were presented with a view of our enormous dried-out field and bare treetops and hills as far as the eye could see. The Ganaraska Forest seemed to stretch on forever, at least at night. The sky was starless, meeting the thin branches on the horizon in some blended, imperceptible mess. We knew we'd have a better view during the day. Still, it was a triumph.

Then we heard a voice behind us.

We turned and saw Maaz poking his head through the door. We'd assumed he was right behind us the whole time.

"I found something weird. You guys gotta come and take a look at this."

If the outside world could not tempt him to venture even a few steps onto the roof, we knew he must've found something truly alarming to call us back indoors. We walked back and re-entered the storeroom, immediately feeling the difference in temperature.

"Bro why'd you pull us off the rooftop!? The view was amazing."

Nawaaz was exaggerating. We couldn't see much from the edge, and the view was amazing only because it wasn't through a window. So perhaps it wasn't too much of an exaggeration.

"For this." Maaz tossed a brown leather book at us. Farid caught it and opened it up while Nawaaz and I peered over his shoulder on either side. We saw handwriting in blue ink.

"You found a . . . notebook?" I asked.

"No. Well, yeah. But look at it carefully. It's like a diary. A journal or some shit."

"Wait what?" I peered back at the notebook. At the top of each entry, every few pages, there was a date. Farid randomly picked an entry, and we all started reading in silence.

1/15/78

Dear Mark,

You might reach a point in your life where you're feeling low and sad and doubtful about your purpose. I go through days and weeks where I feel like everything is perfect and life with Catherine is all I could ever want or need. And then one morning, I'll wake up and want Sacred Heart to burn to the ground and for all of us to die. I mean, why should I care? Every morning, it's the same old business. Every day, it's the same shit. This morning it was, "The Devil—possessed with envy at the thought that we, beings of clay, would possess the inheritance that he'd forfeited forever through his sin—came to the woman, the weaker vessel, and poured the poison of his eloquence into her ear, blasphemously promising her that if she and Adam ate of the forbidden fruit, they would become as gods. Nay, as God Himself. Eve yielded to the wiles of the arch-tempter. She ate the apple and gave it also to Adam, who had not the moral courage to resist her. The poison tongue of Satan had done its work. They fell."

"The weaker vessel." Except I don't feel weak. I don't feel weak at all. I feel like I could challenge any man's faith and devotion to God. Maybe not the clergy, but I just mean a boy my own age. I know it's pride, but it's not pride against God. I just don't think I'm weak. It's strange. Women are too weak to resist Satan, but they're strong enough to convince Adam. Adam is strong enough to resist Satan, but he's too weak to resist women. Who's really weak and who's really strong? I feel like these are blasphemous questions, so I hope God forgives me. If you feel like this too—full of doubts and all that—I want you to know that it's important to turn to God and pray in those moments. Pray and talk to Catherine, haha. They're the only two ideas that make me feel anything at all. I can't really ask Father Michael after what happened the last time. Honestly though, why is Jesus always shown as white? Even in my own damn house, Jesus is white for some reason. Tsche! (That's the sound of me kissing my teeth.)

—Cyn

Something fell from a high wooden shelf, distracting us before we could read the next entry together. Our eyes had been focused on the diary, so we heard the loud clatter before we spotted a base-ball rolling in and then out of view. We looked at each other wide-eyed.

"*Wallahi* fam, this is *kabira*," Maaz said. "We can't be doing this. It's a sign."

He took the journal and chucked it against a wall. He shook his head, performed a quick *tauba* by touching each cheek with a few fingers in a mock slap and walked towards the stairs. Nawaaz followed. Farid quickly dove after the book, and I joined him. Maaz and Nawaaz turned to look at us.

"Those people are complete *jaahil*, man! Ignorant! *Kaafir!* Allah is going to strike us where we stand if we read that stuff and get influenced by it!" Nawaaz said, falling back on his faith with his brow furrowed.

Farid and I looked at each other. We would've laughed if the situation wasn't so serious.

"Who said anything about being influenced?" I asked. "It's just interesting is all. This is a thing from the past. From someone who used to be here."

"So what? None of that matters. Leave that shit there. Let's go before we get caught." Maaz gestured for us to follow him. He looked like he was running from a rolling boulder and had no time to spare. But it was the middle of the night, and the boulder was nothing but a baseball that had rolled through the storage room, reacting to the changing chill of a shrinking shelf.

Or perhaps his fear was founded. Finding the journal set into motion events we would all regret. Everyone except me. Maybe Maaz had a premonition then.

As we all walked back down the stairs, I noticed Farid still had the journal in his hands.

—

Over the next few days, Maaz and Nawaaz wanted nothing to do with the journal. They didn't even want to talk about it. They clammed up whenever we mentioned it, as if it were some sort of necromancy guide. They tried to pretend it didn't exist, willing the memory into darkness, which mirrored their reaction to all of their guilty acts. Don't tell, don't remember. Read no evil is no evil.

For our part, Farid and I refused to read any more of the journal without them. The four of us were together. We were a unit. If some of us weren't on board, none of us were on board. We weren't going to fracture our group into the readers and the non-readers. That would force me and Farid together and leave Maaz and Nawaaz to grow closer without us. We didn't need to discuss any of these repercussions. We were at that age when we implicitly understood how loyalty worked.

It was up to us to constantly badger and press Maaz and Nawaaz to take another look at the journal with us. We were kept so busy between classes and recitation that we didn't have much time during the week to read it, but nevertheless, I knew we were making headway with our incessant prodding.

"What if I read it out loud?" Farid said. "That way you wouldn't be guilty. Since you're just overhearing it, it will only be my sin."

"Are you an idiot?" Nawaaz replied. "If we listen willingly we're still at full fault. Even if we're not aware it's a sin, we're sinning. We can't read anything with *shirk* in it." The falling baseball had really spooked him and Maaz.

"How does that even make sense? That's never made sense. It's not even a sin to read the Bible. It's just some girl's journal," I said, shaking my head.

Rather than suggesting an answer, Maaz ignored my question and made his own case. "Idiot, what if we get caught with this damn thing in your room? What if one of the Heart Attacks or some shit comes bursting in here looking for something, and they see that and read it? They'd kill us! You think they give a shit that it might be harmless?"

This thought did fill us with fear, but Farid had never been one to feel too much of that. He ignored Maaz and continued with an even dumber suggestion.

"What if we tie you up? What if we, like, attack you two and 'force' you to listen to our reading? And you two 'fight back' but aren't actually liable since we're forcing it upon you. Huh? Checkmate."

Farid's proposal was so ridiculous I questioned why I was even on the same side as him. All I wanted to do was read the journal because it seemed interesting. It seemed like a wasted opportunity not to read something neat and new from the past. Plus, to me, Cynthia was kinda like us. It seemed as if she didn't like being at her school. She was questioning things and was clearly missing her old friends or something. Most of all, the journal was something that was not a tome on *fiqh* or a hadith from one of the *Kutub al-Sittah*. This was a glimpse of the world. I imagined that Farid was also interested in it because the diary was new and different and fresh. For him, it was a chance to pioneer and feel light bulbs go on, a spark to inspire some grand caper.

Nawaaz and Maaz were silent for some time, contemplating their answer.

"Honestly, I think in that situation, we'd have to yell and shout as loud as we could to shut out the reading," Nawaaz finally replied.

"Like cause a ruckus or some shit to drown out the sound." He was perfectly serious, rubbing his chin while looking on in the distance.

I should've known that a ridiculous question would beget an equally ridiculous answer. We were at a stalemate.

But not for long. Divine providence was at work, encouraging its agents to push us off cliffs and onto rock bottom so they could drag us and lift us up again while we clamoured for salvation and gratitude through blackened eyes and bloodied lips. If we were to taste the sweet nectar of the hereafter, we first had to taste the foul rottenness of this world so we'd have a reference point. Just a taste, though. Too much and we might come to prefer it.

—

That evening after Isha, Maulana Ibrar delivered a short sermon.

"Here in this place, my dearest youngsters, we are constantly beset by forces from the outside world trying to lead us astray," he began. "I understand. I do. It's difficult at your age to understand, or to repel all these things that are attempting to lead you astray." His tone was that of a man trying to relate to a generation he had nothing in common with. He was asking us to move towards him and meet him halfway in trying to understand him. We did, but it was still too far away.

"Our Lord has created for us a perfect faith to guide us," he went on. "And if we will obey His word we will enter into eternal life; but if, after all that had been done for us, we still persist in our wickedness, there remains for us but one destination: Jahannam. A truly wretched, decrepit pit of despair, with a smell so foul the angels turn their nose in disgust at the *mention* of it. It is said that whosoever smells Jahannam even once feels their nostrils burn and bleed in reaction. This abode of demons and lost souls is filled with fire and smoke and cramped beyond anything you've seen. In the prisons here, we at least have *some* liberty of movement, even if it's only within the four walls of our cell or the dirty prison yard outside. Not so in Jahannam. There, because of the great number of *kuffar*, *jaahil* and *munafiqun*, you are heaped together in a smoking hot pit, the walls stretching on for as long as you can see. Heaping piles of bodies, burning and writhing in pain. The smell of burning flesh will enter your nostrils and force you to retch and vomit while you try helplessly to move, bodies above you screaming in pain as well. Your movement is so constricted that you would not be able to even remove from your eye a small maggot that would gnaw at it. And the deepest spots in that pit are reserved for those in our position, who knew better but neglected to *do* better. People like us, in institutions of learning meant to illuminate our communities, who still entered into partnerships with Iblis. People who had the knowledge and understanding to save themselves but chose instead to waste their time, cavort with girls and carry themselves in a shameful manner, swearing and lying. My beloved youngsters, I understand that you are challenged here. But please stay away and refrain from *kabira*. Don't hide things or bring things into this place that are not allowed. Posters, music, phones, drugs. You have a golden opportunity before you. You will be able to look back on these days in years to come as some of the most blessed years of your life. Don't waste them in mischief with bad company and *shaytaan* amongst you! When you die, you will cry and beg in the grave for another chance while snakes bite at your feet and ankles again and again without the ability to move or stop them, but no excuse will work then. It will be too late, my dear youngsters."

We'd been caught in a captivating reverie, entranced by the words of the maulana, afraid to look away and into each other's faces, horrified of the reproach we'd find in our classmates' eyes. After we were dismissed and headed up to the dorms for the night, I noticed Maaz and Nawaaz following me and Farid to our room. We didn't protest, but I remember hoping the sermon hadn't affected them too much. I, too, was bothered by the timing, by how close to home the sermon seemed, as if the *ustads* possessed some preternatural knowledge of what we'd been up to.

As soon as we entered our room, Maaz and Nawaaz started diving through Farid's stuff—going into his drawers, ripping off his sheets and pillowcases. Unlike the maulanas and Sharmil Bhai, who went through our stuff with heavy-handed ignorance, *we* all knew the best places to hide things, and it showed. Farid and I looked at each other with surprise, shocked that our friends could react so violently to a sermon. But trying to stop them would have caused a noisy fist fight, so instead we just watched them act like invigilators. Even without a word exchanged, we knew exactly what they were looking for. Farid and I were still trying to compose ourselves and our defence of the journal when we were interrupted by the door opening behind us. The creaking sound made us all turn from the messy scene to face the intruder.

Heart Attack One was standing there with a yardstick, a strange grin on his face. His beard stretched from ear to ear, his skin shiny with an after-Isha glow. The hallway lighting illuminating his silhouette.

"Hmmm. What do we have here? Hmm?" He entered and began counting the inhabitants in a slow and methodical manner. The way he was counting suggested that he was expecting to find a whole army of us in there.

"One . . . two . . . and three . . . and four. Let me see. Who else? Who else is in here?" He turned to each one of us.

We stared back, confused. Heart Attack One looked inside the closet and then turned back to face us again, having concluded that there was indeed no one else there.

"What are you doing in here?" he asked of us all.

"Uh, this is our room," Farid said, pointing at me with his eyebrows raised.

"What are you two doing here?" He pointed the stick at Maaz and Nawaaz.

They said two different things at once.

"We were trying to get back some notebooks we lent," Nawaaz said.

Overtop of him Maaz said, "We were just saying goodnight."

Yardsticks in hands beg to be used, but you can't use them if a student is simply retrieving their school notebook. You needed a crime.

"Goodnight? Goodnight!? There is no goodnight!" Heart Attack One said with a leer, seizing upon the Western convention. "You were doing *masthi*. Let me see." He bullied past us, swinging the yardstick to force me to dodge to the side while he shoved through. He poked Maaz out of the way and then noticed all the opened drawers and the mess on the bed.

"I understand. Maulana gives very nice *bhaiyan*, and now you want to be good students. You're hiding it, no? You're hiding . . .

phone?" He turned to us with a knowing smile. The gold cap on his head beamed from the light entering the room from the hallway. We huddled in that half-light, perplexed and scared. We knew we had no cellphone, so we should have been safe on that charge, but the charges hardly mattered at Al Haque. We were now suspects. And this was Heart Attack One.

We had no idea which of us had come up with the Heart Attack nicknames—we only knew that the most ferocious maulana had been so ferocious he'd inspired the first moniker. The other Heart Attacks were added to the club only because we became wanton with membership and wanted a way to classify cruelty. In truth, Heart Attack One was in a class of his own. His name was Furkan, but almost nobody called him Maulana Furkan. It was always "Shhh, Heart Attack One is coming," or "Heart Attack One is gonna catch you." His brown skin bordered on purple, seemingly permanently flushed by insult. His eyes were bloodshot, as if he'd been crying his entire life (though we'd never seen him drop a tear). His long, full black beard did nothing to hide his mottled face. We all had vague ideas on how the man was raised. Things we'd overheard in the conversations between adults: that he came from a small village in Punjab, that his father had been eaten by a tiger, that he used to fight djinns and believed every child was possessed by one. We knew he was married with a young son. It had taken him some time to find a wife. Most *ustads* were married by their mid-twenties, but Heart Attack One was not most *ustads*. He seemed pleased any time he caught kids making mischief. Most anyone else who cared was usually sad, angry or disappointed, but Heart Attack One *relished* mischief. Every time he caught one of us, it seemed to affirm some belief of his. He was one of those people you never needed to be warned about. His aura suggested zero warmth—no one would ever ask him for directions. Even when I spotted him on my first day, I knew to steer clear; the body language of the other students and teachers told me everything I needed to know. He taught one of the younger classes, for first-year kids still memorizing the Quran, and appeared stuck, perhaps comfortably, in enforcing rote memorization. Maybe the *ustads* knew this was all he was good for, but in truth, he wasn't even good for this. His fury was unparalleled. We had no idea how he lived his life at that level every day. Never growing exhausted, never dimming his eyes to a look of lethargy or calm. Instead, his eyes burned until you couldn't meet them. No one could. No one matched that gaze.

Everyone knew that the yardstick perpetually clutched in his balled fist had a nail sticking out on one end. The point was driven into the wood and would never leave a permanent mark. We'd never be cut too deep. Nothing that we could show our parents when we went home for break. They wouldn't have cared much anyway. Everyone was complicit. Parents traded stories from childhood and laughed. Punishments became a creative exercise. Chickens, walls, slaps. Would we laugh too one day?

Sometimes at night, students could hear hammering or weird sawing noises coming out of Heart Attack One's office. The next day he'd emerge with a new instrument of torture in his hand. Steel hangers wrapped and coiled together. Sticks glued and taped. Branches that had been stripped of bark and reinforced with rope. Would we laugh?

Heart Attack One led us to his office. The worst punishments were meted out behind closed doors. This was sanctioned. He'd been kept on a leash, and then Maulana Ibrar had probably had a private word with him, asked him to go through the dorms. "See if you notice anything. I overheard some of the students discussing a phone." And he'd taken to the task like it was his sole purpose in life. Because it was.

Heart Attack One closed the door behind him and turned to face us. "Hold out your hands," he said.

We each held out our right hand as he stood before us. He raised his stick above his head and brought it down first on Farid, who yelped in pain. Then he struck Nawaaz, who let out a hiss. Then Maaz, who screamed. And finally me. I hated that I was last. I pulled my hand away imperceptibly at the last second to lessen the blow, but it didn't do much. It killed.

"Which one of you has the phone?" he demanded, walking back to Farid.

"What? We don't have shi—anything!" Farid protested.

The stick came down again. He was striking us with the nail side. Again, he struck Nawaaz, Maaz and me on our palms, completing another round. My palm was red. I felt the burn of an open cut. Farid was shaking his hand around, trying not to squirm.

"Where did you get it?" Heart Attack One demanded, this time addressing Nawaaz.

"We don't know what you're talking about. We don't have any phone. You can go look—"

He couldn't finish before the stick came down hard. Truth and lies did not matter. This was something Heart Attack One was born to do. The ultimate fury in the hands of its most ultimate practitioner.

"Who has the phone, then? We know you're all troublemakers. Always up to no good. If you don't have it, you must know who does. Who is it? Hmm?" he asked Maaz.

"We have no idea. We would never bring a phone into this place," Maaz replied tersely.

Heart Attack One swung again, harder. We heard the crack in the air, the slap on skin, and Maaz winced and held his eyes shut, though I could tell they watered. No one is the master of their own body. All bodies betray their weaknesses and react unbidden to heavy blows.

I was next. Heart Attack One struck my hand, and I dropped to my knees in pain. This seemed to be the wrong thing to do. I felt the instrument of pain against my back.

"Get up, idiot! You have no right to sit. Up!"

I stood up, blocking out the pain as Heart Attack One beat me into mute submission. After completing another round on the hands of the others, he turned to me with a question.

"Why you hang out with these *banchods*? Huh? You're going to become *shaytaani* like them."

I stayed silent.

"Answer me. Say something." He poked my lower gut with the stick.

"I don't know."

"Idiot. What d'you know? Having golden opportunity here to learn and study and instead you're always up to mischief. You heard Maulana Ibrar's beautiful *bhaiyan*. What happens if you waste time and do mischief here together? *Always* together. Okay no problem. Then show me your *shaytaani* friendship. High-five each other."

We looked back at him, confused.

"Come on. Goodfriendsno? High-five. Come on." There was a wicked smile on his face when he said this, but his eyes remained that bloodshot red, absent of life.

We looked at each other and then back at Heart Attack One. His expression changed, a barely perceptible shift to anger.

"Hey, I'm not joking. You high-five him." He gestured with the stick to Farid and Nawaaz.

They held up their uninjured hands and weakly high-fived.

"Oh! Nonono. Not like this. With your hands." He motioned towards their damaged hands.

My stomach sank into hell. Farid held up his swollen red hand and met Nawaaz's weakly in the air.

"No! Properly! Proper high five. I want to hear the *chhap*! Like goodfriends." He said "goodfriends" like it was one word. Like goodfriends was on a different level than good friends.

Farid and Nawaaz attempted their high five again, but it was no use. Their hands were red and swollen and weak. Heart Attack One didn't care. Their disobedience incensed him. He began to beat them mercilessly.

"I told you properly!" he shouted.

They weren't being beaten over a phone. They were being beaten because they'd disobeyed Heart Attack One and he enjoyed violent correction.

"Again!" he shouted.

Pain was calculated this time. Farid and Nawaaz had a scale where on one side there was a flurry of blows from the stick, and on the other side there was a painful high five. And the flurry of blows showed no sign of ending. So Farid and Nawaaz high-fived each other properly and screamed. They fell to the floor and writhed in pain, holding their wrists at the base of their palms.

Heart Attack One turned to me and Maaz. "You two, same thing. High-five like goodfriends."

We knew better at this point than to deliver a light one. Despite this, our palms were so raw that we failed. We held back. Our bodies didn't want to participate. Heart Attack One's eyes bulged out when he saw our disobedience. I knew how to assuage the man, however. I grabbed Maaz's elbow and made a big show of preparing another high five. I scrambled and knew Heart Attack One would love my performance. It would say so much about his power.

I bit my lip and held my breath and struck Maaz's palm with mine. I felt like my skin was going to split and burst. I fell to my knees, this time permitted, and held my wrist to numb the pain. I could've sworn I was going to lose my hand. How this punishment, this pain, didn't lead to death I couldn't understand. Who had perfected this cruelty how many years ago and then imparted it to Heart Attack One? Or was this Heart Attack One's own divine inspiration saving us?

"Don't ever hide phones from me!" he shouted as Maaz and I rolled on the floor in pain. "I will find it! I know you know!"

With that, he went to his office door and unlocked it, swinging it open. He started kicking us in that direction. We scramble-crawled to freedom and immediately ran to the bathroom to douse our hands in cold water. It was late at night, and the bathroom and ablution area were empty. The four of us sat on stools next to each other, running our palms under freezing water.

Farid had his eyes closed, but he opened one eye to peek at me.

"Bilal has a phone eh," he said.

94

We all suppressed laughter, shaking our heads. The silence of the room was broken only by the torrent of water falling on our hands.

"You still have that journal?" Maaz asked through closed eyes.

"Yeah," Farid replied, without bothering to open his.

"Good. We gon' read that whole shit. Word for fuckin' word."

I shut my eyes too, joining them. I didn't want to see anything. We sat in silence together, four boys in a row with their hands stuck out under taps meant to wash away sin. The water broke on our palms and tried to drown out the pain, parting across swollen skin, droplets running rivers across grooves and creases. It cascaded down our fingertips and crashed onto the tiled drain below, like waterfalls so magnificent they were attributed to angels. This, though, was just four bonded boys—bonded two ways now—making waterfalls so magnificent they could only be attributed to us.

CHAPTER 6

Dogs Gon' Eat

We decided to read no more than one entry every few days so we could ration the diary's entertainment for as long as possible. It stirred something in us, though I didn't know it at the time. Connected us to another world and another life, tethering us to things we had been warned about. Sunbeams and verdant grass as far as the eye could see. Twilight and dusk. What the night looks like from the top of Tokyo Tower. Why Oddjob was fucking illegal to use in *GoldenEye*. What flowers in November meant. But how could you ever articulate these things at a tender age? You couldn't. Instead, we let the diary work its magic and keep that hardy part of us alive. The part that had doubts about being at Al Haque. And as the diary's hold grew, its whispers of another life stoked our desire to escape and discover it. Though there was no path yet, no route to leaving, the cogs were beginning to turn.

In those cold November mornings after Fajr, or in any of the unplanned silent moments we were accidentally given, we'd sneak off to read the journal together, either in the stairwell foyer or, if it was warm enough, on the roof. We eventually figured out that Cynthia was addressing the entries to her baby brother.

9/12/77

Dear Mark,

I know you're too young to read this right now, but I'm going to write it to you anyway. Just things I see, things I think and some advice for you for when you're older. Dad gave this diary to me when he dropped me off at school, and I know girls usually write the names of their crushes in it or something, but I think we're safe from all that here. Hah. So I'll just write to you instead. I hope you won't mind.

—Cyn

"Nah, that one's too short," Farid said one morning on the roof. "Read another one. I can't walk around checking the sky for lightning bolts if it's not nice and long." He spoke through a mouthful of Bubblicious he'd bummed off Nawaaz, who I'd seen extort it from a younger kid.

I flipped through a few pages to find a longer entry.

11/30/77

Dear Mark,

Honestly you won't believe this, but Catherine and Vivian took part in an activity and didn't kill each other. I don't know if I told you about Vivian, the girl at the top of the class. I mean she's nice enough—just a bit stiff and prudish, if you'll forgive my saying so. That's the girl I'm trying to beat this semester anyway. Catherine hates her though. God knows why, but they always get into snarky fights that are awkward for the rest of us. Except today! When the teacher kicked us all out for the afternoon I thought we'd just wander around in the snow 'til dinner. Apparently, playing sockey in the hallways is equal to blasphemy against the Holy Spirit? I dunno. So there we were, on Sacred Heart grounds, knee-deep in the snow because Catherine had an idea I just couldn't say no to. We were making a fort, or at least something with walls, sliding and piling up snow around us, but before we knew it, everyone else had joined in and started helping us. Catherine was like a proper army sergeant or something, barking out orders and getting everyone to follow along. It was amazing. Even Vivian wanted to be a part of it. I thought Catherine wouldn't let her help us, but she laid off and let her pack and push the snow around us 'til we had a little house-thingy we could sit inside. And you know what's crazy? It didn't even feel that cold. At least, I don't remember it being cold at all. When we were finally hanging out inside the fort, watching the white sky turn mauve, it started to feel kinda nice. Like it didn't matter where we were, or that some of us didn't like the others. Catherine didn't bring up Vivian tattling on us last week even once. I think that's what they mean when they say you can feel the Holy Spirit inside you sometimes.

—Cyn

"Wait, wait, hold up! How you building snow forts with a snitch?" Nawaaz said through his own chewing gum, incredulous. "Nah fam, that's wack. How you gon' allow that?"

The rest of us just looked at each other and shrugged. Maybe a different time had different rules? Maybe we were too hard, or maybe they were too soft?

We took turns hiding the journal. Our paranoia meant that every few days, we changed the hiding place—sometimes in my pillow case, sometimes in the lining of Nawaaz's winter coat and sometimes right on the seldom-used bookshelves in the main prayer hall. We believed it was better that way. Less chance the book would be found in a search. Meanwhile, the teachers were all misled into thinking that I had some latent talent, some hidden faith that needed a bit of coaxing. I just needed to be pushed, encouraged. We all knew the truth though: I just didn't want to get beat. I didn't want any bruises. We couldn't all be Farid.

I wanted to fly under the radar, but unfortunately, doing well accidentally put me *on* the radar. Surah Bakarah, Al-Imran, An-Nisa—all were committed to memory, and I was well into the next few chapters. I was knocking on ten. It wasn't too difficult. What else did I have to do? Here, away from distractions like the mystery of the Unown and the solution to the Water Temple, I could focus on *tajweed*, which sounds to lengthen and hold, which prophet came after the next.

I needed to know more about Cynthia though. We all did. The four of us became so curious about what Al Haque was before it was Al Haque, and whether some answers from its past could provide us with a way to escape. Had anyone left Sacred Heart before their time? Were there secret passageways or excuses we didn't know about? We decided to ask the longest-tenured maulana, Maulana Hasan—the one who taught our *hifz* class, and whom Farid had locked out of the prayer hall during his first week at the school.

"Maulana-sab, what was Al Haque before it was a madrasa?" I asked one day after everyone had finished reciting their lessons to him.

"This was a full-time Catholic madrasa for girls, which makes it a good fit for us," he said.

"Why does that make it a good fit?" Maaz asked.

"Once a place has been used for a religious or spiritual purpose, it's better for it to stay that way, even if it was for a different faith. I remember they didn't have many students left when the committee bought it. There were some incidents too—kids skipping class, up to all sorts of nonsense. *Alhamdulillah*, it's in much better hands now."

Clearly, he was more clueless than Maulana Ibrar and the other maulanas, who were more aware of how deep our mischief ran. Maaz and I were quizzing him about the madrasa to probe for any path of escape, any weakness in the infrastructure of our existence—building code violations, fire hazards, even ghost stories—that might give us some ammunition as we built our desire to get away. If Farid or Nawaaz had asked the maulana these same questions, it would have been an immediate red flag. By then, everyone knew Farid to be what he was, concerned only with this life. And Nawaaz was Nawaaz, the myth that never went out of style, the eternal banger, the scary reminder that violence motivated, that fear could inspire respect. The true face of man, focused on dulling pain by causing pain. Where creation and destruction were synonyms.

—

One morning during review, we were all humming through our respective chapters when we heard a loud thud. Everyone stopped to see where the sound had come from. Maaz and Nawaaz's bench had broken. A leg had somehow come off, and the plank had fallen to the carpet at an odd angle. The Qurans and *kitabs* slid down to the end where Maaz was sitting. Nawaaz was at the front of the class with the teacher, going through his chapters, but the noise had forced them both to look up. Maulana Hasan looked around for an extra empty bench that wasn't there. He spotted me before I could turn back to my pages and gestured for me to come nearer.

"Nabil, take Maaz to Maulana Furkan's class and get an empty bench. I think he has few spares. Don't take long."

He dismissed me with a wave and returned to Nawaaz's *Qirat* to immediately correct him on a mispronounced word. Even while hopping in and out of a conversation, Maulana Hasan was able to identify where Nawaaz was and correct him accordingly. Our *ustad*'s dedication to teaching and commitment to the word of Allah was resolute and unwavering. Sure, he was quick to anger and maybe a little less personable than Maulana Ibrar, but these weren't flaws that counted. That's why we lived scared.

I motioned for Maaz to follow me, but as we walked away, Farid latched on to my leg and slid along the carpet while I tried to shake him.

"Take me with you!" he demanded.

"Fam we're just getting a *patla*. We'll be right back," I answered.

"Let me come too!"

I rolled my eyes in annoyance. "Lemme go before Maulana-sab sees!"

"Please . . . I'm dying." He let go though, and soon his voice trailed off. We could only afford enough sympathy for two.

Through the main hallway, we took the basement steps to Heart Attack One's class. We followed the sounds of children coming from an open doorway, and we could also hear the chaos and ruckus and what we thought was the recitation of Arabic as we neared the bottom of the stairs. We weren't really afraid because we were on official business, protected by Maulana-sab's mission. When we entered the room, though, we were met with a scene that instantly changed how we felt.

The faded teal carpet matched the one in the principal's office, but it had odd, intermittent stains across the surface because the room did double duty as the dining area. Like a monarch, Heart Attack One sat at the far end of his throne room, facing the entrance and whoever came through that doorway. The class benches were positioned around him in a giant U-shape. Maybe thirty or forty kids sat around him, and in the middle of the U was dead space. Or what should have been dead space. For Heart Attack One, however, it was a stage. The small bench directly in front of him was reserved for students presenting their memorized material. There was a kid there right now, but he and Heart Attack One were not paying any attention to each other. Like the rest of the class, they were both transfixed by what was happening on the stage. They'd barely registered that Maaz and I had entered the room and were instead watching the two kids in the middle, locked in a pitched fist fight.

Maaz and I exchanged a look. I had no idea what the fuck was going on, and we both gave the stage a wide berth as we slowly made our way towards Heart Attack One.

Kids were cheering and laughing, and I couldn't spot a single one actually reading his *kitab*. No one was sad or despondent. I was desperately searching their faces for the same concern that I felt, but I couldn't find anyone in the raucous audience who looked worried. The kids were enraptured, and I could see why, but I couldn't understand what was happening. Why were these kids fighting? Why was Heart Attack One doing nothing? What was this?

When we reached Heart Attack One, he motioned for us to sit down next to him without breaking his deep red gaze from the fight.

"*Beto!*" he commanded.

We sat and faced the fight, uncomfortable but a comfortable distance away from Heart Attack One. It was too far for him, however. He leaned over and slapped my thigh, grabbing on to it and pulling me closer to him while still watching the fight.

"*Areh*, come. You won't get hurt. Get a nice view!" He pulled me in even closer, and our thighs touched, mine burning from the heat of his contact. I cursed Maaz's luck.

We watched the two kids exchange blows, holding and grabbing on to each other's kurtas for leverage. They looked to be about the same age and were pulling and shoving each other to cheers and jeers. One was a black kid—one of the few at Al Haque, and the only one in this class—and the other was a pale Middle Eastern kid. The black kid somehow managed to grab the Middle Eastern kid with both hands around the waistband of his pants. The second kid tried to detach himself from the first kid's grip by raining blows on his back. It wasn't working. The first kid wouldn't let go. He started swinging the other boy around in circles, around and around the carpet, then slammed him down, rag-dolling the kid across the floor. The pale boy's blows were growing weaker and weaker while his assailant's strength showed no signs of relenting. He kept picking the kid up and slamming him down. Then he swung him around one final time and shot-put him into a bench with finality.

The bench tumbled, sending the word of Allah flying and kids scrambling out of the way. All the kids laughed their approval while the loser lay over the bench, tired, immobile and hurt, his chest heaving with exertion. If he got up, the fight would continue. He wouldn't get up. He was exhausted. Sweat covered his face as he lay on his back, one arm draped over the upturned bench.

"Come on, Pathan-bhai!" Heart Attack One's voice boomed out over the class.

The kid didn't move. Heart Attack One shook his head.

"*Sala*," he muttered. "We bring them here and they go soft—"

He slammed his hand on the leg of the bench twice, and immediately, on cue, the entire class went back to their *kitabs*. Reading the Quran, learning or memorizing *du'as*, *fiqh*. The room was filled with recitation and learning, holy deeds and prayers. Angels were among them, just like that, vouching for them in the eyes of Allah. It was as if there had been no fight. No perform-ance. No respite. No violence. As if they'd been reading like that for the last thousand years and were ready to read for a thousand more. As long as you didn't address what had happened, as long as you didn't turn to your neighbour to say, "Hey, that was kinda fucked up, right?" as long as you weren't allowed a second, a grad-ual moment or a gradual anything, you could treat it as a blip in time. We were reading, there was a blip in time, and then we were reading again. Did something happen? Did we scream? Did we laugh? We're reading now though.

The only indication that anything had occurred was the lop-sided cap on the Pathan kid's head. He was reading softly, a little tired but otherwise acting as if nothing had happened. The black kid was right beside him, doing his own reading. No one noticed or cared that the cap was falling off the Pathan kid's head at a strange angle.

"This Abdi is a real fighter," Heart Attack One said. "Those Somali *kallus* are tough." He slammed a fist into his hand and turned to us with a glib smile.

We stared blankly back at him, unsure of how to respond.

"Okay, what do you want?" he asked.

"Maulana Hasan sent us here to get an extra bench. We're wondering if you have one. We have to take one up if you do," I said.

Heart Attack One granted our request with a dismissive brush of his hand. As we carried the bench out of the lair, we heard two more loud, sharp slams from his direction and we froze. Had we done something wrong? We turned to face him. We were lucky. He wasn't even looking at us.

"You. And you," he said, pointing to two kids.

He said it like he'd deliberated upon the decision for days. Like he was pronouncing an appointment that he'd been mulling for some time. Like he'd done the math, and not come up with two boys at random. This was an equation. And honestly, maybe for him it was. Maybe he had a ranking in his head. I know those kids did. The S tier, the A tier, the B tier. You know damn well they had a leaderboard. KOs, wins by decision. No contests. What else were we to do? Watch each other fight and *not* notice that someone was undefeated?

If this was to be our national sport, then by God we would own it. And if you didn't like it? Too bad, you lost. No one gave a shit, least of all your parents. I mean, they sent you here after all, to be placed on Heart Attack One's roster as you woke up in cold sweats all week and wondered if this was the day you fought for him.

"You. And you." He said it like he'd known for days that it was going to be those two. How could it have been anyone else? His *salat* had been disturbed, his *zikr* interrupted, his teaching cut short—all by the images of who should fight next. What would make for a great match? How long would it last? Trading blows. Could there be blood? Did names like Khan and Abbas mean anything anymore? He probably knew these were bloodthirsty thoughts, full of desire and therefore forbidden, but he had them all the same. I'm sure he treated them like his very own blips in time when they happened. I'm sure he convinced himself that the fighting league was just upholding a *sunnah*. After all, even the Prophet had wrestled. How different was this from kabbadi or pehlwani? And even if the other *ustads* wouldn't approve, was this not a blessed endeavour as long as he was there to make sure no one got seriously injured? I knew he thought like this because we thought like this. There wasn't much separating us.

Two kids who'd probably been nervous wrecks all week stepped into the ring to thunderous cheering and bench slapping. Heart Attack One pretended not to hear the shameless excitement. In a weird way, the two kids seemed relieved. No one ever knew when they would fight, just that at some point they would. There was no preparation for this. Their time had come. Anxiety was gone and their sentence was delivered. There were no more nightmares of fighting naked. No more questions of when. The answer was now.

Maaz and I couldn't handle it. Fighting was one thing. An organized contest run by older kids was something too. But a brawling league run by a maulana out of a religious institution's basement was a whole other thing altogether. And run with no fear. Heart Attack One knew he was untouchable and believed his endeavour to be small mischief. If he was caught, he would get a talking-to, and then he'd obliterate the rat who sold him out.

Of all the crimes I'd been a part of, and all the ones I'd continue being a part of, this would not be one of them. We were not whatever Heart Attack One was. But that knowledge did not help us feel lighter on our walk out of that room; our silence was a burden that made the bench we carried even heavier. We'd be no rats about the fight league, but that meant leaving the boys there in that room to die their first slow death. Something about sacred bodies moulting into the profane. Borrowed bodies. Dust returning to dust. The murder of something that was once respected. We'd say nothing, just as those kids would say nothing. Fear motivated. And Heart Attack One made Cletus Kasady look like a Teletubby. Sabretooth was Barney compared to him.

That night before Isha, Maaz and I attempted to explain what we'd seen to Farid and Nawaaz. We were in the warm prayer hall waiting for *adhaan*, strewn about on the red carpet in small groups of three and four. Our morality groups. We could tell just by looking which group was what. There was the stupid but pious group. They never knew their lessons and suffered for it, but they also never snuck out and were generally well-behaved. There were the fucked-up time-wasters. They didn't bother studying, and the maulanas had stopped beating them or even calling on them to recite their material. They were lost causes and would most likely be sent home at the end of the month. They were here due to behavioural problems, had bounced around from madrasa to madrasa and would eventually disappear into some backwater province and never see an escalator again. There were the four of us, believing we were better than we were. And then there was Hafiz Abdullah, near the front, alone, always alone. His head buried in a Quran making fools of us all.

Farid had once tried to flash Hafiz Abdullah an MP3 player under a bench with a shit-eating grin. Mostly just to flex, and because Farid was Farid. Allah knows how Farid had even managed to sneak it into the madrasa, and I doubt he had any reason for it other than to flaunt it. Farid wiggled his eyebrows and Hafiz Abdullah twisted his wrist in a "What the fuck is that?" gesture, and we knew we were done. Even if you didn't know what it was, the absence of both interest and condemnation told us we spoke two different languages entirely. Here, where there was nothing but scripture, no scenery other than tired carpets and tired looks, anyone would be interested in any electronic device. Hafiz Abdullah was not anyone. His slicked-back hair tucked neatly beneath his black cap gave him the lean and learned appearance that he earned every day. That was one of the reasons Hafiz Abdullah was left alone.

After Isha was finished, we hung around in the prayer hall, speaking quietly in small groups as people finished *sunnah*, *nafl* and *wajib* at their own paces. Maaz, Nawaaz, Farid and I held a whispered consultation.

"He's making kids kill each other," I repeated. It needed

repeating because Farid, Nawaaz and even Maaz didn't seem to take it seriously. "They're beating on each other like it's some sort of fight club. It's not right."

"So what do you want to do?" Nawaaz asked. "Snitch?"

"No, what the fuck? Is that what I said? *Wallahi* don't cheese me." Even the suggestion of snitching had to be met with vehement rejection.

"I don't think the other teachers know though," Maaz said softly. "And I don't think they'd want to know."

"Yeah, and they won't know," Farid said. "I don't know why you guys are acting surprised. Heart Attack One *been* doin' this shit his whole life prob'ly. You guys are acting like you found out something new about him."

"So that's it then eh? We just let these kids kill each other?" I asked.

"Listen man," Nawaaz replied, "maybe things were soft for Mr. Bengali boy growing up, but it's not a big deal. You just joined this year. Mans grew up in this. Did the kids even give a shit?" He was perplexed, and he'd pissed me off. My credibility was being questioned once again.

"Oh please, I've probably taken worse beatings than you," I retorted.

Before Nawaaz could respond, Maaz chimed in. "Honestly, this typa shit been happening since I was in that class too. Nawaaz and Farid prob'ly seen similar shit. And kids beating on each other while teachers watch is one thing. It's whatever. I'm here for it. But now that I think of it, this shit *did* look like some messed-up league. Some organized shit. I don't think anyone would be okay with it. Shit, we might even get in trouble cuz we knew and didn't do shit."

"League shit?" Farid asked. "Like winners and losers?"

"Yeah man," I replied.

"So who's on top?" he asked.

I looked around the room to see if the black kid was still there and spotted him.

"That kid."

"Eyy . . . 'mali gang!" Nawaaz whispered.

"Gang gang!" Farid's words did not come out as a whisper though.

We were immediately hushed by a stern look from Sharmil Bhai, who was trying to do some *zikr* on a *tasbeeh*.

We held on to each other, silent but shaking from mirth. We couldn't help it. I knew I was getting nowhere that night. We all hated Heart Attack One, but kids fighting each other was actually sickly entertaining. Yes, most of me hated it, but we were slowly dying and could see the entertainment of the dying now. If we were going to take on Heart Attack One, our argument about children's suffering wouldn't hold up; we'd need to bait the man into a graver crime. We could see right into each other and knew exactly how black our hearts were. And whatever was left, we'd find out about.

Nawaaz

It was my turn to read from the journal, even though I wasn't really 'bout it. But that's how it is. If your boys are down for something, you do it.

9/22/77
Dear Mark,

Sometimes I wonder why would you be allowed to become a priest and not me? Father Michael says it's because Jesus was a man, and so a man would be closer to understanding his struggles and would be closer to him. I guess that kinda makes sense. But it's still . . . unfair. Mary Magdalene was twice the disciple any of the men were. When Catherine suggested the only reason the other disciples didn't like Mary was because they couldn't have sex with her, I was mortified.

I hope Catherine's all right. I haven't seen her in a while and I'm worried. To be honest, life without her here would be awful dull. I know the other girls think the same, even if they won't admit it. They're way too happy just to parrot along and graduate, to get out of here. I wonder if she'd like to be friends though. I feel like I could help her y'know?

The other day I walked in on her and a couple of the older girls smoking grass in their room with the windows open. They didn't give me too much trouble, though—just made me promise I wouldn't tell anyone, which isn't an issue. I'm no rat. But it got me thinking. Wouldn't you be able to help a parishioner better if you shared the same experiences as them? If they're struggling with drug addiction or marijuana use or whatever, wouldn't relating to them maybe give you something to say that they could connect to? I feel like Catherine would be able to give better advice than a lot of the Fathers cuz, y'know, she's actually been there. That said, if I ever catch you with grass, Mark, I will personally murder you.

Oh, and remember that if you ever want to become a priest, you'll have to show me you know more than me. Otherwise I won't let you. Don't care, sorry.

—*Cyn*

"Damn that's kinda deep," Nabil said.

I rolled my eyes in front of him. I wasn't getting into it with him again after he'd already flipped out seeing the fight club that day. Was he not there when we regulated Bilal? Nabil always thought that we were better than we were. That there was more to *ghuna* and the girls nonsense than there was. Like Cynthia's words weren't betraying the tormented suffering of a girl who knew, deep down, that her desires were wrong. When we went our separate ways for bed and I was alone in our room again with Maaz, I turned to him. "Bruh, that dude is soft, I don't give a shit what you say." Referring to Nabil.

"Why are you measuring dicks with mans?" Maaz snapped back at me. "Why does it matter who caught a worse beating or who's hard and who's soft?"

I kissed my teeth. Mans didn't get it.

"This guy's just actin' all surprised seein' madrasa shit and tryna control us with it. Why don't you see that?" I said. "Some random-ass fight league isn't that surprising. You know that."

"Maybe it should be. Maybe that's what Nabil is saying. Maybe it is more than a little fucked up. Hard, soft, doesn't matter. When we see some twisted shit, we should still be able to see it and say it's twisted, no?"

I didn't know what I was, beyond guilty and ashamed, and gross, and desperate. An argument between us would create distance, at least for one night.

"Bro, me and you been in the game for too long," Maaz said, softening his voice.

"Nah man, fuck all that. I'm cool with him. He's a homie, don't get me—"

But Maaz cut me off. "Nah, wait. Just listen. Me and you, we been in this shit too long. We don't remember what shit looks like on the outside. We think this is all normal, right? Anything and everything that's for white people is bad and shit. And listen, I fuck with that. We've all seen too much wack shit out there to really be like 'Oh, they got it all figured out.' *Nawuzubillah*, they don't even wipe they ass when they take a shit. But you remember years back, Hafiz Suleiman? Remember how wild his class was?"

"Yeah that's what I'm saying! A fight league was nothing compared to the shit that was happening there. Yo, he'd let *us* beat on kids who were misbehaving and—"

"And you remember what would happen if he found out you had a cut or a bruise or some shit?"

I couldn't say anything. I knew where Maaz was going.

"You remember how he'd lean over the bench and grab you by your cut or bruise or whatever? How mans would just clutch you by your cut and twist it when you forgot something? When you didn't know your *sabaq*? How he'd grab your bruise and squeeze it? Or how he'd hang you upside down by your ankles and beat on you?"

"I was a dumb kid," I whispered. I couldn't say it any louder than that because I knew how wack it sounded. What could I say? We put that shit behind us and it turned us into whatever we were.

"Maybe a fight league is fucked up. Maybe Nabil has a point. Maybe soft isn't bad. Maybe he's actually a different kind of hard."

Valuing our bodies so much that he stood up for them. Feeling a sad tenderness when we saw our skin as cheap. How could he survive here though with thoughts like that?

"He can come at us different though, is all I'm saying. He can just straight up say he's not tryna act different or white or anything. Sometimes I don't know. He acts different," I said.

"He was in public school awhile. Forgive him. And what's he supposed to do? Explain to us that he wasn't there when Hafiz Suleiman would hang you upside down by the balls?"

I shook my head.

"You know, all this uppity shit won't get us nowhere." I punched my pillow, fluffing it up again, and turned to Maaz, who was looking up at the ceiling. "Even if Nabil wasn't there, *there* was brought to him. You know what I mean?"

Maaz was quiet. He was starting to get it.

"Trying to tell us we gotta do something won't get us nowhere. We're here. Al Haque, fam. Where this shit happens. And if we call our parents, you know exactly what they'll say."

"'Maybe they'll knock some sense into you. That's how we were taught,'" Maaz said, parroting our parents.

"If there's ever another way—to punish them, or to make them stop—*wallahi*, you know your boy would be about it."

"You don't have to tell me man. I know how Flema mans deal with things," Maaz replied.

"You already know." I thought for a minute in silence. I looked at him again, his face lit by a stray moonbeam that had snuck in through the window. His eyes and lips and nose all still pointed at the ceiling. I turned away, unwilling to give in to the darker temptation.

"I ever tell you how we dealt with the pedo?" I said over my shoulder.

"Huh? Nah."

I'd piqued his interest.

"This was when I was a kid, a *while* back. I think I'd been at Al Haque only a year, if that. Maybe it was before I even started. Anyway, we used to play ball at the court, right? In the summertime, when school was out or madrasa was out, it was like a jungle out there. No summer camps or anything like the white kids had. The weather was nice, our parents were sick of us by that late in the day, and earlier in the afternoon, it was way too hot to let us outside in the sun. They were paranoid we'd get *darker* or some shit. So around like six, they'd kick us out and we'd ball out with the other kids and just chill and shit. Mandem reached all the time, right? Running their own game on the court. From like everywhere. You know how it is. Some kids were new-new right? Like fresh from Afghanistan, Pakistan, whatever. Even if they didn't know English, they knew what a bunch of kids on a court looked like. So they came too and whatever. It was easy buckets on them, so of course we let 'em play. My boy Juned was one of these new kids. His English wasn't perfect, but that's whatever y'know? He'd come to the court every day, and he'd have to bring his sister Maryam with him. They were the same age as us, but usually the girls would go off and do their own thing on the soccer field or some playground nearby or some shit. I dunno. So one day we're playing ball and one of Maryam's friends comes running up to the ball court and is talking to Juned. We stop playing cuz it looks serious. And she's talking some wild shit. Saying some guy came and talked to Maryam and took her, saying her parents were looking for her. And Maryam's English wasn't the best, right? This was some white guy who came, probably looked scary and official and shit to her, and took her. Her friends knew it was weird, so they came to us. So you know us—we go *crazy*. We go running to the playground and see she's missing. We go looking for her everywhere. *Everywhere*. We're panicking, we don't know what to do. We're just kids, right? We go into buildings, corner stores, every street, every backyard, parking lot, whatever. Finally, it's getting dark, we think, Oh shit, we gotta tell Juned's parents. Juned's scared as fuck his parents are going to kill him. So we go with him even though he's going to die. We get to Juned's place . . . and we find Maryam there. She's at home. Their parents are confused too. Everything looks fine to them—they're just like, 'Why are all these kids in our house?' So we're just about to leave but we notice something is off. Maryam isn't talking. Juned is trying to talk to her, but Maryam ain't talking bro. She's not talking. Juned is like, just trying to be gentle, talking to her quietly. But the girl had some random toy in her hands and was looking down, sitting on a bed. She's not saying shit to no one. Not to her brother, not to her parents, not to us. Juned's trying to ask her what happened to her and she won't say. Anyway, we can't stay there forever so we leave. But the next day, Juned meets us and he has a fucking cricket bat with him. We're like 'Okay what's going on?' He says when Maryam finally talked to him she said that the white guy took her into his building stairwell and did something to her. And now Juned's hunting this motherfucker down. So we're like, 'Okay that's fucked up but let's chill. We got police here. They can do something. They can take care of this.' We manage to calm him down, right? He wants to wild out—some village justice type shit. So we call the cops and report what happened. The girls saw him. Even if Maryam and Juned couldn't explain what happened or who they saw properly, I know the other girls gave a proper description of this guy. Not a lot of white guys in the hood, right? Shouldn't be hard to find this fucker. But we don't hear anything. We're thinking, Okay, maybe he got arrested. Maybe the cops took care of it and we're safe. But Maryam, that girl just . . . didn't go out anymore. It was the summer, she should go out *sometimes* right? See her friends or something. Finally, I think Juned convinced her somehow to come to the park and she actually came. We were low-key kinda happy to see her not gonna lie. She was trying to have fun. So she goes off with her friends and right when the sun's coming down and we're all about to leave, Maryam and her friends come running towards us. We're frozen, and we're thinking, 'Oh shit, please not again,' but Maryam's with them at least, so what can be wrong? They're saying they seen this white dude again at the schoolyard. This same pedo motherfucker the cops didn't do shit about. It's been weeks. So what do we do? Do we call the cops again and tell them the same shit we told them the first time? They gonna come rushing into our hood to arrest this fucker before he leaves? Nah. Do we just wait and see if he'll be arrested? Trust the pigs to take care of us? Nah. Trust the Canadian justice? Nah. We look at Maryam and she's frozen. Right there in her eyes we see the fear and horror as she follows our conversation with panicked desperation, eyes roving from one person's lips to the next. What are we gonna do? Who's gonna protect us? We just turn. One, maybe two feet away from us the older mans are finishing up their game. We go up to them and we tell them. We tell them everything. They stop playing immediately and then all of us, we go to the schoolyard where the girls were playing and they point him out to us. He's smoking by himself by a huge wall. Some big polo and like office-guy slacks. He sees us but turns away and pretends he doesn't. The older mans turn to us and tell us to go home. To take the girls and go home. They tell us in a way we can't say no. So we leave. But I'm me y'know? I get halfway home and I'm like, 'Nah I gotta see this shit.' So I run back. I go back into the schoolyard and now it's dark. The only thing you see is what the streetlights show you now. Orange pools on the pavement where I can see this pedo just having the shit kicked out of him. He's not moving—maybe he's dead. None of us care. I just remember being really far away, seeing his back, his dumb polo all red with blood, and the older mans who did something fucked up. But they did something. They did *something*."

"Mmm," Maaz mumbled.

He was drifting off to sleep. This was a meek bedtime story to him. He knows all this stuff. He's not the one who needs to hear this. But I wanted to say it anyway. They're too full of hope, the rest of them. And honestly if I'm keeping it real, in a way, maybe I am too. I believe in Nabil, Maaz and Farid. But I know it's never going to be a phone call to the cops, or telling the teachers or our parents, that would ever solve all the wrong shit around us and see our hope turn into something real. If we're ever going to end that nasty, bully sick-violent shit around us and see our hope actually grow into something, I'm going to need to protect it with nasty, bully sick-violent shit too.

CHAPTER 7

Hold You Poison or Grapes?

When I got to class the next day and the sounds of recitation filled the air, I was worried. Any dream I had of a different life outside Al Haque had so many barriers I didn't even know where to start. Faking sick wouldn't work—they'd see through that the way they'd seen through that for hundreds of years. Getting expelled also wouldn't work, as all four Heart Attacks would probably go super Saiyan on our asses before sending our dead bodies home. And plus, the weeks at Al Haque had compounded my guilt. My selfish desire to escape was beginning to exact its cost, and every misdeed and want weighed heavy on me. So I did the only thing I could do: I threw myself into prayer.

With no other option to turn to, I chased the succour that all sermons told us would come. The more faith you had, the fewer spiders you killed. The more faith you had, the more faith you had yet to have. Maybe I'd find an answer. I learned what you could learn too. You can only raise your hands up to God in a mockery for so long before it's a mockery no longer. Try it. We'd sit there, leaving our hands up so the maulanas would see, and ask for things in a parody of asking. One by one, we'd file off to bed. A few of us would remain, lost in thought. And then a "Ya Allah, please help the Leafs win the Stanley Cup this year" would turn into a "Ya Allah, help me be good. How do I be good?" A "Ya Allah, please help me find a way to leave this place" would turn into a "Ya Allah, please help me accept this place and be happy."

I saw that same search for faith in the next entry we read from Cynthia's journal that night from the room I shared with Farid.

9/30/77

Dear Mark,

If you're ever scared walking down a dark hallway, you should remember that you're in a holy place and nothing will harm you. Don't be scared! I mean if you are in a holy place. Sometimes I'll walk down a hallway and hear something through the walls or in a room, but when I go inside, no one's there. There's like a murmur, and I can't tell if it's inside my head or somewhere else. It scares me, knowing there are so many rooms here that are empty and unused, but you can hear things sometimes that suggest otherwise, y'know? When I walk by myself down the hallway and all the students are on another floor, I find myself tiptoe-running like some goofy bank robber who has to be fast and quiet.

Classes aren't half bad though! We spend the morning in Mass and Bible study and do the regular stuff in the afternoon. I'm learning a whole lot that I think Mom and Dad would be happy about, but I just wish I could ask questions about it, y'know? I found out why we're always asking for forgiveness and why we have confession. It's original sin.

Original sin is really interesting. Basically, if I understand it correctly, we're flawed. Like from day one. Less than perfect, weak and with a "proclivity to sin," according to Father Michael. Father Michael says it is our natural condition. Our instinct to betray Jesus Christ is the same instinct that leads us to live sinfully. We're born this way, and there's nothing we can do about it except try really hard to be good and beg for forgiveness for just . . . being that way.

We ask forgiveness for something out of our hands and out of our control. Something Jesus Christ our Saviour died for. Decisions made thousands of years ago by Adam and Eve or the Apostles are being paid for by us. Father Michael says this like it's a beautiful thing. He says, "Just as sin entered the world through one man, it entered us all. Every one of us that is born is born with that blackness, and it's the same blackness that plagued Adam and Eve, dear children. We struggle the same struggle, fight the same fight. And only through the grace of God can we die in a virtuous manner." This lifetime of struggle is meant to be a beautiful, desirable thing.

Not that you'd get any of that right now. And I don't care what anyone says either, you're absolutely perfect and without sin. Anyway Mark, I wanted to let you know I'm safe here, and I'm learning. And if Mom and Dad send you to a place like this, you'll be safe too, and I'm sure you'll learn lots, so don't worry about me!
—Cyn

"So she's learning, but she wishes she could ask questions about some of the stuff that seems more sus?" Farid asked us, looking around.

"She's making the best of it," I replied, but not to his question.

Even to me, my words sounded more like an attempt to convince everyone that making the best of it was what was happening.

"She'll learn. We'll all learn," Nawaaz said, nodding his head at us.

Maaz was quiet.

After Maaz and Nawaaz left our room, I realized my mind was too distracted to sleep, so I wandered down to the main prayer hall. If it was still early enough, the room was left unlocked so anybody studying or performing acts of worship late into the night could still get out when they were finished.

This was where we would beg and tears would fall. When we couldn't sleep, this was where we went for answers. Where we would shake with asking, pleading, coughing. Our bodies would tremble with the desperation of the sick. Most of it was selfish but there was never a night we ran out of things to beg for. It always started at better grades, better health, fewer beatings. Salvation for the *ummah*, health for our parents and grandparents. When we were done being selfless and thoughtful, we'd be confronted with the only thing left to ask for. The only thing we hadn't begged for. The blackness inside us. We'd beg for a light, some hope, some happiness, or death. We'd beg for respite or relief from the pain. We'd beg for it all to go away. We'd beg for stupidity or intelligence, but never both. The strength to accept or the weakness to capitulate. We'd beg for it all in the hopes that we would turn into good people. For the ability to stop, to start, to accept, to forget. By Allah, I begged with sincerity. By Allah I begged.

This wasn't my first night praying and pleading for these things after hours. I just wanted to feel *good*, to be without pain about my life. So I would beg for that honeyed wisdom. Sometimes, I noticed Maaz would be there too, and tonight was no different. More often than not, he and I would be some of the last ones left begging. Maybe we just had a lot on our minds in those days.

That night, after praying for some time, I turned to look at him and noticed his hands were raised in the air with his eyes closed, his cheeks red and flushed from crying. I imagined that my own cheeks looked exactly the same. Somehow, maybe he felt my eyes on him because he opened his eyes and met my gaze. We looked at each other longer than we ever had before. Usually, it was important not to stare too long, hold a gaze too long. We were scared, suspicious, wary, searching for some connection in the other. How do we break the silence? We kept looking. Unsure whether to crack a joke about red cheeks, tear stains, deep pits and dark circles. The soft skin, the red eyes, the lines from use. What was the other? It was apparent we looked like each other. A mirror, one brown and crying face reflecting the other. Begging for faith above all. Begging to be able to write about how sweet and wonderful Tahajjud is, and how the West is just shackles and chains. How we're three-dimensional because we struggle with faith by struggling to wake up for Fajr, not how we're three-dimensional because we struggle with faith by struggling with Fajr itself. Fat asses in Baby Phat and diamond rings. Sean Paul promises. Snake on a Nokia and the voice of a faraway nymph asking to borrow a pencil. That three-dimension three dimension.

"I'm tired," I said finally. It was not only true, it was safe. It could be interpreted in multiple ways.

"Me too," Maaz said in a response that was much the same. "I wanna get outta here."

I was quiet for a long time. I'd run out of tears and my cheeks were sore. I couldn't believe someone could feel the same way. We were all caught putting on a face for each other every day, doing what we were asked to do every waking moment. Could this be something else? Or was this someone just saying what I wanted to hear so he could help me not be alone for one night? I was too young and dumb to think that far ahead.

"I don't want to be here either man," I replied. "This just . . . isn't me. I can't do this."

"I'm just . . . fuckin' tired," he said again.

"I'm exhausted. I'm sick of crying. I'm just sick of begging."

"I want . . . but I mean, how? This is us. This is our life now right?" he ventured.

"You ever seen anyone . . . not graduate?"

"They all graduate man. We all get out of here the same." His reply was solemn.

"What happens when someone is expelled?" I don't know why I asked the question when I already knew.

"They'll go somewhere else if they keep, I dunno, wanting. And then they get sent away. India, Pakistan, Bangladesh. Wherever family is. If they don't cut it out there, they can do some farming shit their whole life. When they're old, this shit will just be a distant fake dream from another life. They probably won't even think their first fourteen years were real."

He was right. We all knew it to be true. Here or there, both places were the same. You were sent away to somewhere more remote, back to Port Colborne, back to Chandigarh.

"This country wasn't just to fuck around in. Not for our parents and shit. They tryna build something," he continued.

"Including us," I finished.

"Including us. Plus I'm double fucked. I can't even drop out with my uncle watching my ass." Seeing my confusion, he added, "Maulana Ingar."

"What!? Heart Attack Three is your uncle!?"

Maaz nodded. We didn't interact much with Heart Attacks Two or Three, as they taught other classes adjacent.

"Damn bruh, you should've said something. That's so weird. Makes sense though."

"Yeah."

"Well shit, how come you're not flexing for an extra pillow bro? You gotta use the connect."

Maaz didn't see the humour. "It's not funny man. I can't screw this up. I can't fuck this up. Our family shit is on the line. Honour, reputation. That typa shit. They need me."

"But aren't you like, one of us? Wouldn't he have already stepped in to correct your shit?"

"This is nothing. Nothing. As long as I know my *sabaq*, know my *dor*, know my shit, there's no trouble. This is just kids being kids."

"Goddamn . . ."

"It wasn't always like this. I remember when I was little, my parents were different, even when my uncle was around. When I used to draw, my dad would come home from work with these huge stacks of office scrap. All typed on one side, and the other side blank. I'd think, Holy shit, how am I gonna get through it all? But I would, quick. And then I'd beg for more. And he'd bring more, like clockwork. A big-ass heavy stack tied together by plastic string. He'd come home after work and just sit in the corner of the room

126

and watch me draw. I hated it. But after a while I stopped noticing. I'd draw on the floor with a book underneath my page to stop it from tearing, and he'd just sit there quietly. He never cared what I drew or bothered to judge anything, but he'd be there, sweaty and smelly, tired from work, staring off into space while I scratched some shit in pencil onto a page without a word exchanged between us. Sometimes I'd show him the drawings, and he'd just grunt and give them back. His shirt would be unbuttoned, his sleeves rolled up, his eyes somewhere else. I know being a janitor isn't easy. My mom would be in the kitchen, heating something up for him, and he was right there in that room with me, even if a part of him wasn't. I'd be at his feet with just the sound of pencil and crayon scratching on the paper. Then, when Maulana Ingar moved closer to us, he came over one time and saw me drawing. He asked me what I was drawing and I showed him the Ninja Turtles or some shit, I dunno. He just said, 'Hmmm,' and smiled and handed the page back to me. In his head, I think he was probably like, Wow! Something new. This can't be right. It's new. It's different. I don't remember anyone drawing in Gandhinagar. They can't possibly draw in Gandhinagar, so in this new land full of evil, this new thing must be evil too. This is exactly what we have to protect our children from when we bring them here. He saw a slippery slope. Something new like drawing Ninja Turtles led to more somethings new, like alcohol and sex. All three were addictive. And if none of it is sanctioned by Quran and *sunnah*, then none of it can be condoned y'feel me? I knew something was wrong. After that night, my dad stopped coming into the room as much when I drew. Soon the paper shipments slowed down. And then one day, after I'd been begging again and again for paper, he finally snapped."

"What happened? What did he say?" I asked. This all sounded familiar.

"'*Beta* the *worst* torture from Allah on the Day of Resurrection will be for those who imitate in the act of His creation! We cannot mimic Allah's creation of life. If you draw faces, you will be told on the Day of Judgement, 'Give life to that which you have created,' and you can't. You can't. Don't be proudy. Drawing face is copying Allah. Don't do these haram things anymore.'

"I didn't know what to say," Maaz continued. "I could argue with my dad. I couldn't argue with a hadith. I saw the way we were around the stories and narrations. With my uncle around, my parents changed. My dad grew a beard, and my mom wore her hijab tighter. We got rid of the TV. Anything with a face on it was thrown out. Every picture book. My dad cried a lot more. My mom too. But it was a different kind of crying, full of calm and peace. They didn't really laugh as much. They found a happiness without laughter, a joy without enjoyment. They found it all. Fear for the *ummah*, for my brother and me. Alarm and concern for all of us. My uncle had come and introduced us to *tauheed*, and now we walked around checking the sky for signs of calamity when we went out. Soon after that, I started at Al Haque. *Alhamdulillah*, my uncle had come and helped to save us. Even from drawing."

I was quiet for a long time.

"Do you still want to draw?" I finally asked.

Maaz was crying now. "Of course," he whispered through tears and gritted teeth. "Of course. Yes. But every time I try, I can't. I'm . . . scared. I'm just . . . so scared."

I couldn't help him. Pork, alcohol, music, pre-marital sex, unrelated women, murder, art with a face. Haram is haram. At that age, I had no idea Muslims were celebrating their faith while holding wildly disparate values. Or maybe I did.

"Maybe if we can't . . . get rid of that . . . shitty part of ourselves, we have to run away," I said to no one in particular.

"Where? Are we really that weak?"

"Yeah . . ." There was nowhere to go. The fear would always be there. "I'm just afraid," I said, before I realized what I was saying. "Allah as my witness, I'm trying. I'm trying to be good. Even if it doesn't look like it, I am. I want it all to end and to be clear-eyed and shit. I'm trying to forget all that other shit. I'm trying to learn. I'm trying to kill all that old stuff inside me, but I'm afraid of losing it too."

"What do you mean?" Maaz wasn't following.

"Bro, I just . . . this isn't me. I love baseball and hockey. I love Pokémon. I love my friends. I love reading. *Lord of the Rings*. *Redwall*. *Rumble in the Bronx*. *Drunken Master II*. I'm forgetting. I'm forgetting it all. Is Arthas Menethil ever brought to justice? Sundin had eighty points and forty-one goals last year. Ivysaur evolves at level 32. Cut is still a useless fucking move. There's a Rare Candy hidden behind someone's house in Cerulean City. I'm trying to lose it all. How the fuck do I get out of the Water Temple? Will I ever hit a real home run? How many times has Martin's sword been taken down to be used and returned? How many more times will it be used? Is it even possible to beat someone spamming Blanka's electricity move? Cheesesteakjimmys. Poweroverwhelming. Fucking twenty-minute fast Gryphon builds. Begging Allah not to let these bitches on the ladder find my hidden base. Dust and Dust_2. The time I pitched an immaculate inning. The time some older kids came to fuck up our team in ball hockey and we beat them, and then beat the shit out of them. And they bladed away swearing racist shit the whole time. I'm forgetting . . . I'm losing it all. All of it. And I'm terrified."

It was Maaz's turn to be silent for a minute.

"You know . . . the Prophet knew this," he said finally.

"What do you mean?"

"There's a hadith. The Prophet came home one day, and in front of his entrance, hanging from his door or something, he found a curtain with a bird on it. When he saw Aishah RA, he said, 'Remove it from here. When I enter and see it, I am reminded of this world.' The bird on the curtain was his Charizard I guess."

I thought about that for a minute.

"I'm trying to get rid of the curtain. Allah knows I'm trying."

"If we fail though . . ." Maaz said. "I mean, I don't want to go back to no butt-fuck country where I can't even fit in. Maybe we do need to run away."

"Bro we don't even fit in here," I added, trying to build up our consoling idea.

"No. We fit in *exactly* here," Maaz said, using his finger to gesture at the few feet separating us. "Right here. Me, you, Nawaaz and Farid. We fit in with each other."

"Yeah, like how Cynthia fit in with Catherine," I said quietly.

"Exactly. You think we should stop reading that journal? Is it actually, like, having an effect on us you think? Adding to whatever keeps us up at night?"

"Bro I don't know. Maybe it is. But it's nice reading about something else for a change right? In a way, I can't help thinking it's keeping us sane, building us up. Don't you wanna find out what happens to her?"

Maaz let himself smile. "How about this? If Cynthia ever escapes or makes it out at the end of the journal—if it's obvious she left it all behind—we'll make a run for it too. But if she picks a Christian life or whatever, then we . . ." His voice trailed off, but I knew where he was headed.

"Deal," I said, before he could take back his words. I knew Farid and Nawaaz would be down for anything Maaz and I led. Those guys would follow us off a bridge if we jumped.

"We should head up. It's mad late," Maaz said, ending the conversation before things got even more awkward.

He got up and I turned off the light in the prayer hall, then followed his creaking footsteps out of the darkness, each of us lost in our heads, mulling over the idea of leaving, having just turned an abstract desire into a real one. I wondered though if our resolve was abstract or real. If it was abstract, Maulana Yusuf would soon ensure it became real.

CHAPTER 8

The Strikeout

The next morning at breakfast, Maaz and I were happy to find a distraction laid bare before us on the mats. By daylight, our own nighttime whisperings couldn't be forgotten fast enough. We were just scared kids, all abstract desires and no means.

In front of us, instead of the cream cheese and honey and eggs we were used to, was chana and haleem. Good too.

"Hey, don't you guys think this is a bit weird? Every single day we have the same breakfast, but all of a sudden today, on a normal weekday, they give us this?" Nawaaz was looking at the rest of us, refusing to touch the roti at his knees.

The rest of us were stuffing our faces with food. Farid's cheeks bulged, and his head was just a few inches from the plate he was sharing with Nawaaz. We had no idea why there had been a change to the menu, but we wouldn't question it. We were trying to sop up every last drop of this rare treat of a meal, stealing chunks of brisket from one another with the help of elbows and knees. And we were not alone. Everyone in the drab food hall was doing the same. Stuffing ourselves with something different. We didn't know why or when there would be another meal like this, so we ate without question. The food could have been poisoned and it wouldn't have mattered. It was not cream cheese, honey and scrambled eggs. This is all it took to make us rabid.

As a matter of fact, the only person who was not rabid was Nawaaz. He was sitting high on his knees like a meerkat, looking around and studying everyone hunched over their meals on the carpet, wondering why no one was as suspicious as him. His suspicion was two-fold. He knew something was up. Ninety-two days in a row we'd eaten nothing but cream cheese, honey and scrambled eggs, and now, finally, on a random Tuesday in early December, we were presented with haleem and chana, the scent filling the air when we filed in. Nawaaz, though, smelled an ancient ruse. We were being fattened up and softened for something. There was no good thing in the universe that gave without expecting in return. Seeing that his friends were unaware, Nawaaz scanned the room for others like him, people who saw how much the universe cared. Everyone was heads down in their troughs. Seeing only one exit, and no exit that would lead anywhere substantial, Nawaaz concluded what the others like him must have concluded. He joined his friends in the meal, ripping off a hunk of roti to collect the treacly gravy. If this was their fate, there was nothing he could do to escape it. He joined the hunched bodies in their sacrament, grinding his teeth with industrial sentiment. Somewhere in the room, someone else's head popped up to repeat the same ritual Nawaaz had just performed.

After breakfast we joined our *hifz* class. We were reviewing new material when we were interrupted by two sharp slaps of Maulana Hasan's hand against the bench.

"This week is a special week," he said. "We have someone special joining us. A returning graduate. Someone who studied here and is now a big Maulana-sab in New Jersey. He studied here in Northumberland County just like you guys. Same place and everything! He'll be here for a few days, and he'll give a talk for us too. You guys should spend some time with him, learn something from him. He was born here, a very good student. *Alhamdulillah*, we're happy to have him back for a time."

We shot each other covert smirks when the maulana said "born here." That generation always thought it meant something. Like we were all bound together, just as those who were not born here were bound together. Of course, we actually *were* bound together, but in another way. Shared silence and rebellion, the search for a space with empty space behind us. That we'd look around and find it or search for it in our peers was laughable for now. Smirkable.

We had some time before our next class, so we decided to read another journal entry. It was a crisp December morning, with the bright sky and biting cold serving to wake us further, and Farid was wrapped in a giant blanket he'd dragged to the roof. The wind ruffled his hair, and only his face peeked out to listen to the next entry. Maaz and Nawaaz squatted close to me as I read.

10/3/77

Dear Mark,

Catherine and I are friends now! It's so wonderful to have someone like her here. Things were starting to get awfully lonely. Even if I was learning a lot and doing all right in my classes, it's better having a friend you can rely on and share everything with. We sat together at lunch, and she almost fell off her chair laughing when I called Sister Frances Father Frances instead. I swear it was an accident! I just heard the other girls do it—Catherine too—because of the way Sister Frances looks, and I let it slip. I feel horrible, but Catherine thought it was funny.

Sister Frances is meaner than she needs to be though. Especially when it comes to Catherine. Catherine's not ashamed of laughing. And it doesn't strike me as a . . . fake laugh. Oh yes, fake laughs are a thing. Just wait till you get older, Mark. You'll run into tons of people with those. Like Father Brendan. He tries a bit too hard, you know what I mean? He's the new priest here, so he's supposed to be easier to talk to and like "cool" and all, but ugh! We know it's him during confession! He knows it's us. He can't just expect us to blurt out that inappropriate stuff right? Some of the questions he asks are just weird. Like, "Do you ever think of boys touching you?" I'd rather talk to Sister Frances about that stuff. Learn to detect those fake laughs as early as possible Mark!
—Cyn

When we got to *hifz* class, we found Maulana Yusuf sitting next to Maulana Hasan in the teacher's spot. Who was this new person who looked so similar to us? His smell reached us even in the back rows, the wafting fragrance of Jannat-ul-Firdaus floating back to bless us. I found myself stealing glances at him and had trouble focusing on my *kitab*.

He was a little taller than us, in a long white jubba and a pristine black sweater vest. The jubba ended high on his calves, and we could see his socks pulled up over his pants, creating a small bundle. It's how some of us wore our socks as well. He had a dark green cap on, and long oiled locks peeked out from behind it. A hand on his knee revealed the silver glimmer of a fashionable ring on one finger. His full beard was bright and black, and his fair complexion was flattering to his light brown eyes.

I, of course, was immediately suspicious. Call it my survival instinct. You weren't going to get far being open and trusting. Was this poison or grapes in the open hand? But at the same time, I was curious to learn what would be different about today's class.

I wouldn't have to wait long. When it was my turn to present my lesson, I sat in front of the two maulanas and opened my Quran at the appropriate page. Al-Anfal into At-Tawba. I tried not to be nervous or let the presence of an extra teacher bother me. My first few verses were choppy, but as I got into the flow, I became more comfortable and felt the sweetness of *Qirat* help me. This was something Maulana Hasan mentioned frequently. The honey of *Qirat*. How, even if you don't understand what you're saying, the power of Allah's words can carry you, lift you as you worship and commune, and send the *ayat* somewhere. Angels, *shaytaan,* djinns, whoever, whatever, it becomes easier. When we hear something beautiful, we know.

I was jerked out of my recitation by another voice.

"*Khaiyraminkum,*" Maulana Yusuf said, correcting me. He wanted me to emphasize and elongate the letter *meem*. Even though I had.

My opinion of the new maulana was immediately soured because of this bullshit behaviour. Something rubbed me the wrong way about him. Here was a teacher who didn't give out perfect grades "just because" and was proud of it, or a teacher trying to justify his title when it wasn't necessary. It was okay to just listen. He was supposed to be perfect, or close to perfect, or at least abundant with virtue. This type of pettiness was unbecoming. I continued reciting my lesson to the end and went back to my desk.

"Yo," Farid whispered.

I looked at him.

"How is he?"

"He's fine. But he's being extra."

"What do you mean?"

"Like he's trying to find mistakes—stuff Maulana Hasan doesn't even do."

"Oh dry. Think he gets angry?" Farid asked.

"Farid. Don't."

"I don't like how proper they're tryna be. You think I can get him to beat me?"

"Farid you fucking idiot, don't do it."

As if on cue, I heard the two bench slaps and looked up to see Maulana Hasan beckoning Farid with an open hand.

Farid adjusted his golden cap, stood up and walked forward into the trenches. I was growing worried for him. In our own ways, Maaz, Nawaaz and I were breaking. Dying, forgetting, whatever. All our bullshit was just a lamentation. Farid though, didn't know how to break. He knew only how to endear himself to all of us. Even the other kids in the class loved him. He kept things light. If you got beat for one reason or another, Farid would find a way to sit with you during the next meal and pretend not to be hungry so you'd eat more. If you were homesick and quiet and kept to yourself for too many days, he'd stand next to you during prayer and wiggle his butt and hips to encourage a laugh. We all pretended to be sick of him, of course. Our Yorick, burdened with all our tension and melancholy. I watched him reciting up front with his back hunched over. Even over the hum and drone of *Qirat*, I could see Maulana Hasan's expression change. Blinking, kissing teeth. I saw Maulana Yusuf correct Farid a few times. He kept plowing along. Maulana Yusuf looked incredulous. His brows were raised and he had a half smile on his thin lips as he continued to correct Farid. I hated that smile. It was the smile of the superior, the in-the-know, of someone who thought they were better without ever saying "I'm better." A smile that seemed to say "Look at this *jaahil*."

The smile though, was not what I'd expected.

Maulana Hasan reacted more accordingly.

"Get out! Get back! Go back!" he shouted, putting an end to Farid's farce.

Farid stood up and sheepishly walked back to our bench. I don't think Maulana Hasan knew it was a ruse. We all knew that he dreamed of travelling back to Makkah and Medina to sit in Masjid-al-Haram and Masjid-an-Nawabi and listen to the beautiful recitations of all the diverse Muslims congregating from different parts of the world. He would frequently tell us of this great dream of his, and he wished for us to share in it too. Farid was not someone Maulana Hasan could understand. To him, Farid was only and ever only disrespecting the holy word of Allah. The machinations of a kid would not be calculated next to that. Maulana Hasan loved the Quran more than anything else. Though he was short-tempered and distractable, I could respect his devotion, and he was easier to understand than Maulana Ibrar, who acted both above everything and aloof, though he had begun trying to ingratiate himself with us in the weeks after the missing car keys incident.

Farid looked a little annoyed when he came back and sat next to me.

"Man, I couldn't even get Maulana Hasan to touch me. I wanted to at least show the new Maulana-sab the old one hasn't changed."

No doubt that's why Maulana Hasan had shouted. Normally, as a beater, he'd prefer to lay hands. But in the presence of his esteemed student, he wanted to present a cooler demeanour. Which was strange. Laying hands was sanctioned, after all. Boys were animals and could be course-corrected with violent steering. So it was an interesting choice from Maulana Hasan.

Maulana Yusuf was given the lofty privilege of leading us in prayer for the rest of the day, and that night after *Isha thaalim*, when Sharmil Bhai had led the younger kids off to bed and the older kids had gone to study their own thing, Maulana Yusuf asked several of us to stay back before turning in. I noticed that those asked to stay were mostly kids in our year, our class and Maulana Ingar's class. We sat in a circle, unsure of what to expect, but I knew that at the very least, I would much rather be upstairs studying.

"I don't think I ever got the chance to talk to you guys proper," Maulana Yusuf started. "I was in this exact same place—exact same—just a few years ago. Room 203. On some real talk, man to man, I just wanted to tell you guys not to waste your time messing around. I know what it's like. I know where you're at. You're here only a few years, so make the most of that time. These can easily be the best years of your lives, seen?"

This was all stuff we'd heard before, but never at this distance.

"They were for me. I miss those days man. I miss them! Such simple days. I took 'em for granted." He kissed his teeth and shook his head. "May Allah forgive me. And those brothers who didn't take it seriously—may Allah forgive them. I know y'all are struggling. Be strong. Fight *fitna*. Focus on each other, be around each other. Help each other. Don't worry about what's outside here, and don't bring what's outside here into here."

We all nodded like we understood.

"Which one of y'all has a phone in here?" He said it with a wide, disarming grin.

We all smiled back with politeness as if we had no idea what he was talking about.

"I know people do it. It's okay. When I was here, we used to sneak out and take a cab to Sahan's in Scarborough. To this day, *wallahi*, I haven't had better goat stew. We were just so sick of the food here. My boy from back in the day, Ikram, got the runs because of Sharmil Bhai—"

"He was still here back then?" Maruf asked.

"*Akhi*, when they bought this building from the Catholics they probably found him inside sweeping or something."

We all laughed at Sharmil Bhai.

"One day Sharmil Bhai meant to add salt to the *tarkhar* and instead went off with the chili powder. Of course we had to eat it. Honestly, may Allah bless Sharmil Bhai for his service to the madrasa. I'm not complaining, but after that meal, we didn't last half an hour before we all had to use the bathroom. There was a queue outside to use them upstairs, yeah? We all had the runs but Ikram had 'em real bad. There wasn't much we could do though right? We're all in line, waiting to use the bathroom, when we hear the *adhaan* for Isha go off. We're all rushing to use the bathroom and make it for Isha so we don't get handled right? We make it to *namaaz* on time, and right in the first *rukooh*, five, six people just let it rip. Huge farts." Maulana Yusuf was laughing with us. We couldn't help it. "*Astaghfirullah*, I don't know how many people's *namaaz* even counted that night. May Allah forgive us."

When we finally stopped laughing, Maulana Yusuf continued his story.

"Anyway, Ikram was really hurting that night. Empty stomach, homesick, in pain. So we snuck out to get some food. We take a cab to Sahan's and what do we find? Nine or ten classmates who'd also snuck out for the same reason!"

Everyone laughed again, except for me. What was the point of this story? These were mixed messages. If what he'd done was forbidden, why not tell it as a cautionary tale? Where was the beating at the end? Where was the bit about eternal hellfire to suffer as a result of these transgressions? Why endear himself to us? This was a respected *ustad* telling us about a sin he was not supposed to have committed. Admitting that he had meant that we could do the same and come out just as unscathed as him. A respected teacher in nirvana, holier than thou. It was difficult to believe that someone who looked like us, talked like us, was once like us, came out of the tunnel alive and dead at the same time. Maybe that was the only route to salvation? Cry, die, give up the rebellion, and then remember it fondly and beg eternally for forgiveness for our misspent youth. Every other maulana had seemed too pristine. I mean, we could see no one other than Hafiz Abdullah turning into one of them. But this was something that gave us hope. I didn't like it though. If the *ustads* could be just like us, what did that make us? Some kids who'd never got a chance, out of control and under the control of someone else, being told being bad may be a route to being good. But then also being told that being bad can only lead to being bad. I hated the hypocrisy. Like, "Bro you don't want to do that stuff. I've been there, it's not worth it trust me," and at the same time, "Look at me now. All the bad shit I did, but I found my way." Did you have fun or did you not have fun motherfucker?

It was clear that Maulana Yusuf fancied himself one of us. He was just a better dressed version. Crispy jubba, fresh *itr*. He was once where we were, felt a little of what we felt. Was not from another land with other problems. Would not look at our country and say "this country." Maulana Yusuf was bartering. Giving us a misdeed and hoping we'd divulge one in return.

"I know someone has a phone. Someone's got one. I don't really care who. I just wanna see it."

He glanced around, thinking he could catch the culprit with a look. He gazed into the eyes of a number of us.

"Is it you?" he asked me, his light brown eyes glimmering with mischief.

"No," I scoffed, genuinely amused by his failure. No doubt if he'd been correct, he would have said something about how a maulana from the same place can always tell when a kid is hiding something.

He slapped the thigh of the kid next to him.

"Is it you? You have one don't you?"

"No, no," the kid protested.

"Who has one?"

He wasn't letting it go. Things were getting awkward. He wouldn't let us get away with our deception. We wanted to move on, but maybe Maulana Yusuf knew that if he didn't let us, the only way out was the way forward. We wouldn't snitch though. It was on the kid, whoever actually had it, to move us along the chessboard.

"Yeah I have one. But only for emergencies," Bilal finally said.

"Emergencies? What kind of emergencies? Emergency Popeyes? Or emergency *fitna*?" Maulana Yusuf laughed at Bilal with the rest of us. We were so grateful it wasn't one of us being judged, we covered our anxiety with mirth, all of us flashing that same smile I hated.

"No, it's to call my parents."

"You can use a phone here for that! What emergency is there that you need the cell?"

Bilal was silent.

"Don't say emergencies. I know what it's for fam. Send it." Like he was owed some time with the phone now.

Bilal was scared, but he was even more scared of refusing. He pulled the phone out of a discreet pocket and slid it over to Maulana Yusuf. I was scared too. I guess we all were. We all held our breath while the maulana pressed some buttons and stared at the screen with mild curiosity. A faint light illuminated the slight smirk on his face. He finally put the phone down in front of him and ran a few fingers through his beard, turning his gaze upon all of us.

"Be patient. Do you guys know what's waiting for you in Jannah? Does anyone know? Can anyone tell me what's waiting for us in Jannah?"

We were all silent.

"Come on. Someone say something. What's waiting for us? Why do we do all this?"

"Uh, everything. Riches, rest . . ." Alif said.

Maulana Yusuf was asking the question in a way that suggested he was looking for a specific answer, but we didn't know what answer he wanted.

"Yes but what else? Do you know about the *houris*?"

We had no idea. But I noticed Jalil and Maruf, the two older kids who'd helped us beat down Bilal, grinning.

"The *houris* are the most beautiful creatures in all the heavens. The most beautiful things you've never even seen. They're not even human. They've been specifically set aside and reserved for us. If we can last—make it through these mere sixty, seventy years in a virtuous manner—we have awaiting us a beauty you guys can't even comprehend! They're shaped like hourglasses, curvaceous yet slender, virginal and yet insatiable. *Insatiable.* Breasts that don't sag, that are a perfect handful, so that when you grip them, they fill your hands and you can see them between your fingers trying to pop and squeeze out. Nipples as big as cherries, pointed up with youthful desire. And they have the most magnificent colour. They are a perfect tan, smooth olive-gold skin eager to serve and please. They'll never annoy you. Their asses will be amazing, nice and round and juicy. They'll be crazy for you, devoted to your every desire. They'll have no hunger except the hunger to have you in bed with them. The *houris* will have you in fits. You'll be so hooked that your slaves will enslave you! *Subhanallah.* Your first few days in Jannah will be a complete write-off because of them. When you first catch the barest whiff of their fragrance, feel the first few strands of their hair on your fingers, taste their pure skin with the slightest press of your lips, behold the sight of their wild curves slowly undressing for you, you will know. You will know you've been rewarded. And all you are asked, simply asked, to do in return . . . is be patient. Here we have a saying, don't we? Patience is a virtue. Think about that."

We were enraptured. Almost all of us, anyway. Whatever I was, was something else altogether. If we were finally getting answers, I would venture a question. That's all answers ever did for me. Led me to more questions.

"What about women?"

My question broke the trance. If we had been in some sort of drooling stupor, I'd snapped us to attention.

Maulana Yusuf zeroed in on me. "What?" he asked.

"Oh I just mean like what about women? What do they get? Are there *houris* for women?"

I couldn't help myself. I just genuinely wanted to know. I was too damn curious. And if I was in an environment full of knowledge, then maybe I would finally get some.

"Look at this guy, asking about women," Maulana Yusuf said. "Why are you asking about women? What's wrong with you? I'm talking about *your* rewards, not theirs, man!"

"Oh I was just thinking. I guess . . . I assume they get the same thing? Like there's men like that?"

"No. They get us."

"What?"

"You want your wife to be with other guys?"

"Uh . . . no."

"They get to be with us in Jannah."

Get to. I looked around. Everyone seemed unperturbed. Like this made sense. Like getting to be with one of us was a reward and not a punishment.

"Don't worry," Maulana Yusuf said reassuringly. He'd seen me look around the class and could tell I was bemoaning the fate of women everywhere, destined to be with the likes of someone like Khalid, who we called Pepperoni Pizza behind his back because of his acne. "We'll be perfect in Jannah. Not like this. Healthy, young, unblemished. Of a perfect eternal age. Youthful, strong, handsome. We won't look like we do now. We'll get to be with our loved ones, and even our wives will be beautiful. Glorious."

"But we'll still have at least two *houris* right?" Pepperoni Pizza asked.

"Of course."

"And they'll have . . . one husband?" Maaz asked. He was doing the math in his head. One wife and two *houris* versus one husband.

"*Astaghfirullah*, what are you asking? You want your wife to have more than one husband? Look at this idiot." Maulana Yusuf pointed at Maaz.

We all laughed because we were supposed to. How preposterous.

"Women would not be able to handle more than one partner. Especially not more than what you will give her in Jannah. They will not be resurrected like that. That is what the *houris* are for."

"They'll be resurrected without the same desires as us?" I asked.

"Men and women are different. Tell me. Are your desires the same as those of a woman?"

"I don't know—"

"They're not. It's simple. Allah created men and women different. Don't listen to what they tried to brainwash you with in

146

these schools here. Equal sure, but different. Men and women were created differently by Allah, with different desires."

"And when our wives ask us what awaits us in Jannah, what do we say? Do we tell them about the *houris?*"

"Joke. Tell them we'll be happy with just them in Jannah."

We all laughed again at the ridiculous idea of integrity in heaven. The idea of positing a lie from a knowledgeable-all-knowing-answering-truth-giver.

Cynthia and I had a lot to be confused and miffed about. This whole conversation reminded me of when she wondered why Mary Magdalene wasn't allowed to be an Apostle. There were a lot more questions than answers, but as I looked around the circle, I realized everyone was content and satisfied with the answers they'd received. Two *houris* and a wife were enough to purchase their patience, and they had no spare empathy left over to extend to the other half of us. We'll just say they're different. But numbers didn't lie. Half is half and three doesn't equal one. What were they getting to compensate for the one? What were they getting in place of our deficiency?

It didn't matter that night. Women were faraway creatures and everything was for us. I get it. We hadn't seen a girl in so long that they seemed like an idea that was easy to smile at in that *thaalim* circle. We were dismissed, and I thought I was alone with these burning questions in my mind. Weird for having them.

At the top of the stairs, Nawaaz, Maaz and I saw Hafiz Abdullah coming out of the bathroom, freshly showered, hair still wet, with a towel around his shoulders.

"Not your type of thing?" I asked, realizing that he hadn't been with us downstairs.

Maaz and Nawaaz leaned in, eager to hear his answer as well.

"Nah it's fine. I just have to make sure I know tomorrow's *sabaq* as well."

He disappeared down the hall, a silent beacon of guidance, showing us what true virtue looked like.

He knew—he always knew—what was right and appropriate. When you stacked one good deed against another, he always knew which one you were supposed to pick. And now we knew too. Side with learning the lesson a maulana-sab had assigned you over listening to something sus from another.

I smiled and shook my head, and Maaz chuckled softly at our new-found wisdom. He elbowed me before he headed down his hallway with Nawaaz.

"Yo meet me at the landing in thirty," he said. "Let's chill for a bit."

Our conversation a few nights ago had drawn us closer together, and Maaz and I were enjoying the new level of friendship we shared, even if we rarely got a chance to express it. We were on the same page when it came to most things now; that was evident in the way he asked questions too.

When I got to the landing, I found my friends already waiting. The dim light creeping in from under the door did almost nothing to illuminate their faces.

"What the hell was that?" I asked to no one in particular, letting out a huge sigh.

"Lemme say somethin'," Nawaaz replied. "If the *bhaiyans* and lessons were more like that, your boy wouldn't doze off as much."

"I can't believe they never told us!" Farid whisper-shouted.

"I don't know. Don't you guys think it's a little weird?" I asked.

"What do you mean?" Farid asked.

"Isn't it weird that girls get nothing?"

"Man what's wrong with you? They don't get nothing. They get us!" Nawaaz reiterated.

"Who wants *us* man? And plus, even if we're perfect and they get us, we're still getting more than them, no?"

"They probably don't want any more. You heard Maulana Yusuf. They're happy with just us. That's their nature. Men and women are different," Farid said, trying to placate me.

But I just had too many questions.

"Yeah but *we're* saying that. We are! Not them. If they say it, it's one thing, but we haven't even seen a girl in months. How would we know their nature at all? What they want? What they're like?"

"You're actually being so dumb right now. Don't cheese me."

I could see Nawaaz starting to get angry. Questions with no answers questioned authority. And how could you doubt the authority of God?

"Maulana Yusuf *told* us what their nature is," he said. "*Bhas.* That's what their nature is. We trust him. He's a learned scholar."

You have to put your faith in something, sometime. And I still had a little bit of faith in myself. I wasn't the only one.

"They're half of us though," Maaz began. He'd been silent the whole time. "In all that half, I'm sure there are some women who are different. Some women who have a different nature or the wrong nature or some shit. Not everyone's the same. Not everyone's perfect. We've seen it. Some women might want more, or none at all. One wouldn't be good enough for everyone."

Farid yawned but furrowed his brow and crossed his arms across his chest, willing to hear Maaz out.

"And what about us?" Maaz continued. "We're told right? About what we'll have. What if we don't want that though? What if we like skinny women or thick women or black women or white women? I heard the words 'perfect' and 'beautiful' tonight, and I heard 'nipples as big as cherries.' I didn't know that shit was beautiful! What if . . . let's say we don't have that, and instead, we have what we want in Jannah. You know how it is. Every wish come true and all that. What if . . . what we want . . . is this shit right here? Not Al Haque, obviously, but, like, this. Us, chilling in the stairwell but feelin' good cuz we're around each other. Struggling, doin' whatever . . . you know. In Jannah, it wouldn't be the same. There's no struggle. This . . . tastes so much sweeter right here, right now, because we're all so fucking exhausted. The words, the days. We collapse here, and there's no need to collapse there. So . . . how would it ever compare?"

"I don't know what you're asking man," Nawaaz said. "You're questioning the nature of Jannah. These are the questions Maulana Ibrar tells us to stay away from. For these exact reasons. Maybe we're not ready to know yet."

"Actually, I've thought about this too," Farid said, surprising us. "You guys know how I am. I wanted to know why I couldn't . . . I dunno. I wanted to see the point of it all. Something Mufti Abbas told me sort of helps to calm me down once in a while. When I get really crazy, it helps." He paused for a second. "What we have awaiting us in Jannah is so sweet, we'll forget about sour. It won't matter anymore."

I knew exactly what he meant, and the thought haunted me as well. But I could see that Maaz and Nawaaz looked confused. Luckily Farid could also tell and offered them an explanation.

"Basically, whatever they tell us is 'perfect' and 'beautiful' is so perfect and beautiful that the great feelings of struggling here with each other, or the kinds of girls we actually prefer, don't matter anymore. Good will be so good that we'll forget about the good we've had and dared to compare to heaven's."

"That does sort of help," Maaz said after a moment.

It was kind of true. If these *houris* were so good that I'd forget variety existed, then so be it. But that wasn't *just* what we were told.

"Yeah but then why go into all these details about what the *houris* will look like or how many we get and how girls get none? Why talk about what perfect looks like if it's not perfect for everyone? If it doesn't matter because it's so good, why do numbers exist? Why are we getting two?" I asked.

"Yeah . . ." Maaz had his thin eyebrows raised in the half light. Nawaaz was playing with a hair on his chin, and Farid scratched his head.

"The shittier things are here, the bigger the promises get right?" I said. "It's like we hear exactly what we need to hear."

"It doesn't sit right," Maaz concluded. "They're putting us all in a box—girls too. Telling us how it is."

"Isn't that what they're supposed to do? Since they know!?" Nawaaz asked.

"Oh for sure," I said. "But it's not adding up. Like, are we that stupid we don't know shit? I know Maulana Yusuf says women have a different nature and don't want more but I *feel* like if they want two lovers they *deserve* two lovers."

"You gotta trust Maulana Yusuf fam," Nawaaz replied. "You gotta listen to them. We all do. They're tryna help us. They know better. Our questions are being answered."

"No they're not—"

"They are," Nawaaz insisted. "All your follow-up questions are just a giant version of 'But how do *they* know that?' Maulana Ibrar told us to stay away from that question. Trust the *ustads*. We have to. All of us. They only spit truth."

"Except when talking to their wives," Farid said.

"That was a joke!" Nawaaz protested.

"It was a lie," Farid said. "From a truth-spitter. If you want to joke, joke. But did you see him correct us afterwards? Did you see him tell us what we're *actually* supposed to tell our wives after? . . . That's what I thought. What are we *actually* supposed to tell them then if that was just a joke?"

"It doesn't matter," Nawaaz began. "Joke, truth, whatever. I know a little. I know life sucks right now and I know this gets easier the more we listen. The more we accept. The more we trust. The three of you could stand to do that a bit more. There's a lotta peace where I'm at." He jabbed at himself with a thumb.

"I'll tell you what," I said, "I'm glad we're reading that journal right now. It's nice knowing that at least someone else had questions that they weren't getting answers to." I looked around at the group.

"Man, bun that journal. I ain't losing sleep over that shit," Nawaaz said.

"Oh please," I said. "You're not in bed right now. You're right here with us, losing the same sleep as our sleep. Staying up late, asking the same questions with answers you don't like."

"Bruh, I'm not in bed right now for the same reason I'm not in bed other nights when I'm over here. You won't stop asking some damn questions!"

We all laughed. It was true. But Nawaaz knew he was right there with us. That's why he laughed along. And before retiring for the night, we elected to read another entry in Cynthia's journal.

11/5/77

Dear Mark,

I sincerely hope you love sports and sweating, if only to spare you the biblical pain of exercise. Seriously. I'm not sure how Catherine and I managed to get out of PE, but we did. I was sick as a dog and she faked it, but they let us sit out. We just sat around and talked instead, playing board games. I found out she used to live with her grandparents in Quebec, and they were the ones who sent her here. They were too old to make the trip down for the parent-teacher thingy, and she doesn't sound like she misses them much. I'm not sure if that's good or bad. There's so much to feel guilty about, so much out of our control, that it all feels kind of pointless sometimes y'know? Like, yes, it was probably a sin to finagle our way out of phys ed, but it was so nice not having teachers or kids around. I forgot how quiet things can be when it's just two people. I found out Catherine and I have a lot more in common than I thought! We both love salty snacks, we both love reading and we both love rainy weather. Looking out the window from the classroom we could tell it was sunny and cold, and we could see them all hanging out down below in the afternoon sun, messing around in the dead leaves and stuff. I felt like a tiny thing part of a huge thing. Closer to God even. So was everything Cat and I did (gonna call her Cat now) to get out of phys ed really a sin?

I'll say another thing too. All the nuns and teachers have told me to stop hanging out with Cat because she'll be really distracting for me. They're all saying things like, "I've seen this happen to good kids like you a hundred times. You don't want to be friends with someone like her." And "I had a friend like that before. Trust me, it wasn't worth it." But they all had so much fun didn't they? And guess what else? I've convinced Cat to stop smoking dope. Now if I had listened to everyone's advice, we wouldn't even be here. She doesn't even hang out with those older girls anymore and is trying harder in class. So much good has come out of following my own heart. Anyway Mark, I really hope you find a dear friend like this one day!

—Cyn

We fell asleep that night much easier than we would have had we not stayed up late to discuss the nature of it all, and had our hearts not rung with Cynthia's words and her reminder that there was more to life than the afterlife.

—

The next day, Maulana Yusuf had an entourage. I was a little surprised, though I should have seen it coming. People prayed near him, sat with him, fought for the honour of performing ablution next to him, jockeyed for position next to him at meals. During *bhaiyans*, his words were drunk with the fervent expressions of the parched. Faces glowed. Half smiles played on lips and jokes were laughed at extra hard. I was annoyed to see Nawaaz and Farid as part of the entourage as well. Maaz and I tried to ask them about it after Isha.

"Yo, why you guys dripping off his nuts?" Maaz asked.

"Fam are you dumb?" Nawaaz was bristling. "Maulana Yusuf has so much *ilm*. We're just trying to learn."

"Y'all don't see any . . . problems?" I asked.

"I'm just trying to be good," Farid said. "To learn something. He tells us stuff no one else does. And it's not boring. We don't have to lose ourselves to become an *aalim*."

"Ugh, what does that even mean?" Maaz said to no one in particular.

"The hadith he drops are fire!" Nawaaz added.

"He's just . . . a person," I attempted to say.

"Nah bro. Mans are like a mutant hybrid. Galloway mans meets Wali-ul-lah," Farid said.

We all laughed at the stupidity of it. As if a Galloway man could ever be a friend of God's. Maaz and I watched our two companions tail Maulana Yusuf over the next few days. Playing that weird "acceptance game," where you try to be good, accept, trust the words of a mutant hybrid. We watched from the sidelines, wondering if it would ever fall apart. Most of the kids in our year were enamoured of him. He delivered sermons in words we could understand, in a way the other maulanas could not.

Soon, Maaz and I noticed we were not the only two kids on the outside. Hafiz Abdullah was often by himself, studying or reading the Quran on a prayer mat, unbothered by the commotion or laughter around him. Maybe he had a problem with the language, or maybe he saw something else. Maybe he saw no merit. Maybe he didn't believe in compromises or sacrifices. Maybe he was waiting for it to fall apart too or something. Maybe he wanted to focus on other stuff. Maybe you had to pick sides, and mutant hybrids were lacking as a result. Whatever the case, he wasn't about it.

One night after Isha, after the maulanas had gone home and the kids had been sent to bed, I heard quiet footfalls passing by my doorway again and again. I tried to ignore the noise, but I saw Farid get out of bed and pull on some socks, making like he was going to join the commotion.

"What the hell is going on?" I asked, sleep in my eyes.

"Oh we're sneaking out to the basement to play some baseball. Khalid has a tennis ball and Maulana Yusuf's down. He said he wanted to see if anyone could strike him out."

"Aren't you worried Sharmil Bhai is gonna wake up and murder us all?"

"Nah bro. Maulana Yusuf stayed up late with him to work on his *tilawat* and mans are out like a light right now. I'd be surprised if he wakes up for Qiyamat."

I shook my head and buried myself in my pillow again. I heard the door softly click as Farid exited. I had no interest in joining their exercise. It was less baseball and more build-a-legend. I could hardly drift off to sleep, though, before I heard the door softly click again. I sat up in time to see Maaz leap into my bed.

"Yo, you heard what they're doing?"

"Yeah, sounds kinda dumb," I said.

"Yeah but could you imagine? If he was utterly wrecked and couldn't get a single hit?"

"Yeah but why? Why would anyone do that?"

"For lying to his wife."

I smiled.

It was dumb as hell. The concept of punishing a well-meaning, helpful mutant-hybrid Galloway mans-meets-Makkah-*pakka aalim*. A weak reason. No beating was suffered. No betrayal endured. A weak hypocrisy at best. But that's what we were suffering from too. Punishments due to weak hypocrisies. And maybe, maybe, Maulana Yusuf's mutant-hybrid hypocrisy wasn't actually all that weak. I wouldn't know. I'm not a girl. But Cynthia was. Plus, there was another secret reason he needed punishing: I'd never be able to talk about my dream of escaping and move it forward as long as Farid and Nawaaz were enraptured by Maulana Yusuf's words.

"All right, let's see."

Maaz and I hurried through the dark madrasa, which we now knew by heart. We were the last ones in the basement and we could hear a bit of the ruckus before we got there. When we opened the double doors, we were greeted by the sight of the students postured throughout the room in some disorganized pattern resembling an outfield. At the far end of the room, Maulana Yusuf was standing with a makeshift branch that looked pretty good for a baseball bat. Maruf, who was kind of a dick, was throwing the tennis ball at him and Maulana Yusuf was launching the ball into the waiting crowd. I also noticed Abdi, the fight club champion, diving for loose balls and hurling them back to Maruf with ease. A bunch of kids who were just content to watch were leaning against the walls with their hands behind their backs, in a kaleidoscope of coloured pajamas and tufts of hair sticking out or buzzed down. Maaz and I joined them.

We watched Maulana Yusuf jack another ball into the crowd, and it hit the ceiling first before bouncing towards a tangle of rushing teenagers. It was quite a feat because the ceiling in the basement was incredibly high. I nudged Alif who was standing beside me.

"What kind of baseball is this?" I asked, confused.

Alif shrugged his shoulders. I'd forgotten that he was fairly new to Canada and couldn't be expected to know the sport very well. He turned and nudged his friend Jara, who was focused on the one-sided sparring match between Maulana Yusuf and Maruf.

"Hmm? Oh it's a home-run derby," he said.

"How?"

"Maruf is tryna strike him out."

"What are the rules?" I asked.

"You strike him out you win. Nothing else counts. Maulana Yusuf said he's good at baseball and no one could probably strike him out."

"Has anyone struck him out yet?"

"Yo, he's killing it. He could play for the Jays. On his Carlos Delgado shit."

I tried to exchange a look with Maaz, but he wasn't paying attention. He was surveying the carpet of random fielders with a goofy grin he'd learn to hide in the coming years. He'd found an opportunity to gain leverage and get something, with no one any wiser.

"I'll bet you any money my boy can strike him out," he said.

We heard a 'Woah' from the crowd as the ball went whizzing over our heads and slammed against the wall, making us all duck for cover.

"Aite say no more," Jara said, sniggering. "What do you want though? I don't have money like you."

"I know your mom sends you those expensive cookies from the UK every month. Lemme box dat."

"How you know about that?"

"Mans are a likkle soft around the middle."

"Whatchu mean dog?" Jara grabbed Maaz in response and tried to playfully headlock him for the insult. "Fine. One box of cookies. But if I win, you gotta do my towel service and laundry duty next week."

"Seen."

They dapped up in agreement. I didn't like being used as a pawn in Maaz's games but I cared more about humbling Maulana Yusuf. I was studying his swing, and it was pretty good. In another life, maybe he could have honed that natural swing into something. Maruf really was trying to strike him out, and he could throw the ball hard. But Maulana Yusuf was crushing every pitch into the crowd or ceiling. And it had been so long since I'd thrown a ball. So long since the sweat and grime of a pitcher's mound had lived under my fingernails. A lifetime ago, there had been summer heat and sun, the cacophony of young voices and racist smirks, wondering what a weird-looking brown kid was doing. So long since I'd drawn in a deep breath and gripped seams without mercy. All I'd seen was an invisible batter's box, a visible brown void of a well-worn catcher's mitt and a fight between me and the hitter. Most people who hated baseball still loved the hitting aspect of it. I loved pitching. They couldn't see the value in watching a pitcher. They wanted home runs. They didn't get it. Every pitch was a fight. Me against him. What am I thinking? What's he thinking? What's he thinking I'm thinking? It didn't matter if we were winning by a lot. My job was not done. I still had to go up there and give the man his shot. I had to take him out. That's the only way the game would end. Speed, control, hiding grips and wind-ups. One versus one. Who can best whom? In the case of Maulana Yusuf versus Nab Nasty, the answer was me, always me.

And it wouldn't even be close. That much I knew. Despite having been off a baseball diamond for so long, I knew. Too many afternoons spent cooling nerves, hacking loogies, massaging elbows. He might have been good for a madrasa-borne hitter but I was not that. And once the game was in me, it seemed as though no amount of worship would exorcise it out.

Maruf's pitches were starting to slow down. Maulana Yusuf was hitting them so hard they were firing right to the back wall now with oohs and aahs. He was making it look easy. Build-a-legend shit.

Maruf waved a hand to signal that he was beaten, then dropped the ball where he stood. Maulana Yusuf turned to address us, branch outstretched.

"Is anyone else left? Is there anyone remaining who's brave enough to test me?"

Everyone was silent.

"Come on now. Don't tell me Al Haque's gone soft. We used to go 'til much later in the night."

Maaz and Jara grabbed me and flung me forward onto the carpet where I fell on all fours in front of Maulana Yusuf, but still some distance away.

"*Acha.* You think you can strike me out?" he asked, looking down at me with a playful smile.

"Yeah," I replied quietly, standing up slowly and brushing the dust off my knees without looking at him.

Maulana Yusuf tossed me the tennis ball and walked back to take up his batter's stance. His kurta sleeves were rolled up to his elbows, and the pants were bunched around his calves. He swung the bat and tested his weight on both feet. He lifted his chin a little so he was looking down the length of his beard towards me. It was dead quiet. I looked back and saw Nawaaz and Farid among the scattered fielders. Maaz was leaning on the wall with an evil glint in his eye. I closed my eyes and took a deep, slow breath. I felt sorry for Maulana Yusuf.

I lifted my left leg, wound up, coiled, cocked and released. There was a loud bang like a gunshot as the ball hit the back wall behind Maulana Yusuf. Even out of practice, I still had it. The ball slowly rolled back in front of Maulana Yusuf, who remained frozen, trying to process what had just happened. No one moved. Maaz rushed forward to pick up the ball and throw it to me, then resumed his position along the wall. Maulana Yusuf focused his eyes on me, narrowing them and resting the bat on his shoulder lightly. It was no use. I wound up and threw another ball. Another swing and miss. Another loud bang. The ball bounced and rolled towards me, and I picked it up again. I walked back to my pitching position and faced Maulana Yusuf once more. His eyes were dead set on me. He wanted to hit this ball. He *needed* to hit it. The saddest part was he really believed he could if he focused hard enough. I took a faltering breath, sad for two people, exhaling all that emotion, and wound up again to put him out of his misery. I released the ball and watched the green blur whiz by Maulana Yusuf, who swung furiously, throwing his whole body behind it. He'd started his swing a little earlier, but he was still too late. There was another deafening bang, and this time he stumbled and almost fell over, using the bat as a crutch to stay standing. It had been quiet the whole time. Even now, post-immaculate strikeout, it was still silent. This wasn't supposed to happen. This wasn't part of the script. Instead of build-a-legend this was break-a-legend. I walked away. I could be sad again. And those three pitches reminded me why. My baseball dreams were dead. My dream dreams were dead and this was all that was left.

"Wait. Wait!" a voice commanded.

I turned around to see Maulana Yusuf a little out of breath.

"Again. Gimme one more. Keep throwing."

"No, I'm done. I'm tired."

"What do you mean you're tired? Just a few more pitches *yarr*."

"Nah, Maulana-sab I'm really tired. I gotta go to bed."

"What are you, afraid? You afraid cuz I was getting close eh? A few more and I would've learned the timing and started cranking them out of here. C'mon don't be scared. Just a few more."

"I'm done."

"*Bacha*, you're really that scared?"

"Sure." I walked away.

He needed to save face. He didn't know—hadn't known—what he was contending with. Years later he'd complain that no one had told him I was that good at baseball, like he was owed knowledge for the challenge. Like I'd duped him. Like there wasn't the chance that when I walked into the basement, he'd be Mohammed Mantle. This story could have been so different. A lesson learned for me instead of the teacher. I knew nothing. Just that I'd thrown my heart out. Every time I picked up the ball it was the same. Throw my heart out. How could he hope to match that with what he didn't have? He was just buying time 'til death. So buy time, say that and own it, don't make excuses. Don't try to make mutant hybrids a thing or lie or act like you were cheated. You threw down a gauntlet without reservation. And now you learned. Evolved. He'd add some clauses next time, and hope to avoid the dumbfounded silence of the crowd so he could continue building a legend and convince kids that being a mutant hybrid was a thing. Not that it would do much. Someone, somewhere, would always continue to best him. *You* could never be that blessed at something.

Maaz

I don't know what I'd do without the roof. It's so easy, so nice, to get away from the wild bullshit down below. Even away from Nabil, Nawaaz and Farid. Just to clear my head sometimes and get a breath of fresh air. It's so fucking bright up here after Fajr. I'd killed my breakfast and left them to squabble and argue and out-eat each other and shit. I just needed a little bit of time before they got up here too. To pine for some paintbrushes alone, I guess.

I see everything this place could be. If the maulanas knew us— like, *really* knew us—it would be so easy to grow and for them to help us if we could speak without fear. We're so close to a place like that, *here* in the West. Could you imagine if Alif was able to tell Maulana Ibrar he was homesick? And if Maulana Ibrar would react by getting him on the phone with his family, or getting Sharmil Bhai to cook some special food he'd know? I'm trying to change things a bit to make stuff like that happen here, but Nabil thinks it's selfish and manipulative sometimes. But I know it's not two sharp slaps that will fix Farid but two sharp lessons on niche things, like djinns and space exploration. I know Nabil shouldn't be here. I know Nawaaz is in pain and needs to sit next to Hafiz Abdullah and not me. And me. I know I need a path, a way to speak about the *nafs* inside me. Some way to purge the loneliness. The desire. That *shit* between Nawaaz and me. We're just . . . that desperate for touch. I want I want I want. Wanting is dangerous. It's better to live simply, live virtuously. I know this. These painting and drawing dreams are almost dead though, no worries. It's only when I look up at this sky that I remember.

It doesn't even make sense how bright it is. There's no sun in sight, not even a glowing orb behind the clouds. Just light shining across the blurry, imperceptible sky. I can't even look at it for too long without rubbing my eyes. And out across the ledge, all the snow in the world, covering dead branches and green pine trees like it will never melt. The land behind the madrasa just stretches on and on forever. There are a couple trees here and there to mark boundaries, but honestly, I'm surprised the most anyone could dream up was a dumb rumour about a field phone at the other end of the white wilderness. I feel like Farid probably has a few other ideas in his back pocket for what's across the land though. Does it ever end? Man, what I wouldn't give for a piece of paper and some pencils right now. Landscapes are okay, right? Glorifying His oneness by portraying the beauty of His creation. So where's my art class? Where's my time to worship? It's like Nabil says, our people just err on the side of caution all the time. Better safe than sorry each time. If a version of something is haram—if something is even slightly wrong—then all of it is better to stay away from. And this is what you get because of it: me sitting on the edge of the roof, feet over the side.

Nabil and I get into the deepest conversations now. It's so weird.

I hope Farid and Nawaaz don't feel left out when we're talking.

Right on cue, the door to the roof banged open behind me.

"Ey, what's good?" Farid yelled, hopping over to me.

He was with Nawaaz, who slapped me on the back hard, then grabbed the collar of my sweater and jiggled it, almost throwing me over the edge. His grip was stronger than most, and at that moment it showed.

"What the fuck? You trying to kill me?" I looked at him, wondering if he seriously knew what he was doing. The edge of the roof was slippery, good grip or not.

"Chill fam I had you," Nawaaz said.

"No man, you can't play around with shit like that! You gotta know where the line is. You coulda killed me."

Nawaaz kissed his teeth in annoyance.

I turned to open Cynthia's journal, which had been lying in my lap while I waited for them to show. It was my turn to read, and I was worried. We were nearing the end. If Cynthia ran away—or quit or was expelled or whatever—would we have the guts to follow through? I didn't know. We didn't even have the guts to discuss it properly. Nabil and I still hadn't mentioned it to Farid and Nawaaz yet. But I felt that reading it—knowing that it was real, that maybe someone got away—would help us in some way. And even if she didn't end up doing it, that would help us too.

11/17/77

Dear Mark,

You're not going to believe this, but we actually did it. We pulled it off! I got a letter from Mom and Dad excusing me from PE. I just told them I hated it and felt like my chest was going to explode every time (not entirely untrue), and they blessed me with a letter to the principal. I guess they're much easier to get stuff out of now that they sent me here. I'm doing all the tough teeth-pulling for you, you know? You're probably going to have the easiest time in the world. Well, I'm glad for it anyway. Better than Cat calling the school and pretending to be Mom, putting on a Ja-fake-an accent to try to get me out of class. She was seriously going to do that! And where would we have even found a phone? I'm not about to walk across the Sacred Heart grounds on the off chance the field phone is real. It's been fun just hanging out in the classroom with her. Father Frances kind of looks at us funny sometimes, like she's after something. The hunger in her eyes is gross. The way grown men leer when our parents aren't around. Not a big deal. I'd be looking at girls that way too if I were as ugly as her. Nothing but hate in that one. It's like when Mom says, "Wen cocoa ripe, im mus buss."

Cat talks about what she's going to do when she gets out of here like this is a prison. Me, I'm not so sure. There's both good and bad to Sacred Heart. Obviously, people like Father Frances and Father Brendan are trying so hard make life here hell, but I am learning an awful lot, and I found Cat. I feel like maybe if I become a teacher later, I can help people? Cat says I'd make the most annoying teacher, but she says it in a way that doesn't sound like an insult, haha.

—Cyn

Nabil had his hands up against the edge of the roof during the reading, gazing out at the countryside.

"Yo, you know mans are saying that we're running terrorist training camps and shit out here eh?" he said.

None of us knew then how the hate would compound, to be heard louder and louder over the years, and thereafter used against eighteen people, and then every other lone gunman with dark skin. Back then it was just a whisper.

I rolled my eyes, knowing exactly which "mans" he was referring to.

"Let 'em say that," Nawaaz shot back, clearly unfazed. He stuck his foot out, knocking over a squatting Farid, who'd been scribbling into the snow with a twig.

"That's not funny shit. White people use that shit to be racist and bully bare kids," Farid said from his ass, looking at us.

"Bro, who's getting bullied?" I asked. I had my reservations. In Scarborough, there were so many Muslims, it made no sense to try that shit. Even in the hood, there was too much of a mix to hear any of that. We knew better.

"You got bullied?" Nabil asked Farid directly.

Farid didn't respond.

Nabil turned to me. "You got bullied?" he asked.

"C'mon man," I said. "I mean . . . heard about it though. Like you know how it is. Parents and teachers always telling us, 'Watch out for the racism, watch out for the hate. White people think we all terrorists!' I don't doubt the bullying happens to someone in like Barrie or whatever. But I remember, in Cataraqui one time, right after 9/11, one of these little white kids tried that shit, right? Came up to us and was like 'Yo, are you guys Muzz-lums?' And we were like 'Yeah what's up?' And he said 'Yo, y'all did 9/11?' And we're like 'What the fuck? Is this kid joking?' We didn't think he was serious. So we didn't say anything, but he kept going like he was for real, really about this. 'Yo, y'all did 9/11? Why? Y'all blew up the Twin Towers. Y'all going to attack us here too aren't you? You're gonna blow up everything!' And we got pissed so we were like 'Ya, we did 9/11! The fuck you gonna do about it?' And he was quiet. 'Yeah we did it. We killed all those people and we're gonna blow up all your shit now too. What the fuck you gon' do? And what?' Mans were real meek after that; he was outnumbered. This was Scarborough. So no . . . I wasn't bullied."

The others laughed and I smiled, picturing the incident.

"You know we had to throw out a box of Jos Louis this morning cuz Sharmil Bhai didn't know they were haram," Nabil said, pivoting.

"Wait! I don't understand why we'd have to throw them out," I said.

"Allah, is this guy dumb?" Nawaaz stretched his fingers out at me, palm saluting the sky.

"Jos Louis have marshmallows or some shit in them," Farid said without looking at us. "We read the ingredients and they have glycerine."

"How did he not know that?" Nabil asked, shaking his head incredulously at Sharmil Bhai's error.

We were trying to convince Sharmil Bhai to let us go grocery shopping with him so we could pick out nice snacks and things we actually wanted to eat, but he didn't trust us. I don't blame him. But his desire to still buy something nice for us had backfired.

"You know technically gelatin isn't haram?" I said.

"*Astaghfirullah*, how can you say that?" Nawaaz said back.

"What do you mean?" Nabil bit. Nabil always bit. Since that night at Tahajjud when we'd stayed up late praying, we indulged each other while our two friends watched.

"Well it's like this. The ruling on a thing changes when the thing changes, right?"

Nawaaz rolled his eyes and walked away. Farid joined him. I was losing them. They didn't want to argue about something they had no say or power over. Even if I was right, there was no way any of us could convince our community. But in class a few days ago, Maulana Ibrar himself had said that something haram can be turned into something halal. Me referencing a class they'd dozed through probably hadn't helped maintain their interest. But I loved learning. And so, too, did Nabil.

"Sure," Nabil said. "Over time, a ruling can change. But gelatin's always been haram."

"Fam you're not following. Listen. Remember what Maulana Ibrar said? Alcohol is haram. But alcohol can become what?"

"Vinegar," Nabil answered.

"Yeah, and we can have vinegar right? It's changed from alcohol. Because the harmful thing is not there anymore. There is no harm, no risk . . . in that new thing. And we all know gelatin is a protein that comes from inside the animal, right? But it goes through so much processing—so much shit through the manufacturing process to make it into Jos Louis and Jell-O and whatnot—that by the time it becomes gelatin, it's no longer the animal, the pig or the improperly slaughtered cow. It's no longer the thing that was decreed as haram anymore. It's transformed. It's no longer the animal."

Nabil was looking at me like I'd blown his mind, but he quickly composed himself.

"Okay that's amazing, and it makes sense, but I'm going to play devil's advocate here—"

"Of course you are," I said.

"Even with that information, all of the scholars here—every *aalim* and *ustad*—has said, and continues to say, that gelatin is haram. Look at any website. Isn't it better to be safe than sorry later? If a ruling ascribes gelatin as haram just in case some piggly part of it survives in the Jos Louis, isn't it better to stay away? Err on the side of caution? Just like with the dyeing-your-hair-black thing. Better not to, just in case. Same with music. Preserve your faith."

"Oh for sure. No doubt. No doubt no doubt." I was ready for this argument. I'd thought a million and one steps ahead, and I knew I was right about at least this. Time on the roof, reading, thinking, really paying attention in class had prepared me to see through hypocrisy and nonsense. And only Nabil was around to hear it. Farid and Nawaaz had begun wrestling each other a few feet away, clearly bored with us.

"If it's better to be safe than sorry, why don't we stay away from vinegar?" I countered. "Why don't scholars make the same proclamation towards it? I'm just saying, why don't they pass judgement on salt-and-vinegar chips the same way? Or grapes? If it doesn't matter if even 0.000001 percent of a thing has gelatin for it to be haram, why is the same not true for grapes and their 0.000001 percent alcohol content? Shouldn't it be haram? I'll tell you why. We've been eating grapes and vinegar for forever. We've been doing it forever, so these things have never even been under the umbrella of things that could be haram. But processed shit and microscopes have been around for only a little while. I dunno, maybe the 1950s or whatever. But someone had to ask some maulana or mufti about it at some point right? And the man had to say something. *Something*. So he did what you said. Better safe than sorry. If it's new, it's bad right? Made the first ruling. And every other maulana's and mufti's job got a lot easier. They put together a scholarly consensus. And now, even as we keep coming up with questions, we have a 'safer than sorry' world, hypocrisies and all."

Nabil was nodding his head and looking down at the thin layer of frozen snow at our feet.

"Maybe we'll learn something in another class or another year that might show us it's deeper than that," he said. "Maybe it's not hypocrisy but something we're missing."

"Maybe. What do you think happens if we ask Maulana Ibrar about it right now though?"

Nabil just laughed. "Probably the exact same thing that happened to Cynthia when she asked questions of Father Michael. Answers . . . that led to more questions."

The journal had been gnawing away at me, and clearly at Nabil too.

"We should, like, try to find her somehow y'know?" I suggested.

"Definitely. I mean, I've thought about it. But it's like, impossible. We don't have anything besides a name," Nabil said. "Maybe if we had access to a library or like, at least a phone and a phone book or something. We couldn't find anything else in the storage closet remember?"

A few nights ago, we'd gone back in to where we'd found the journal and done a more meticulous search for clues on Sacred Heart. We found nothing of any true importance except some old hockey sticks and other sports equipment. So at least Cynthia and her classmates were kept more active than us back then. My mind lingered on Nabil's mention of a phone and phone book though.

"Hmm. I mean, it's not impossible to get some of that stuff in here," I replied, rubbing the few hairs on my chin, thinking of some of the more creative ways we'd snuck contraband into Al Haque. My mind also wandered onto what a phone would mean for us if Cynthia ended up leaving Sacred Heart. Could we really do the same? Nabil and I were having this conversation by daylight now, about leaving. That tiny difference made it seem all the more real.

"Well, let's see how the journal ends. Y'never know, maybe she's still locked in a storage closet here or something," Nabil said.

I chuckled and turned my head, and my face froze. Nawaaz was dangling Farid over the edge of the roof by his feet, jerking him up and down, swearing about something or other. I scrambled up and sprinted towards them, Nabil by my side. I slid to my knees and grabbed Farid by the waist while Nabil pulled him from the opposite side. Our games were beginning to go way too far.

"What the fuck is wrong with you?!" I turned to Nawaaz, disgusted.

"You could kill him that way! What the fuck is wrong with you guys? You need to know your limits and shit. You can't be acting like complete animals all the time," Nabil said.

Farid and Nawaaz cracked up. They lay on the snow, rolling their heads back in dark laughter. Unconcerned about their mortality, apathetic about their lives. Their jest filled the sky. They weren't bored—they'd proved something, they'd made a difference, they'd entertained themselves. And we'd rushed over with such ardour when they'd been so careless.

I loved those two. I needed them in my life. Hanging out on the roof on a Saturday morning, we made our own cartoons, even without pen and paper. But in that moment, Nabil and I could see the difference between life and death, and Farid and Nawaaz couldn't.

CHAPTER 9

Alexander Graham Bell

My strikeout seemed to break the trance Maulana Yusuf had over most of the other students. There was a much looser group that followed him around now, and Nawaaz and Farid were back with us. The strikeout had freed the rest from his thrall, to attend to whatever priorities they'd neglected, like my budding escape plan that was going nowhere. In some weird way, my scheme had been threatened by Maulana Yusuf's false promises. After all, how could I ever get Nawaaz and Farid to take the idea seriously if they were captivated by higher ambitions? After Maulana Yusuf's unceremonious departure, life returned to normal, save for one major thing.

The guilt. It grew like a wild fractal, infecting every fibre of my being. It had already been growing prior to my late-night musings with Maaz, and my conversations with him had quelled the guilt a bit when we'd first explored the idea of leaving. But now, I began to wonder, Should we really leave?

Of course, there were lots of reasons to go: the fight club, the Heart Attacks, the poor meals, the corruption. The rampant bullying, *Grand Theft Auto*. But now, there were also some reasons to stay.

There was the night when Maulana Ibrar ordered Popeyes for the whole class when Khalid was able to recite a hundred different hadiths from memory. The maulana sat with us at dinner, across a plate from Farid, and watched us feast and gorge with abandon. He didn't admonish us once, and when we wondered if he was ever going to eat the crispy golden thigh in front of him and share in our pleasure, Farid forced him to reveal himself. Reaching over onto Maulana-sab's side of the plate, he clutched the thigh, assuming our teacher was content to sit and watch us eat, but Maulana-sab grabbed Farid's wrist and gave him a death stare. We broke into tides of raucous laughter, comforted by seeing Maulana Ibrar behave like Popeyes meant something to him too. We weren't so separated in that moment. How could we call him Heart Attack Four after that?

That wasn't all. How could you sit in a *zikr* circle and not feel the holy magic of its recitation? This is important to understand—this will be the guilt you carry forever. Proof of something and the nature of our existence. Sit. Cross your legs and close your eyes. Or keep them open. It doesn't matter. Recite a memorized phrase in a language deemed divine, words you understand and yet don't understand. Again. And again. Every syllable and sound. Again. Now you'll ponder, feel yourself stir while you lie still. Move and shake and tremor as you all worship at a different pace and tone. Your soul moves. Noise fills the air. Darkness falls and still you're there. Feel yourself connected by others, and Others. Why are your cheeks wet if there is no magic to be measured?

That wasn't all. We watched each other grow. It was September no longer. Maaz and I, even Nawaaz, were beginning to learn and feel and find warmth in our community. We didn't need Sharmil Bhai's reminder to water the plants on the windowsills anymore; we wanted to keep them alive. It wasn't just about forgetting our old transitory loves—it was beginning to remember our transitory existence. We were removed from so much pain when we saw tears in the eyes of our teachers. You wouldn't smirk forever.

Cynthia's diary made the guilt grow as well, but as its hold on us grew, so too did the peace it provided. We had no intention to stop reading it, and we knew that in some way, its companionship was leading us towards an escape.

This was the guilt and haunting that held me the week after Maulana Yusuf left. We were at breakfast one morning when we noticed the servers were few and far between, and flagging one down wasn't particularly fruitful. We were still hungry, so Farid and I wandered around the hunched bodies and into the kitchen to see if we could gather a bit more food. But we came face to face with Jalil and Maruf.

Though they were only a year ahead of us, we seldom saw them share smiles or meals with the other students in their class. Instead, they were attached at the hip, not unlike me, Maaz, Nawaaz and Farid, but with a key difference. While the maulanas were not afraid to beat the everlasting crap out of the four of us, they never touched Jalil or Maruf. Maybe it was an age thing. Perhaps they were expected to know better because they were older, and if they didn't, it was their loss. Or maybe Jalil and Maruf had something over the maulanas. Perhaps Jalil and Maruf were among the soon-to-be-expelled and not worth wasting energy on. Maybe they would soon be shuffled off to another madrasa or shipped back to Afghanistan on some farming shit. Whatever the case, we tried to give them a wide berth as they'd made their disdain for us known and weren't shy about making life difficult for the younger kids, yanking and ordering them about. They saw things in us that didn't exist—things even Heart Attack One wouldn't accuse us of.

On that morning, Jalil was hunched over the giant basin doing dishes while Maruf sliced blocks of cream cheese and spooned honey onto plates. There were a few other kids also helping out in the kitchen, plating honey with a giant spoon or standing near the counter to take full trays of food back out into the rowdy basement. Maruf was in the middle of a story when we neared him.

"I told her like I wasn't down for shit anymore y'know?" he said. "Like she was ran through already and still chasing me down. She was cheesing me I can't lie."

Jalil was laughing really hard as Maruf continued.

"Fam, this girl *been* battried at jams and shit. I would tell her to reach the bathroom at Yonis's place, and then the mandem would go in there one by one just for a taste, y'know?"

"So what happened at school? You got away?" Jalil asked in a tone that implied he was starving.

"Bitch was chasing me! How the fuck you think I'm gonna get away?"

Jalil laughed even harder while the younger children continued to wait and work away.

"I'm running down the hallway, she's calling my name behind me. I pretend I can't hear her 'til finally I'm behind the school and I think I got away and shit. This bitch pops out of nowhere and says 'Please, please, I'll be quick. C'mon let me give you some.'

So I'm finally like 'Fuck, okay.' I pull out my dick and she starts sucking it but I'm not getting hard cuz this is wack and I just want it to end. She's going crazy, and I'm like 'Okay I'm close. Get ready.' And she's like 'Really?' And I'm like 'Yeah watch out watch out.' So I pull out and I start pissing all over her face. She started screaming and swearing at me and shit, and then I just turned and walked away."

Jalil started loudly slamming the wall next to the sink with his hand as he doubled over in laughter, and Maruf chuckled at his own ingenious prank.

"Taught that bitch a lesson for chasing me around like that."

Farid and I exchanged a shocked look. Maruf turned back to his cheese and spotted us, flashing a malicious smile.

Farid turned to leave, unwilling to continue the unsavoury encounter, but I pulled him back, holding on to his elbow.

"Uh, we need more roti and cream cheese," I said.

Jalil and Maruf pretended not to hear us.

"So like can we get more roti? Y'all are supposed to give it to the servers, and we're not getting any. So can we get some?"

"Yeah we told them not to give y'all any," Jalil said, looking up from the basin, one yellow rubber-gloved finger pointed at us.

"Why?"

"Bruh we don't serve fags."

"What?" Farid and I both laughed.

"Fuck atta here before I smack the shit outta you." Maruf returned to the cheese.

We didn't know what else to do, so Farid and I left. I was confused. Insults had explanations, even dumb ones. Where the hell had that come from? Rumours spread, and nothing was a secret at Al Haque. Nothing. Had someone seen Maaz and Nawaaz up to some shit? I'd never talked to them about it since I saw them that day.

Farid seemed unfazed though. I tried discussing it with him a few nights later in bed.

"Yo, remember when Jalil and Maruf called us fags?"

"Yeah?"

It was dark, pitch black. Dead quiet. Both of us were looking up at where the ceiling probably was, speaking so softly that neither human nor djinn would overhear.

"Why'd they do that?"

"Who knows? They make shit up. They need a reason to stay hatin'."

"Nah, but like, why 'fag'? They coulda said wack. It's weird. They coulda said *kutha, madher chod*, whatever. Why that?"

"Why does it bother you so much?"

He didn't know what I'd seen.

"I just mean . . . do people do that haram shit here?" Part of me was fronting of course, but another part of me really thought it didn't happen.

"Oh sure."

"What?" I bolted upright.

"Bro it happens. What do you want me to say?"

"Uh . . . that it doesn't happen?"

"Fam, wake up. You can't stick a whole bunch of kids into a building without girls in this day and age and expect nothing to happen. You pull them away and out of classes with girls with booty, away from Newgrounds and all that internet shit. No more miniskirt, slinky, strapless, spaghetti-paghetti bullshit—" I started laughing while Farid continued. "Crop top, drop top, belly button, cheek peeking, collar-shoulder-showing-ass nonsense and tell them, 'Hey, save yourself for the *houris*.' It's not gonna work."

"But yo, you were so into Maulana Yusuf when he was here."

"Fam, I was bored. I'm dying of boredom. Cynthia's diary is nice and all, but it's not enough. He was new. Told good stories. I just wanted to see if someone, something new could keep me hooked."

I was quiet for a minute.

"So . . . do you think there are fags here?"

"There are gay people everywhere. I don't know. I don't care really. In Cornwall, I slept in a room with four guys who'd do that shit to each other all the time. I know they're gonna have wives one day. I know if they had nothing to beg for forgiveness for, they guaranteed themselves something forever. I know if you ignore the world the world won't ignore you. If someone pretends to have all the answers your body will tell you if they're right or wrong. You're gonna have shit bouncing around in your head and heart, and if all they say about it is marriage and shame and obedience, some other shit *entirely* is going to go down at night. Can't feel shame without the shame. Maulana Yusuf's good, but even *his* words can't compare to the shittiest jpeg of Jessica Alba. With all due respect."

Talking to Farid was like that. Sometimes a kid and sometimes Gaspar the Guru of Time.

———

The next day brought tidings of escape, though we didn't recognize them as that at the time. After Fajr, Maulana Ibrar made an announcement.

"The provincial ministry of education has recommended that we start an exercise program. We're doing well, *Alhamdulillah*, but it is something we are in agreement with. You can use the activity and this is important. Once or twice a week, you'll be sent outside. Stretch, play football, whatever. Use that time to stay in shape. You need to keep your minds fresh by keeping your bodies fresh as well."

This was news to us. We had mixed feelings about the province's recommendation. Perhaps if it wasn't the middle of winter, we'd be warmer to the idea. But we hadn't realized the government could influence Al Haque at all. Try as it might to exist in a timeless void, to ignore the world, the world would not ignore it. A property tax would be paid, go into a coffer, be used to fund pipelines that would fuck up Indigenous lands, to police refugees and to support a bill to surveil Canadians. That bill would tell an angry Quebec motherfucker, 'Oh shit, we have to kill the Muslims. They're taking over if our government says they're taking over, so we have to surveil them. They must be up to evil shit if they warrant surveillance.' He'd go on to kill six inside a mosque. And then another animal would put that Quebecker's name on a gun and kill fifty-one others in New Zealand. They could find you in the middle of the woods and force you to exercise, monitor your every movement, log your every action online, but they wouldn't do the same for someone with a Dutch last name who'd go on to drive over a family in a quiet Ontario city. Can't win.

Exercise was a welcome change, though. Change was a welcome change. That we were now allowed—decreed—to spend time outside was strange and uncomfortable. After Zuhr, we were told to bundle up and not come back until Asr. By the time we got outside, we found most of the students already there. Sharmil Bhai and Heart Attack One were supervising the chaos while the younger kids rolled each other down the hill towards the madrasa entrance. Other students dotted the yard, wandering around, huddled in groups. We underestimated the effect of light. As I stood under the bright heavens observing the scene, my mind wandered back to escape, stoked now by snow and chill.

We slowly started up the hill, not really sure where to go or what to do, trudging through the snow while others tried to figure out the same thing. At the top, away from the cleared path, the land was covered in white, the grass and weeds of the field completely blanketed. As far as the eye could see, there was white, with a row of trees and dead bushes visible every once in a while.

"Yo, what about the phone booth across the field?" Farid asked.

We all groaned. We'd heard this story before. It was the oldest rumour at Al Haque, meant to enthrall us in our most bored moments. Even Cynthia had known it to be a dumb story. With cellphones banned, it was common to suggest the "field phone" to students who wanted to call somebody. "Yo, use the field phone." It was a stretch to imagine that there existed a payphone set up by Mr. Alexander Graham Bell himself, in Northumberland County, to assist Muslims and Catholics in reaching their loved ones. He could never have known that there were community courts where judges winked at fathers and returned sons and daughters to slavery in the year 2027. As if he'd ever known people beat people like animals, tied them to bedposts with balls and chains until their spirits were broken and their tears were spent. When visitors came calling, grand tours of the property would skip that person's room. They weren't feeling well or had a mental illness. The way kids had been kidnapped from families here and put into "schools" with no escape was the same way they left, because they'd learned that there was a town just *that* way, or that their home was just a few hours back *this* way. Or that the phone was just across the field.

"Ey man, even Cynthia knew that shit wasn't real," Maaz said. "This dumbass wants to find a phone booth so he can enter a SpongeBob cereal contest or some shit." He turned to Nawaaz, and both of them cracked up, amused by the idea of Farid still possessing the childlike wonder of the SpongeBob-obsessed.

"Ey you have a better idea?" Farid shot back. "Plus if there really is a phone, we can prob'ly cop a car, no? Call one of your connects and link up."

"We're walking in this direction anyway," I muttered. "It's not gonna matter much."

Maaz was incredibly defensive about intimacy, about close-ness, about the hearts of matters. If he saw too much tenderness too close to him, he'd cut it with a gibe. If he could glean that you were a daydreamer without having to divulge that he was an artist, he could use you, play you, or simply position himself somewhere he'd have a better life. A dream-seller in this instance. A master shrew, full of promise, determining which life would bear the most fruit. The religious one or the worldly one? It was disappointing because he was our brother, our blood. He didn't have to be better than us. He didn't have to put one of us down, or create distance where it wasn't needed.

But no one objected to Farid's idea about trying to cross the field. So we walked. All we heard was the deep crunch of our footfalls or the momentary caw of an unfamiliar black bird in the sky. Our eyes were focused on the ground, watching where our feet were falling. We walked single file with no snowshoes or mink pelts or Hudson's Bay Company promises. Just hand-me-down Timbs and Payless boots, escaping boredom and tradition. Snow rode up our jubbas and kurtas and made our calves shiver. Our holy book, which predicted black holes and the earth's revolutions, had neglected to tell us that snow was a thing that could attach itself to our ancient garb.

Lost in my thoughts, I bumped square into Farid, who'd stopped walking.

"Guys keep your eyes down," he said.

"Why?" I asked.

"We could go blind. I read it in a Farley Mowat book. There's too much snow, and it's all white and bright. It's called snow-sick or something. Be careful."

"This guy's so full of shit man. Acting like we haven't been in a field of snow before—" Nawaaz started to say.

"No I'm serious! This is different. It only happens when you walk in a huge field for a really long time. Just keep your eyes down, look at the shadows and shit."

"Bruh you'll fuck up your eyesight if you look at haram shit, unclean stuff and *fitna*. How you gonna tell me I'm gonna go blind from snow?" Maaz asked. "I've seen mans get snuffed in the ball court in Cataraqui and I didn't go blind. I've seen fiends do the nastiest shit to their families for a li'l hit. Snow is snow. Forget all that Farley Fuckwad shit. Look. Look around. Appreciate the beauty and splendour of Allah." He looked up when he said this, then surveyed the land with widespread arms and did a twirl.

A snowball hit him in the back. We turned to Nawaaz, who had a playful smile on his face.

"You haven't seen *shit* in that soft-ass hood. They use plastic knives in Cataraqui. Flema runs your shit."

"The fuck this bitch-ass say? You tryna catch these hands?"

"You couldn't. Maulana Ingar's good boy. Sitting in his lap and—"

He couldn't finish. Maaz tackled him and they rolled around in the deep snow. Farid and I laughed and whooped and egged them on. This too, was history. What hood, what era, what part of Toronto, when part of Toronto, would have the right to a story. What hood was hard, what hood was soft. What went into building a city, a country. Instead of on pavement in a dilapidated housing complex, we were in a field of snow, with evergreen branches as our silent jeerers. All that shit Mowat wrote about. Our own Wolfe and Montcalm, determining the fate of a nation.

They grew exhausted rather quickly. Even with Farid and I fuelling them with insults and yells, the weight of the snow and the chill of the temperature took their toll. We didn't know the old taught lessons that let some people walk barefoot in the cold. Maaz and Nawaaz lay on their backs, side by side, looking up at the sky, enduring our insults in three different languages.

I tried to pull Maaz up by the hands, but he was way too heavy, and I fell on my back into the snow instead. Upside down, the world looked like it made even less sense than it had for the past few months. I closed my eyes briefly for some relief in the dark, and when I opened them again, I noticed something on the horizon. I turned around, right side up, and looked closer. Farid saw my gaze and followed it. His eyes lit up.

"Holy shit. Is that . . . a phone booth?" he exclaimed.

"No way," I muttered.

Maaz and Nawaaz followed our gaze. There was something sticking out of the snow in the distance, no doubt about it. We wandered over, and as we got closer, we couldn't believe what we were seeing. The decades-old rumour was true. Even Cynthia and her friends hadn't believed it. The phone booth was adjacent to a road that bent around a thicket of pine trees in the middle of nowhere. As it came into focus, we realized there was someone actually in it. A small figure huddled over the phone, and as we crept up slowly, we realized it wasn't just a mirage due to snow blindness. We realized we knew who it was too.

Farid stopped. "Oh shit, that's Khalid."

Khalid was a kid in our class who was kind of quiet around us. He was difficult to be friends with. He loved showing the teachers how hard he studied, how much he prayed, how helpful he was. Generally though, he left us alone, so we never bothered talking to him. Maybe he was afraid of us. Instead, he tried really hard to be Hafiz Abdullah's friend. Sometimes he succeeded and sometimes he failed. Often he would sit alone on the eating mat, or with a younger kid he could boss around, because no one else would suffer it. Who knows where his heart was. His ass was in a phone booth in the middle of the road in Northumberland County though. Not a soul in sight, or a car, or any clue as to how or why a nice young boy would be there with a nice young reason.

"Shh! Stop stop stop," Nawaaz whispered.

We froze. Nawaaz crawled low to the ground, unseen. Khalid was facing the entrance of the phone booth with Nawaaz right beside him. I had no idea why we were trying to sneak up on

Khalid, but I was game. What the hell *was* he doing at a phone booth in the middle of nowhere?

Nawaaz twisted his big body, entered the booth through the gap under the door, rose up and grabbed the receiver. Khalid, to his credit, was not a folding chair. Though he was shocked and caught off guard, he was raised at Al Haque. Anything could happen at any time, to anyone. As soon as Nawaaz had appeared, Khalid, not knowing what the hell was happening or who was assailing him, tried to hang up the phone before he faced his Qiyamat. While they wrestled with the handset, Maaz went into the booth to help, grabbing one end of the phone. Khalid had a panicked look on his face. He thrashed with his legs, trying to kick both of them away, but to no avail. The palpable fear in his brown eyes gave him freak strength for the bout. Every jerky move bled desperation as his bloodshot eyes focused on his life. He grunted and gritted his teeth as Nawaaz and Maaz tried to twist the phone away from him. They banged and slammed each other against the walls of the phone booth but couldn't get him to let go. I moved towards the phone booth to help.

"This isn't right," Farid said.

"What?"

"He hasn't done anything. Why're we doing this?"

"You don't wanna know why he's on the phone?"

Without waiting for an answer, I rushed into the booth. Rather than grabbing the handset or laying another pulling hand on the phone, I attacked his pinkie finger. It gave way, and then, like a house of cards, the rest of his hand went with it. He let go of the phone and shoved us all forward like a beast in the throes of death. We all tumbled out of the booth and fell onto the road, Khalid included. I bounded back up and ran into the booth again, grabbing the hand-set, which was now dangling down on its cord. Khalid leapt up too, barely a second behind me, but Maaz and Nawaaz, still on the ground, reached forward and grabbed one leg each, tripping him up. He fell, and they both sat on him while Farid watched.

They lifted Khalid up and held him so he faced me. Maaz and Nawaaz had him by either arm and were forcing him to watch me. Now Farid had his eyes on me too, asking. I knew what he wanted me to do. Hang up. This was none of our business. It had nothing to do with us. I tried looking into Khalid's eyes. He looked a bit like Maaz, stocky and fair. His sideburns were light but stretched down to his jaw, even if the rest of his beard hadn't started coming in yet. His acne-prone skin was flushed with embarrassment. But he wasn't begging. He wasn't even looking at me. He was looking down at his feet, defeated. His parents hadn't emigrated from Afghanistan for this, and it showed. Snow and sand could be flipped, and though the Quran would make no mention of the former, it wouldn't matter. Shame would travel. Call snow its home and enjoy your public browbeating whether it was warranted or not. These feelings, mentioned or not, held more truth than any lesson that neglected to mention snow. This was the world, after all. Where you couldn't be on the phone with whoever Khalid was on the phone with.

I brought the receiver up to my ear and listened.

"Hey there! I'm Krystal. How's it going? I *really* want to talk to you tonight. I'm kind of lonely, and I'm looking for someone I can try something new with. I bet there's *so much* you can show me, can't you? I'm getting so wet and horny just thinking about it. You'll never . . . guess . . . where . . . my hand is right now. What are you waiting for? Dial 1 and then put in your sixteen-digit credit card number to get started, followed by the pound key . . . Hey there! I'm Krystal. I *really* want—" And so it repeated.

My jaw dropped in fake condemnation. Even if the shock was real, we were all sinners, and I had no right to look at Khalid that way. But it was grossly gratifying to look down on someone. I'd never been able to before.

"*Astaghfirullah!* This is why you leave the madrasa?!"

I held the phone away from my body like it carried a plague and tried to catch Khalid's eye, but he wouldn't look up. My friends were dying to hear what I'd heard. Maaz and Nawaaz dropped Khalid's arms and rushed over to take the phone from me. I squeezed out of the booth and looked at Khalid, who was frozen in place, eyes turned down to the pavement. Farid stood some distance away, watching us all. I heard Maaz and Nawaaz snickering behind me, huddled over the phone as they listened to the message a few times.

"*Astaghfirullah innallaha gafurur rahim.* I can't believe mans came all the way out here for this. You come to the madrasa, push around the younger kids, pretend to learn . . . for this?" Maaz said.

"What if we tell the maulanas?" Nawaaz suggested. "I think we have to. This is some next-level haram shit."

"No, no! Please! Don't tell them. I won't do this again. Just don't tell them. I'll do *tauba* and beg Allah's forgiveness!"

Maaz, Nawaaz and I laughed, but I felt a lump of guilt in my throat. Repentance wasn't a joke. But when it was performed at the frequency and pace it was at Al Haque, it lost a little meaning.

"We'll think about it. Where did you find the number?" Nawaaz asked.

"I saw it in the back of a newspaper once, and I just . . . remembered the number one time."

"You should be memorizing *siparas* that way, not phone-sex chatlines," Maaz said.

"Get atta here," Nawaaz commanded. "Go back to the madrasa! Farid, walk him back, make sure he doesn't get up to anything else. People should never be alone out here." He studied the trees like he knew what they hid.

Khalid walked off through the snow with his head down, Farid some distance behind him, neither of them talking. The silence and cold air soured our glee from what it had been. We were forced to think about what we'd done.

That night when we hung out in the foyer, I asked Farid why he'd been so quiet for the rest of the day. I poked him in the ribs, and he swatted my hand away.

"He didn't get to call SpongeBob." Nawaaz laughed at his own dumb joke, but Maaz was watching Farid and didn't join in.

"What we did today wasn't right. Whatever Khalid was doing on the phone was his business. We should've just let him go," Farid said quietly.

"Did you see what he was doing? Phone-sex chat is on another level man. *We* aren't even doing that shit!" Nawaaz said.

"Oh, are you kidding me? Look at us. Look at all of us. How much shit we have going on. Taking food off kids' plates? Beating on Bilal and Khalid? Are we really even that much better than people like Jalil and Maruf?"

We were quiet.

"You're right," Maaz said at last. "About the Khalid thing. But we don't have to be here to suffer through it anymore."

"Exactly," I said. The outside air and the discovery of the pay-phone had emboldened me. "Now that we have access to an actual phone, can't you guys use one of your connects to get us a car?"

"Hmm, it's possible," Nawaaz responded, scratching his chin. "We'd have to hide it somewhere though."

"I know, I know," I answered quietly. *One step at a time.*

Some of us went to bed that night dreaming of escape. I went to bed thinking of Cynthia, and how I wished I could tell her that the field phone had been real all along.

CHAPTER 10

Build-a-Legend

Farid liked to wake up a little earlier than everyone before Fajr. He'd open his eyes around thirty minutes before anyone else and just daydream. Sometimes he'd lie in bed, but most times he'd drag a chair and his blanket over to the window, wrap himself up and sit propped up, looking out at dreary Northumberland County. The all-white fields served as a blank canvas, the perfect page for his mind to wander away from Al Haque. Later, he'd tell us. That he'd dreamed about being an NHL star who wears a dark visor or a mask, and never speaks. He just catches bodies and scores goals in overtime and skates off the ice immediately while the rest of his teammates celebrate around him. The media would go crazy. Every day, they'd ask his teammates and anyone else close to him what his real name was. Who was he? Why doesn't he speak? Has he taken a vow of silence? Why does he skate off the ice instead of celebrating? How come he never smiles? The Problem wouldn't say anything. That was his nickname: the Problem. He just scored goals and led the Leafs to their first Cup in a zillion years. He'd stand in front of the cameras with his visor or mask on and only answer yes-or-no questions, and never tell anyone his name or why he was so badass and merciless. Other times, he'd dream about a girl taking a special interest in him. That he, Maaz, Nawaaz and I had snuck out of the madrasa and gone to Pickering Town, and a cute white girl had seen the way he'd made us all laugh or slid down the stair banister and she just had to say hello, like in the movies. She'd try to admonish us for our unruly behaviour but was secretly really curious about him and couldn't hide it. He'd be taken aback at first, but we'd all hang out, see a movie. She'd hold his hand, give him her number, and he'd conduct an illicit affair through the field phone while his friends supported him. The girl would be patient, she'd understand life at Al Haque *some-how*. Understand that phone calls might occur only once a month, that she might not hear from her crazy lover for a long time. She'd just get it. The price for hilarity was never knowing if he was okay miles and miles away. She'd be real stylish and have a last name like Mc-something. She'd be filthy rich. And when Farid would show up with bruises, she'd break down and beg him to run away with her. She'd tell him that she had an extra house, or that her parents were never home, or that they were really nice and stayed out of the way. She'd tell him there was a way out and another life waiting for him. He'd tell her that he couldn't leave without us, and she'd tell him we could come too. She'd have that rich-people glow, that never-missed-a-meal-and-only-ate-the-best-vegetables glow. Knew what a parsnip was. And she'd seen Farid, fallen in love with his face, and thought, I want to help him. A real white sav-iour complex. Farid would add details to his dreams every once in a while. Like her name was Olivia or something, and she had five extra bedrooms in her house and wore a beret. Or she was somehow sad and needed him to save her too. Other times, when he looked out over the field, he'd dream that it was the olden days, and he was in a forest, fighting the *kuffar* with the Indigenous people. He, Nawaaz, Maaz and I were new settlers who hated beavers, fur trapping, maple syrup and all that bullshit. But when they'd landed, the *kuffar* had been asshole racists who had banished us into the wild, where the Indigenous people found us, close to death. When we were brought back to health, the four of us decided we were going to help the Indigenous people fight back and make sure their land wasn't stolen. We started a guerrilla campaign, attacking and looting the *kuffar* settlers anytime they got close to settling near the Ganaraska Forest. Of course, because Farid didn't need the West or the love of the white *kuffar* settlers, he was comfortable being a free multi-dimensional Muslim, trying to bring guidance and light to the Indigenous people. The Indigenous people wouldn't mind, and they'd establish a free colony of unapologetic, merciless, badass Anishnabeg Muslims. Farid thought living in a place meant you were multi-dimensional and multi-faceted, and you could just do things and convert people and it wasn't colonialism or genocide. But at least he had an excuse. He was just a kid who didn't know any better. Either way it didn't matter. None of this was real. It's not like any of this would ever happen right?

—

It was on one of these mornings that I woke up to Farid leaping off his chair and jumping onto my bed, his face a few inches from my own.

"Merry Christmas," he said in his best wheezing Dumbledore voice.

I shot up, head-butting him in alarm, unsure of what was going on.

"*Astaghfirullah*, the fuck is wrong with you? Quit hanging out at the window," I said, rubbing sleep from my eyes. I was no stranger to his routine now.

Outside in the hall, I could hear kids rushing down for morning prayer.

"Shit, let's go. We're gonna be late!" I threw the blanket off myself.

"I know, I know." He followed me out of the room and down the hall to wash up.

"Why you always by that window in the morning? It's so dark this time of year anyway, you can barely see anything before Fajr," I said.

"Fam it's still nice to look outside. Just . . . been thinking about that thing you said to Maaz. About leaving. Escape. I mean, if things don't work out and we can't cut it here, we should have a plan, you know?"

"You're right. I just can't figure out what the next step should be."

"Well, maybe I can help with that. If it's for a car, I have some money. My parents gave me a credit card to use for emergencies, and they've been real generous with Eid money since they don't see me much anymore cuz I'm here."

"Yeah but how is money supposed to help?" I was perplexed.

We sat next to each other on the ablution stools and washed up quickly.

"Are you dumb fam? We can buy a car. I can drive. If we ever wanna get away, if we ever have to, we can just dip."

"I dunno man. I think you've been staring out that window for too long. And who the hell is going to sell a car to a fourteen-year-old who looks like an eight-year-old?" My anxiety was making me poke holes in the idea.

Farid splashed water on me. "I'm fifteen next month."

That was a surprise to me. Farid looked young for his age and was small in stature. Even his beard hadn't started to come in yet.

"You really have that kind of money?" I asked.

"Better than spending it on the phone-sex chat line with Krystal," he said, winking at me.

"What do you mean? How would you even do that?" I asked.

"Khalid told me the number on the walk back."

"What?!"

"I just asked him straight up. For the number. I was curious. He told me he was ashamed, and I told him that giving me the number would help him get rid of it from his head. Like those confessions Cynthia is always talking about."

"You're impossible," I said, breaking into a laugh.

My mind then went back to the other thing Farid had mentioned. About the car and a plan for escape. My own rudimentary idea had always involved calling a cab maybe, or finding a room to rent in the paper and putting some money towards that. Then maybe we would get jobs in restaurants or delivering papers or something. But a car would be a game changer. Thoughts of actually getting one would now poison any attempts to really focus at Al Haque. But where was our focus anyway? Newspapers and cabs. It was already too late.

"Okay let's talk to Maaz and Nawaaz about this," I said.

That day after Fajr, as we headed downstairs for breakfast, I prepared myself to broach the topic of leaving the madrasa. The four of us were together in a throng of people headed towards the basement, so I wonder what Sharmil Bhai saw in me and Farid that morning. Did he suspect something? He saw us in that crowd and called out to us.

"Hey, you!"

The four of us turned as other kids elbowed past us on the stairs.

"Come here!"

The four of us started up the stairs again in synchronized disgruntlement.

"No, I just need two. You two." He pointed at me and Farid.

Maaz and Nawaaz went down the stairs, and Farid and I followed Sharmil Bhai to the front of the madrasa.

"Go upstairs and get your coats. We're getting a delivery of fruits and vegetables, and I need help carrying them down to the kitchen."

Farid and I moaned but went upstairs to put on our coats and gloves. When we returned to the shoe room, Sharmil Bhai was putting on huge winter boots that went almost to his knees. The ends of his salt-and-pepper beard tickled the front of his boots as he squeezed into them.

"*Challo*, hurry!"

We followed him into the bright morning. Our eyes hurt, but when they adjusted, we noticed a big truck in the distance at the bottom of the hill.

"This area has so many farmers! Lod-ov farmland, so many vegetables and fruits for sale from different farmers." Sharmil Bhai spoke in the tone of a teacher. Like we didn't know we were in the middle of nowhere, and he was imparting something important for us to remember. Normally, he was so incredibly fed up with our shit that he spoke in commands, glares and grunts, but the prospect of fresh fruits and vegetables clearly excited him enough to speak to the spawn of djinns.

"Really?! Then we should give them *dawat*," Farid said with a hand twist in his best Indian accent. "Make a biryani that's so good they take the *shahadah*! Use the fruits and ve-ge-ta-bles towards the service of our *deen*."

I smirked, but Sharmil Bhai's eyes immediately fell and he stopped talking. He'd been attempting to communicate with us, even if it was from the perspective of teacher and student, but when he saw that he was the butt of the joke, he clammed up. We weren't sorry though. Maybe he needed a reminder of how we felt, where our heads were at. Fruits and vegetables might have been enough for him, but it was a cold winter morning, and we were not about it.

We caught up to the truck and a man got out of the driver's side. He had a huge belly covered by a thick green-and-black flannel coat, and he jutted his hand out to shake Sharmil Bhai's.

"Hey, so I gotta couple bales and buckets of stuff in the back. It's the dead of winter, so it's just some surplus I have lyin' around from the harvest."

"Yes of course. Steven, right?" Sharmil Bhai said.

"Yep." The man tapped the hood of his truck. "My daughter's gonna help hand off some of this stuff."

A girl popped out of the passenger side. Her red ponytail poked out of the back of her toque and her cheeks were red from the cold, but still not red enough to hide her freckles. Farid and I followed her around to the back of the truck. We didn't dare say a word. We weren't awestruck or anything—more awkward and pious. We hadn't talked to a girl in so long, we weren't sure we knew how. Both literally and religiously. What were the rules again?

To our credit, Farid and I tried to be professional about the whole exchange. Keep our faith intact. We knew *zinat* when we saw it.

The girl jumped into the pickup and turned around to face us. We had to look up.

"Hey," she said. "I'm going to hand these boxes off to you guys."

She lifted a couple of boxes and put them in our hands. We had to look at her. She had eyes the colour of beryl. I suddenly recalled a narration.

The Messenger of Allah (peace & blessings of Allah be upon him) said: "O Ali, do not follow a glance with another, for you will be forgiven for the first, but not for the second."

We could argue the first was accidental. We carried away boxes of potatoes to the shoe room and headed back, wondering how we'd avoid the sin. Sharmil Bhai and the truck driver were also lifting boxes, talking about how best to store vegetables through the coldest months. Their mutual love of quality produce was enough to draw them together, even if every other trait was wildly disparate.

"You guys don't talk much huh? I'm Del," the girl said.

I looked at Farid and sort of shrugged my shoulders.

"It's fine." She dismissed our piety as modesty. "What is this place?"

She surveyed the building, and Farid looked up at her.

"It's a madrasa," he said.

"Oh. Is that a . . . religious thing?"

"Yeah."

"All boys?"

"Damn, that obvious huh?" Farid replied, scratching his head.

She laughed and handed him another box. I accepted the box she handed me, making sure to keep my eyes averted. On our way back from dropping them off, I saw Sharmil Bhai receive a box from her and I saw him look at her. If it was an accidental glance and his first, he would be forgiven. But if he'd looked at her even once before, or if that first glance was on purpose, he'd committed a sin, regardless of intent. I both did and did not understand the reasoning behind the sin. Even if two looks during a business transaction didn't incite lust, eventually lust would or could follow. If you don't enforce a cap of one accidental look, then looks would lead to more looks. But not looking was also about obedience, devotion and discipline. Could you control yourself, follow the rules and prevent even indulging in desire? At the same time, this was straight-up dumb. This was another human being. You should be able to look at a girl without lust, and without even the risk of lust. You should be able to recognize where that edict came from, and how necessary it was today. Two looks was never arbitrary, but neither was geniality. We would never connect with half of humanity if we didn't look. Al Haque was pretty convincing, though.

When we went back for the last few boxes, Del handed them to us and hopped off the truck, dusting off her hands.

"That's all of them."

"Thanks!"

"You guys are here, like, all the time?" she asked, looking up at the giant building.

"Yeah, year-round," Farid said. "Well, sometimes we go back home for Ramad—for holidays and stuff."

I was staring at the slushy snow at my feet, wishing Farid would hurry his pace. It was so easy to be pious away from the rest of the world.

"Where's home?" the girl asked.

"Oh, Scarborough."

"Where's that?"

Farid and I looked at each other in surprise.

"Uh . . . Toronto?" Farid said.

"Oh! Yeah. Of course. I have an aunt who lives in Toronto."

"Where do you live?" Farid asked.

"Oh, just out in Port Campbell," she said pointing north.

Farid and I looked at each other again.

"Uh . . . I see," Farid said, nodding his head. "Well, thanks!"

When we got inside, Sharmil Bhai instructed us to carry the baskets and boxes down to the kitchen. I silently thanked Allah for preventing another bout with my *nafs*.

"I might be in love," Farid said.

I laughed. "*Astaghfirullah*. One conversation, that's all it takes?"

Farid breathed out deeply. "Fam, you didn't see how red her hair was. She wanted to know about us. She was curious! And I wanna know everything there is to know about Port Campbell."

"Port Campbell is just like every other bum-fuck town around here. White people farming and shit. Get your mind off *zina*. Focus!"

"Nah man, we could not have met a more *different* person from us."

"Farid, you gotta focus man. What are you gonna do, just wild out about every girl you run into? Even if the escape fails and nothing ever happens, we're gonna be *aalim* one day, aren't we? Somehow? So can't you chill?"

"And what if the escape doesn't fail?"

It was too scary to think about. That we could succeed. I didn't know what to say.

"What if the escape doesn't fail and we can do whatever we want?" he pressed.

"I don't know . . . but that's not likely," I said quietly.

"Says you. I say we're going to escape. You're probably going to grow up and become some annoying-ass teacher we all secretly love, and I'm going to find where the fuck Port Campbell is on a map. So just lemme think about her."

In that moment I remembered a painful hadith:

The son of Adam's share of zina has been decreed for him, which he will inevitably get. The zina of the eyes is looking, the zina of the ears is listening, the zina of the tongue is speaking, the zina of the hands is touching and the zina of the foot is walking. The heart longs and wishes, and the private part confirms that or denies it.

Farid's mind was somewhere else as we went down the stairs to join our friends for breakfast.

"Hey, you think Cynthia was hot?" he asked.

I looked at him like I wanted to slap him, and luckily, the look translated. I shook my head. When we told Maaz and Nawaaz about Del that night before our reading, they had a good laugh about the whole thing and cussed out Farid for his impropriety.

1/20/78

Dear Mark,

Sometimes, it's okay to be bad. I think? We snuck out last night to try to make some bannock in the kitchen. I dunno what we were thinking, but Cat was convinced it could be made without water, and she said it's the way her grandmother makes it. I'll tell you what—whatever we made certainly can be made without water, but it sure as hell was not bannock and was not edible. It was fun though! Even Gemma, Emily and Tessa joined us, and I don't even know how we didn't get caught with all the screaming. I hope you get to have that kind of fun with a group of friends someday, but just remember that whatever you do, do not try to make bannock without water!

—Cyn

———

The next day during exercise hours, Farid was nowhere to be found. Maaz, Nawaaz and I hung out on the rooftop, wondering where he was, peeking out over the edge at the kids to see if we could spot him. The teachers still had no idea we had roof access. That night in the stairwell foyer, when we were all hanging out again, he tried to be coy about where he'd been.

"Where were you during exercise?" I asked him.

"Don't watch that," Farid said, smiling.

Nawaaz kissed his teeth.

"We just wanna know, Farid," Maaz said. "We don't wanna be worried and shit. We know Heart Attack One wants that ass."

This was partly true. We had been a little worried.

"I just . . . went to the payphone."

"What?! Oh my God, dude," I said. I was a little disgusted, and secretly a little jealous.

"What?" He feigned innocence.

"Why were you there?" Nawaaz asked. We needed to hear it.

"I got that hotline number from Khalid. I just wanted to see what it was all about."

"You wanted to listen to some li'l thirty-second loop of some fat chick begging for your credit card?" Maaz asked.

"No need fam. I got Papa Patel's credit card," Farid said, flashing a dark card from his pocket.

"And instead of revealing it to us to maybe—I dunno—buy a phone or, like, food or some shit, you spend it on that nonsense?" I was perplexed. I thought he was joking earlier when he talked about the idea of calling the hotline.

"Well worth it. Krystal and I had a nice conversation."

"Oh my God. What about all that shit about Del?" I asked.

"Hey! Don't bring her into this! I just had a conversation with Krystal, that's all. It's not that serious. What Del and I have is something totally different. It's special."

Nawaaz shook his head and rubbed his temples and said nothing. This was so far out of the realm of his understanding, it was giving him a conniption.

"Listen man," Maaz said, "just don't get caught. This is the stupidest thing I've ever heard, but it's your time you're wasting. Don't you wanna try to focus? You're not tryna focus at all?"

"What's with you guys?" Farid asked. "Why you tryna pretend to be all goody-goody all of a sudden? Haram is haram, right?"

We didn't respond.

"Right? Isn't what's haram haram? Halal is halal right? Right?! So that means using this card for a phone, for food, for whatever, is haram right? Because it's being used towards bad shit. Sneaking out? The roof? Beating on Bilal for snitching? All that shit. Haram is haram, right? You can't pick and choose. Once you've crossed a line you can't say 'Oh the line is actually here now.' It's all the same. My phone bullshit, our roof bullshit. Me, Khalid, Bilal—all of us. We're the same. No one's worse than the other. Even the maulanas."

"Not Hafiz Abdullah," I said.

It was true. Every time we thought we were all the same, all the students and teachers, all just struggling to focus, we'd be reminded that the struggle looked a little different for Hafiz Abdullah. He was always there to highlight our deficiencies and shortcomings. He was already on advanced *tafsir*, understanding tracts and passages of the Quran one on one with Maulana Salman, the senior teacher. Sometimes I'd notice Maaz looking at Hafiz Abdullah with envy, and I'd have to remind my friend that if he wanted to be like him, he could. Maaz was smart enough. Hafiz Abdullah though, reminded us that not everyone was a piece of shit. Some of the older kids and the two maulanas who taught them seemed above all the mischief as well. They didn't even interact with us much—just pored over texts of hadith while the rest of us tried and failed to live up.

"Listen I can't speak for them," Farid said. "Maybe some of us are meant to be here. And the rest of us are just . . . *here*."

"Were you serious about having money for a car?" I asked, recalling our earlier conversation.

"Yeah, it's enough. You really wanna do it?"

My eyes were on Maaz, however. If we were ever going to leave, it would take Maaz and I together at the helm. After that night in Tahajjud, we'd opened up a level of friendship I knew people seldom got to experience in life. But I also knew there was a side of him that sat on the fence, measured and judged life on both sides and thought, Maybe things aren't so bad here after all. But we were nearing the end of Cynthia's diary, and I'd need him for this if Cynthia ended up deciding to leave. I'd need all of them. Nawaaz as the ultimate soldier, Maaz as the ultimate strategist, me as the ultimate pioneer and Farid as the ultimate whatever he was.

"Where would we even go?" Maaz said. "There's nowhere for us to go. We have nowhere."

"What about—if shit just doesn't work out here—we'll leave as soon as we're sixteen," I suggested. "We'll get a place some-where. I dunno. But together. We can rent a place, try to make it work." I was talking out of my ass.

"The four of us? We'd kill Farid by day two," Maaz said.

We laughed at the idea.

"We could do it, though. We could make it work, us four," Nawaaz insisted.

Maaz, Farid and I looked at each other. We'd thought we were going to have more trouble convincing Nawaaz to take the idea seriously.

"Oh stop it," he said. "Where you guys go, I go. *Bhas*. Plus, you need me. And we can only make this work together. What haven't we four survived? What haven't we done? If anyone could do it, we could . . . right? We can get jobs, sleep in a room together, save up. It wouldn't take much."

"It's a whole lifetime away though," I muttered. Even if it were possible, living through hell for a few more years sounded like a lifetime back then. Not undoable though.

"You know what we should do? We should find Cynthia," Farid said.

"What?" I asked, surprised Farid was thinking about it.

"Why don't we try to find her? Track her down. I dunno, just try to talk to her. Is she even still alive? Maybe we can ask her for advice or something."

"I dunno, man. Where would we even start?" I asked.

"A phone book?"

"Shit. It can't hurt to just . . . talk," Maaz agreed. "I'm kinda curious if she's still alive, aren't you? What if she's all . . . super religious and a nun now or some shit?"

"Wouldn't that be something? If we found her and she said, 'Convert to Catholic!' Or worse, 'Go back and be good men. Apologize to your teacher and be good little Muzz-lim boys.'" Nawaaz said this in his best old lady voice. We all laughed again.

"It might be worth looking into," I said. "If she left Sacred Heart, we'll leave too. We'll buy the car. How about that? And if she didn't, then . . . yeah."

I didn't want to think about her staying at Sacred Heart. We looked at each other, and that's all it took for us to agree. We didn't even need to nod in assent. The idea was enticing. Cynthia's fate would be a glimpse into the future. If she was a nun, we'd probably end up as religious scholars as well. However, if she'd flown the coop, made it out somehow, then perhaps . . .

There was a huge phone book in Principal-Mufti Abbas's office. We'd seen it before. The only trick was sneaking into the room. But that was a problem for another day. For now, the idea, the vain hope of escape, was enough to entertain us and keep our embers glowing during the cold and lonely nights at the end of that year.

—

One morning, we woke up and saw a piece of paper attached to the bulletin board outside our room at the top of the main stairwell.

HIFZ and QIRAT-UL-QURAN
COMPETITION—BOYS + GIRLS
Pretest Details:
Register from now until January 27 with Maulana Hasan.

The purpose of the competition is to build and strengthen the relationship between the Quran and the youth. In society, it is of vital importance that we strengthen the link between the youth and the Quran to increase the love for the Quran. The Quran is the guidebook for all mankind, and adherence to its tenets will result in success in this life and the Hereafter.

Bear in mind that you are not competing for any worldly benefit but only for the pleasure of Allah (SWT).

Participants must be hafiz and prepared to recite from any section of the Quran.

Judges will be testing hifz, tajweed, proper waqf and lehja.

This competition is hosted by Al Haque and will include Al-Rahmah Islamic School from Cornwall and Darul Uloom Al-Islamiya from Windsor. Even if you are not a part of this competition, please bear in mind that we will be hosting students from other Islamic schools, so carry yourselves with grace and good behaviour. You will be setting an example for Al Haque Islamic Academy.

We didn't think too much about it and continued on to breakfast. We knew we weren't interested and probably wouldn't participate. Beyond types like Khalid and Bilal, it would be difficult to find people who'd want to compete. But Al Haque had something to prove, clearly, as did Al-Rahmah and Darul Uloom.

Before class started that morning, Maulana Hasan made an announcement: "I'm sure you've all seen the notice posted upstairs. There will be a *Qirat* competition hosted by us in March. I remember being part of one when I was a student. This is a golden opportunity for all of you to not just improve your *tajweed* and *hifz*, but also to connect with the Quran on a deeper level. If you are a *hafiz*, I expect you to participate. This isn't about winning at all. This is about representing Al Haque and getting used to reciting in front of a crowd."

I breathed a sigh of relief. I was far from a *hafiz* and thus wasn't too worried about the competition. But I knew that over the past few weeks, many students had joined Hafiz Abdullah as *hifz-ul-Quran*. Khalid, Bilal and our own Maaz were also really close to having the entire Quran memorized. Regardless of the status that came with being *hafiz*, only Hafiz Abdullah was pious enough for the title to become his first name. *Subhanallah*, what an honour that must be, right? We were happy carrying on without it, but alas, these titles and paths were not happy carrying on without us.

That afternoon, we noticed that Maaz had disappeared for a

bit during our *fiqh* class. When we asked him about it that evening during dinner, he told us he'd been speaking to his uncle, Heart Attack Three, who'd told him to enter the competition.

"I don't have much of a choice," Maaz said. "My uncle wants me to compete."

"But you don't even have the whole Quran memorized," I protested.

"I know. But it doesn't matter. I'm almost there, right? Just a few *parahs* off. So even Maulana Hasan wants me to be in it. They put me on the phone with my dad, who pretty much told me I had to do it. For Al Haque, for him. It's not just me though. You guys are lucky. Anyone who's close to finishing is gonna be in it." He sucked on his teeth, clearly displeased by the idea.

"Damn," I said, not sure if I had anything else to offer.

"Well, do us proud big boy," Farid said, slapping Maaz's chest and attempting to walk away from the terrible fate of his friend.

Maaz yanked him back by the arm. "It's not funny man. I'm cheesed. That's it for me. I'm done. No more chilling. I'm just gonna be practising my *tilawat* for the next few weeks. Cuz here's the thing: even if I don't care about my recitation, everyone's gonna be there. My dad, everyone's dads, kids from other schools, the teachers. If I don't know my shit, I'm going to look like an idiot, I'm gonna catch a beating from everyone who knows me. I'm going to make my whole family look bad. I'm fucking . . . forced to read, to memorize, to do this shit."

"Could you imagine though? If you were so bad at it that you got to leave? That they expelled you from Al Haque over *makhraj* and *tajweed*?" Farid said.

"And then what? I'd just be recycled into Al-Rahmah or some

other school, and they'd just know me there as the kid who can't read the Quran properly but had the balls to enter a *Qirat* competition," Maaz said hotly.

"Well, we'll try to help in whatever way we can," I said.

"The best way you guys can help is to stay out of my way."

Maaz got up from the dinner mat and walked away. We felt horrible. We were stuck. I was making promising progress in my own *hifz*, but Nawaaz was a slow learner and Farid was Farid, so it really felt like we were dragging Maaz down sometimes. Maaz was incredibly intelligent, and I'd witnessed him bear lengthy *du'as* to memory after reading them over only once or twice, keeping pace with Hafiz Abdullah and Khalid.

Over the next few days, Maaz made a successful effort to spend less time around us. We'd often find him in a circle with the other kids who were a part of the *Qirat* competition, reciting loudly into the night. They were given preferential treatment, got beat less, received more time in the showers and extra snacks on the weekend. Al Haque knew how to sweeten the deal. If they didn't know their lesson, they were let off easy. There was a competition to win.

I was worried about something else though. My stomach was churning over the possibility that with enough time spent around the Quran, Maaz would abandon our escape plan. Our grand freedom fantasy, where maybe I could play baseball on weekends or read a book and he'd draw or pick up hockey again, seemed to be slipping away. Sleeping in the same room with Farid was beginning to have an effect on me. I was so afraid Maaz had forgotten all about the escape plan that I didn't even bother mentioning it to him in the few moments he spent with us, for fear that he'd shoot it down as ridiculous child's play. I wouldn't be able to suffer that kind of heartbreak, and the rest of us wouldn't dare entertain the idea of escape without his participation either.

The person who appeared the most worried, though, was Nawaaz. He'd watch Maaz across the room with calculating eyes full of both concern and suspicion. Like he was searching for something. Sometimes he'd look at Maaz's walk, or the way he angled his elbows, or the way his lips would form around a word during a conversation.

At the same time, we knew we had to support Maaz and our other classmates because of the stress they were under.

One night, Nawaaz, Farid and I were in our stairwell foyer, discussing what we could do.

"I dunno how long they plan on keeping this up, but I know they can't last right 'til the competition," I said.

"Maaz doesn't even get to bed 'til, like, a half hour before Fajr on some nights," Nawaaz revealed. "I mean, it's one thing if he's doing it like a week before the competition, but for everyone to be this serious about it . . . won't it have, like, the opposite effect if they're all tired and sleepy and shit?"

Before he could answer, the door at the top of the foyer opened and Maaz appeared and collapsed on a pillow beside Nawaaz.

"You're here early," Farid said.

"Actually, I would've been here even earlier, but I ran into Jara and Alif in the hall," he said.

"That's weird," I said. "What's up with them?" It was just past lights-out.

"Nah, I don't think it's that serious. Alif's just homesick and couldn't sleep. I heard them talking, and it sounded like Alif was crying to be honest. I'm horrible with that 'Aww, feel better, poor baby' type shit, so I didn't stick around too long." When Maaz said "Aww, feel better, poor baby," he petted Nawaaz on the head for added effect.

Alif was one of our only classmates who was new to the country. It was one thing for us to be here, born and raised just miles away. We all spoke the same language, cheered for the same teams and understood the sanctity of Popeyes. Although Alif's English wasn't perfect, we thought that he'd been adjusting well. He was good friends with Jara, who shared a room with him and had taken him under his wing. But in truth, we had no idea what Alif faced every day. Away from friends, family, familiar foods and customs. Even if places like Al Haque were inspired by the great madrasas of the subcontinent, the culture was still different. Here, kids could lock their teachers outside of the main prayer hall and get away with it, more or less. Students could sneak out for hours and deceive teachers into believing they'd gone nowhere. In Lahore, your ass would be dragged back by the first public figure who recognized you by your coloured madrasa kurta. The law would conspire with the madrasa to ensure kids turned into men properly. If a teacher got a little too violent with a student, a judge or a magistrate would smile and extract a promise from the teacher to be more understanding. The kids would be returned to the madrasa with a finger wag and an edict to learn their lesson. And even if we preferred January's chills in the wilds of Canada to all of that, we did understand yearning.

"Lemme go see what he's crying about," Farid said, getting up.

"Wait what are you doing?" Maaz asked, his head shooting up from the pillow. He was falling asleep, but Farid had rocked him out of his slumber.

"I'm just gonna go see if there's something I can do. Mans are out here in a nice place, just chilling and shit. He shouldn't be all depressed is all."

Farid disappeared, and Maaz lifted his head from the pillow to face me.

"Remember that journal entry, when Cynthia was talking about building snow forts with Cat and Vivian or whatever? How Cat led them all, barking and shit the whole time, making sure everyone had fun, making sure they forgot how tough it was at Sacred Heart? Doesn't that kinda remind you of Farid? How he is?"

"Even letting the snitch get in on it," Nawaaz added, still with surprise in his voice.

"You're right," I said, not seeing the parallel until then. "That's crazy. But now that I think of it, we should probably go make sure he doesn't burn the entire building down with Jara and Alif."

"Are we sure we want to stop that?" Maaz asked.

We cracked up but followed Farid out. We all knew Al Haque was far from a nice place, but crying was off limits. We had no idea why that was, but you just couldn't cry. It was like admitting that Al Haque was getting to you.

Farid knocked on their door softly, and we waited. Sharmil Bhai slept on the same floor as us, so it was incredibly important to stay quiet. Out in our stairwell foyer we were safe, but here, even a loud whisper would get us killed.

After a moment, Jara let us in.

"Yo, what's good?" Farid asked, jumping onto Jara's bed.

Maaz, Nawaaz and I took positions on the floor. Alif was leaning against the wall behind his bed, his hand covering his face so we couldn't see him.

"Nah we're just chilling man," Jara said. "Y'all didn't need to come through. It's not that serious." Jara was on good terms with everyone. A visit from the four of us may have caused others a bit more consternation, but Jara understood we were concerned. We weren't trying to make anyone's life difficult. Quite the opposite.

"I think I'm going to call my dad tomorrow," Alif said. "I'm going to ask them for a phone call. I'm going to go back to Pakistan."

"What? Why would you do that?" Farid asked.

"I can't do this. It's all nonsense here. So damn cold, nothing makes sense, the food is inedible, the people are selfish. I can do this much better in Lahore." He sniffled.

"What do you mean nonsense?" I asked.

"Someone stole Alif's *soan papdi* from our room," Jara said.

"Ew, people like that stuff?" I said.

"I thought it was safe because I know you guys love the over-sweet snacks," Alif said. "I mean, they're just sweets, but still *yarr*. We just don't do this to each other back home."

"You can't leave over some snack, man. It can't be *all* bad," I added.

"When I told Maulana Ibrar about it, he said I should have left my snacks locked up in my mini-locker. I understand this, but I thought he'd try to find out who did it. Or at least tell me it was the thief's fault. You know? Not look at me like I'm an idiot to be bothering him with such things."

We knew stuff went missing all the time at Al Haque, but Alif had a different perspective. To him, kids didn't do that to other kids. His snacks might have been taken by the younger kids sneaking up for a bit of mischief, but whoever it was, if they were smart about it, they'd rid themselves of the evidence.

"Okay forget the *soan papdi*. There's better stuff you can get here," said Farid. "I have an unopened box of fresh Fruit Roll-Ups. Right now. Let's open it and kill that shit."

"No. Nonono. Man, this isn't better. That stuff is way too sweet. My mom mailed me that *soan papdi*. Fruit Roll-Ups are nothing."

We dropped our jaws in mock insult.

"We're going to pretend we didn't hear that," I said playfully. At Al Haque, Fruit Roll-Ups were currency to jump shower lines and wudhu queues.

"Nothing has any taste here. I don't know how you guys can eat this trash!" Alif complained. My gibe had got him started. "You call cheese breakfast food and have fist fights over deep-fried chicken!"

Alif dropped his hand to make this remark, and we could see that his eyes were red and puffy. He had a long nose and the soft beginnings of a beard on his narrow face.

"I just . . . I can't do it. You guys are nice, but it's too rough to go through this nonsense every day. I just want to taste the good stuff again. The only food you should ever deep fry is *dahi baray*." He said this with a finger pointed to the ceiling in the manner of a true *aalim*.

"All right fuck it," Farid said. "Let's make it then."

"You know what? Yeah. Let's do it," I agreed without thinking. Or rather, I was thinking about Cynthia and the bannock, which I had no doubt was on Farid's mind too. I jumped on board before anyone protested with reason or logic. It was easy to shoot down Farid's dreams, but it was harder now that I'd added my voice too. Maaz raised his eyebrows at me, and we shared a look and a whole conversation in silence. My look told him I was 100 percent about it. Not only was I insulted that Alif could speak pejoratively about fried chicken, but I also wanted to see what *dahi baray* was all about. The Pakistanis at Al Haque swore by it—even the ones who were born or raised here.

"Fine," Alif said solemnly. "You shall *all* taste some real food tonight." He made for the door, but Maaz stopped him with a hand.

"Easy there, *shaheed*," he said. "We'll do this tomorrow night. We gotta pull a few strings first to make sure Sharmil Bhai doesn't wake up and kill us."

Alif wasn't used to raising hell and probably thought we could do it then and there without issue. His solemn tone also suggested that he thought we'd all be caught and expelled for the transgression. His craving for home must have been something fierce in those days.

The next day, word had got out that we were going to be cooking something up in the kitchen. Our plans generally stayed between the four of us, but now that they involved Jara and Alif, two kids who generally stayed on the right side of the law, everyone else on the right side of the law found out. The way they told the story was with muted excitement, however, as opposed to hushed grandstanding. The story grew over the course of the day, with more and more people getting excited about it and wanting in on the plan. Maaz, Nawaaz and I were a little miffed. We just wanted to have some fun cooking as a small group in the kitchen; we didn't want this to turn into another build-a-legend spectacle. Farid was loving it, however, and was inviting everyone he ran into in the hallways.

Sharmil Bhai was a tougher problem to solve, but we figured it out in the end, as dumb as it was. We decided to drag two desks from our rooms and plant them in front of his door while he slept.

If he woke up because he heard something, he'd be unable to open the door and catch us while we cooked the food. Later, we'd return, de-deskify his door and pretend nothing had happened.

We executed our plan flawlessly. Farid and I tiptoed a desk from our room to Sharmil Bhai's and silently placed it in front of his door. We helped Maaz and Nawaaz carry another desk from their room as well and placed it upside down on top of our own. When we crept downstairs into the kitchen and found the light on, we were aghast. Almost every student in our class, and some of the younger kids as well, were waiting around with kitchen utensils in hand.

"What the hell is this?" I asked.

"Tonight, everyone will learn to make *dahi baray*," Alif said with the solemnity of a funeral director.

None of us really knew how to cook, Alif included. I surveyed the room and knew immediately that we were way out of our element. I grabbed one of the younger kids by the elbow.

"What the hell are you doing out of bed?" I asked. I couldn't understand the chaos.

The kid broke free from my grip and ran to his friends, who were leaning against the wall watching us.

"They heard we was making *dahi baray*, bro," Jara said. "People just wanted to be a part of it I guess."

Alif was at the sink, overseeing a bunch of the kids in our year, instructing them to wash their hands up to elbows before leading them to a gigantic cutting board where several tiny knives and piles of ginger and garlic awaited them.

"This is way too risky. We're gonna get fucked up man," Nawaaz said, looking around.

"We can't be responsible for this," Maaz added. "People look at us and laugh or call us troublemakers and shit, but as soon as we do something like this, they want in?"

Farid was watching the people at the fridge when he addressed us. "Ey man, they can't all be like us, and we can't all be like them," he said. He dragged a chair over to the cupboards and began searching them for lentils.

Nawaaz hurried forward and used his height to do the same, no chair required. Maaz and I were unsure what to do. We saw some of the younger kids pulling open the drawers to reveal a bunch of knives and utensils that were never used, and we rushed over to shut them quickly before they hurt themselves.

"Go to bed man. Shit, y'all are gonna get caught!" I tried to shoo them away, but they just writhed free and went to watch the cutting-board action. Alif was leading everyone in a demonstration of chopping, unqualified as he was. The other students grabbed chunks of ginger, garlic, chili and coriander and began chopping with gusto at the large central table. Everything was coming out all mish-mashed, in different shapes and sizes, but everyone was occupied all the same.

"Damn," I said, shaking my head.

"What?" Maaz asked.

"Everyone's loving this shit. It's a horrible mess. The maulanas are going to kill us tomorrow, absolutely kill us, and I think we all know it. But no one gives a shit."

"Al Haque's not so bad right?" Maaz said, looking at me slyly.

"I know, man. I know. It's just a shame that this shit is, y'know, punishable. We shouldn't be here."

"If we could do stuff like this once in a while, it would make staying here almost an option eh?"

"You still thinking about leaving?" I couldn't help myself.

"Was I ever not thinking about it?"

"Nah, not that. I was just . . . worried. You haven't been around us too much, we haven't talked about it really, so I was worried maybe you were gonna drop the idea. Be a good kid and all that. Maybe the *Qirat* competition was having an effect on you."

"Yeah, the opposite effect," Maaz muttered. "When me and you get outta here, we'll enter whatever kinda competitions we want to. Cuz *we* want to."

My heart filled with hope. Maaz turned to look me in the eye.

"You can trust me bro. Me and you, we're the same. We just ask too many questions. Maybe there's something wrong with us—like we're defective or something. We can't think straight or we can't feel straight. But we're not meant to be here, among all this. This shit is fine for Nawaaz, even Farid. Me and you, we just keep looking for what's different. We can't keep our eyes off that other shit. Wondering what's happening outside, what other lives we can lead. I know bro. Trust me. I know."

Maaz had seen the look in my eye and recognized a kindred spirit. He'd given voice to my feelings. My heart filled with love. I'd never had a friend who understood me this way, someone who knew how I felt implicitly. I knew it must have been exactly what Cynthia felt with Cat. I was so grateful that I'd found such a soul in a place I'd had the least hope of finding someone. Maybe Allah had brought us together for that very reason. To help each other escape.

"Let's do it then," I said. "Let's get outta here one day. If shit doesn't work out, let's work it out somewhere else."

"I got you." He held his fist out and I pounded it. And no other seal was needed. Not before and not since. Promises made by fourteen-year-olds would always be pure and dumb. Sincere and naive.

"Here we go," Farid said, lugging a sack of lentils. "Everything we need."

Nawaaz was right behind him with a giant tub of yogurt he dropped on the table. Farid and Nawaaz consummated their own promise, pounding fists while the other kids looked towards Alif for the next step. His thick brows were raised in mild surprise, trying to think, quickly, what the next step was supposed to be. Before he could say anything, Farid dropped a blender onto the table with another loud thud, calling everyone's attention back to him.

"Pretty sure we gotta blend all the shit together in this," he said.

One of the younger kids raised a large shiny bowl onto the table. Rolling up their sleeves, Khalid and Syed began to mix and mash the ingredients in the bowl with their hands while Nawaaz supervised. Meanwhile, we started blending the daal concoction into a viscous liquid. Maaz and I turned on the stovetop and placed the largest, deepest frying pan we could find on top of it, filling it with neon oil. Below us, Farid was fiddling with the oven's settings, but we shooed him away with a sharp foot to his back. *Dahi baray* did not require baking. I spotted a whisk and knew I needed to use it for something. I looked around and locked eyes with Abdi, the young champion from Heart Attack One's fight club.

"Come here," I said, gesturing. "Whisk up everything in this bowl with this cup of water, and just keep whisking."

Our mix was looking ashy and dry, and I was desperate, thinking water might save it somehow. Abdi went to work, both hands wrapped around the giant whisk while he poured water into the bowl from time to time and stirred. Maaz and I started dropping small clumps of the mixture into the hot oil. We jumped back as the oil splashed onto us, searing our skin.

"Fuck! It's so goddamn hot," I said, rubbing my arm.

Maaz was looking at the oil in a stupor, shocked that a pan could be so dangerous. We formed two smaller balls from the slurry and dropped them into the pan from higher up, hoping to avoid the splash back. The oil splashed even higher and harder at us, and we danced around, fanning our arms, realizing we were much more incompetent than we thought.

"How the fuck is it so hot?" I asked.

"Should we turn down the heat? Is oil always like this?" Maaz asked to no one.

"Move," Abdi said, noticing our struggle. "I'll drop it into the oil, and you guys whisk."

He handed us the whisk and started forming small balls of the mixture, then dropping them into the pan low and soft until it was full of the small cream-coloured balls. Somehow, the sizzling had dropped to a soft, compliant murmur with Abdi attending to them. Alif and Farid came over to check on the mixture and helped with turning over the *baray* and removing them from the oil when golden brown. Maaz and I felt less than useless by the bowl, but we whisked all the same.

I noticed Farid fiddling with the oven again. "Yo, what are you even doing?"

"Don't watch that. I'm making something too nice for the likes of you."

I shook my head and continued with the whisking. Soon, we had a huge pile of oddly shaped *baray*. Some circular, some oval, some globular, some in shapes that had yet to be classified. Some were topaz, some were sunlight, some were ruby, some were earthy and some pitch-black; the colours varied depending on how long they'd sat in the fryer. Some were crumbling apart, and some, by the grace of Allah, looked perfect. I looked around and noticed that Hafiz Abdullah was not among us, and I was a little crestfallen. For some people, this was a waste of time. The same way someone needed to be perfect, someone needed to be imperfect.

Once all the *baray* were in the bowl, we brought over the yogurt and dumped it right on top, mixing everything delicately so as not to crush or squish any of the balls. I saw some spare coriander and grabbed a knife, chopping it and then spreading it generously over the dish.

"This won't work," Alif said, suddenly doubtful upon seeing my knife skills. "It's gonna taste horrible. We need the tamarind. *Dahi baray* needs that tamarind."

I looked around for confirmation or rebuttal. *Dahi baray* was not my forte. I just knew that where we were all from, you threw coriander on everything. Had we been making *bhorta*, I would have been able to discern what every ounce and crumb of it should look and taste and smell like. There was silence after Alif's comment, though. They were all in agreement. *Dahi baray* apparently needed tamarind.

"Nah man," Farid said, rushing over to the fridge and pulling open the fruit drawer. He took out a few crabapples. "This shit will do. You need something sour right? Like something real sour?"

"It's not going to work man. Forget it!" Alif was inconsolable and unwilling to compromise. "We need the tamarind, and without it, this is going to taste like nothing. Full stop."

"We don't have tamarind. But we made all this shit," Farid said, "and it's gonna go to waste if we don't eat it. We made it and we gotta do something with it no? What if it ends up tasting great?"

Everyone was quiet.

"This is the best we have—this is *all* we have," he said, holding out the apples in his hand.

He was right. It *was* all we had. I walked over to him, grabbed the apples and began cutting them up on the table. Slowly, people started joining in. The alternative was throwing out the *baray*, packing it up and going home. But Farid had brought us into that kitchen for a reason. To forget the cold, to forget the pain of our lost middle school lives, to forget our worries about *du'as* and lessons, and to help a homesick friend through a particularly rough time. So we mashed up the apples until they were nice and pulpy, halfway to juice. Alif then took the bowl from us and held it over the *baray* and started to pour the liquid out at a snail's pace. He was treating the process like open-heart surgery, with all the solemnity and gravitas that required.

"Oy, get him a chair!" Nawaaz yelled.

Two of the younger kids dragged over a chair out of nowhere. Alif clambered on top of it and continued pouring the crabapple juice over the *baray*. Light glimmered off the trickle as we were glued to the image of Alif, pajama-clad in a T-shirt and cap, standing on a chair above us in a bright kitchen in the middle of the night. I wished Maaz had paintbrushes and a canvas to capture the image in that moment.

When Alif finished, he hopped off the chair and we all stood around the bowl, unsure of what came next.

"Well, we gotta eat it too don't we?" I finally asked the room.

"Time to eat. Who's first?" Alif asked.

"It's gotta be you, no?" Maaz said. "If it's good, you stay. If it's bad . . . well, we'll get it if you leave."

"No, it wouldn't be right if I was first," Alif said. "Everybody helped. Everybody should have it too. We should try it together. Same bite, same time."

We all grabbed *baray* and waited for a signal. Yogurt dripped from mine while I looked at Maaz, Nawaaz and Farid.

"All right," I shouted. "Three, two, one . . ." And then I bit into it.

It was shit. Disgusting. It didn't even qualify as food. I'd never tasted anything so bad in my life. It could only be compared to a car tire or sheet metal or a brick. It just wasn't food. It was bitter, ashy, poisonous and totally unfamiliar. Not a single ingredient we'd put into the mixture was recognizable. I didn't want it in my mouth or in my body. I started coughing immediately and was joined by the rest of the room. We were retching and puking and spitting and coughing all over the kitchen. I went over to the sink to spit out what I could, genuinely afraid of swallowing a single crumb. I turned to look at my companions, and they were straight out of another kind of painting. Maaz was slouched against the table with legs outstretched, *baray* dribbling down his chin, Nawaaz squatting over him in concern. He had a glassy expression on his face, and Nawaaz kept slapping and shoving him for a response. Our own *Death of General Wolfe* was playing out right there in Al Haque. Kids were screaming, puking on hands and knees. I saw Syed slip and fall over a *baray* that Abdi had barfed out.

Alif though, was still standing over the bowl, chewing slowly and methodically.

"Dude, what are you doing? It's disgusting," I said.

The room fell silent. We were all dumbfounded. Why was Alif still biting into the mess?

He had tears in his eyes as he picked up another *baray*. "I knoooow," he moaned as he bit into it, crying hard as the tears fell.

We cracked up. We couldn't help it. We started dying of laughter. We were doubled over, fighting for air. Pounding tables and tiles and fighting tears for breath. Each and every one of us. And then Alif joined us too. Maybe a little less desperate for a place.

CHAPTER 11

Five Hundred Up-Downs; or, The Monkey and the Chicken

We were doubled over in laughter when we heard a distinct ding. The oven had just gone off, and Farid walked over to pull something out.

"What the hell is that?" I asked.

"Behold, my masterpiece," he said. He moved out of the way to reveal a huge pan, and on it was something resembling a pizza. While the rest of us had been dutifully attending to the *dahi baray*, Farid had been off on his own mission. In an act of prescience about our spectacular failure, he'd embarked on a quest to make something that would be edible. We hadn't seen him doing it, but he'd rolled out dough and covered it in mashed tomato purée, chopped coriander and garlic, and whatever random items he could find in the fridge. He put on a pair of oven mitts and carried the pan over to the large central table. We all gathered ourselves and stood around the steaming "pizza." We were afraid. It looked promising, but we'd just survived a near-death experience with another dish that had masqueraded as food. Farid walked back towards the cupboard and came back with a jar of honey.

"Ew, are you sure?" I asked. One innovation had already resulted in disaster.

"Silence, Padawan," he commanded.

He unscrewed the jar and began spooning honey onto the pie while we watched. We couldn't tell if he'd done this before. I thought I'd have to remember to ask him what it was that got him kicked out of the last madrasa. He began cutting into the pizza and handing out slices with my help. The kitchen was packed, but we somehow managed not to run out of slices. No matter how many Farid dished out, there were more to go around. He just kept passing them to me, and I just kept distributing them to waiting hands. I didn't want to look too closely at the pizza for fear there would be none left for me, or I'd somehow ruin the miracle by calculating how many slices remained. Instead, Farid cut and I distributed. Just like the unending cup of milk in that one hadith from Abu Hurayrah (RAH):

> The Prophet said, "O Aba-Hirr!" I said, "Labbaik, O Allah's Apostle!" He said, "Take it and give it to them." So I took the bowl [of milk] and started giving it to one man who would drink his fill and return it to me, whereupon I would give it to another man who, in his turn, would drink his fill and return it to me, and I would then offer it to another man, who would drink his fill and return it to me. Finally, after the whole group had drunk their fill, I reached the Prophet, who took the bowl and put it on his hand, looked at me and smiled and said, "O Aba-Hirr!" I replied, "Labbaik, O Allah's Apostle!" He said, "There remain you and I." I said, "You

have said the truth, O Allah's Apostle!" He said, "Sit down and drink." I sat down and drank. He said, "Drink," and I drank. He kept on telling me repeatedly to drink, till I said, "No. By Allah Who sent you with the Truth, I have no space for it [in my stomach]." He said, "Hand it over to me." When I gave him the bowl, he praised Allah and pronounced Allah's name on it and drank the remaining milk.

When we all had our slices in front of us, we stayed standing, hesitant to make the same mistake we'd made with the *dahi baray* by biting into it together. Instead, we watched Farid venture a bite first and then chew.

"Yo, I'm nice with it,'" he said.

"Bullshit," Maaz said. He bit into his slice, and the rest of the room quickly followed suit.

We had to admit, it was pretty good. At the very least, it was food. It was all we had, and we were making do. Farid had layered the pizza with some beef Sharmil Bhai had been marinating, making for a dangerous combination with the honey spread on top. But compared to the *dahi baray*, this was cutting-edge cuisine.

We were all scattered about, some of the kids cross-legged on the floor, chewing the pizza in silence. The room was bright, the night was old; pajamas, T-shirts and sweaters were our uniform. We were warm from the oven, and there was no indication that it was January, or that we were worried in any way. Maaz, Bilal, Khalid and the rest of the students who were a part of the *Qirat* competition looked relaxed. There was none of the stress or quippy clapbacks we'd had to suffer through in class. They didn't look sleep-deprived or agitated with a slice in hand. Farid was necessary. There at Al Haque, and later with whatever Maaz and I were dreaming up.

Suddenly, the door to the kitchen opened up, and we turned to see Heart Attack One and Sharmil Bhai. Everyone froze, pizza in mouth, slice in hand. The two men both held long pieces of plywood, and Heart Attack One was still dressed in his winter coat and hat. Somehow, Sharmil Bhai had got out of his room.

"What's going on here?" Sharmil Bhai whispered.

The two of them scanned the room, trying to piece together a story that would make sense. Clearly, the students had snuck out; clearly they'd used the kitchen to cook food in the middle of the night. They were calculating how many rules had been broken, how many transgressions had occurred, how many years would have to be spent cleansing sins in hellfire.

"Everyone get out!" Heart Attack One said. "Out! Everyone! Get out of here!" He started beating students, forehand to backhand, until they rushed out of the room. Some on all fours, some crawling, others sprinting, some hopping over his swipes. It was like a nature documentary where lions attack a herd of scrambling gazelle.

We ran into the empty basement classroom, but at the door leading to the hallway stood Heart Attacks Two and Three, also in their winter gear, peering at us through red eyes and preventing our escape. We'd interrupted their sleep and forced the three Heart Attacks to drive through the night to act as reinforcements for Sharmil Bhai.

Some of the younger kids had started crying silently, and my heart was in my throat; I couldn't swallow because of fear. I had no idea what came next and was afraid for my life. I tried telling myself that they needed our tuition, that they couldn't kill us. But to be honest, I wasn't confident. There was no love in their eyes, and looking around at my peers inspired no strength. They had the same scared look. Maaz was on the ground, hands wrapped around his knees, head buried in his lap. Nawaaz was looking around, searching for an escape that didn't exist. I looked for Farid and found him in the middle of a bunch of younger kids, consoling them. Everyone else was crying, holding their heads in their hands, but Farid was trying to make the younger kids laugh and relax. After a few minutes, Sharmil Bhai and Heart Attack One emerged from the kitchen. We sat corralled in a small group, trying to make ourselves seem even smaller.

"Stand up. Stand up!" Heart Attack One bellowed.

We stood up together.

"Spread out. Everyone in a line. One *saf*."

We spread out facing Heart Attack One, lined up across the basement like we were getting ready for prayer. From one end, close to Heart Attacks Two and Three, to the other, near the basement wall where Maulana Yusuf had struck out.

"Reach out your hands. Everyone!"

We complied, knowing what was coming next. Sharmil Bhai started at the far end of the room, and Heart Attack Three started near the door. Wood in hand, they began striking students one after the other, making their way to the middle. The blows were swift and hard, the air singing the journey from hand to hand. Each kid would yelp or cry out or fall to the ground, while the kid next to him stood waiting his turn.

Maaz, Nawaaz, Farid and I were near the middle, and the anticipation was the worst. There were so many of us waiting that it just started to eat away at me. I'd rather be beat and have it over with. But the yelping, hearing how hard kids were being hit, doubled my fear when I thought doubling it wasn't possible anymore. When our turns finally came, Sharmil Bhai struck us hard enough to bring us to our knees.

When they were finished, they stood in front of us with Heart Attack One, watching us writhe in agony. I had the fleeting hope that our punishment was complete, and we'd be dismissed.

"Everyone up," Heart Attack One commanded. "Stand up!"

We stood up immediately, afraid of what would happen if we were slow on the uptake. "Everyone doing five hundred up-downs. Now!"

We started the tried-and-true punishment immediately. It had been around for thousands of years and would be around for thousands more. I had no doubt that whatever future awaited humanity, up-downs would be a part of it.

Our fingers held our earlobes and we squatted and stood, completing one up-down. I'd never heard of anyone getting more than two hundred up-downs before, and even then, it was Farid, months earlier, for repeatedly opening his mouth during a sermon from Heart Attack Four. Still, at least five hundred up-downs was a fate we shared with the other students.

"You four. You four will do six hundred," Heart Attack One pronounced, gesturing to me, Maaz, Nawaaz and Farid.

We looked at him in the middle of our up-downs with perplexed horror.

"I know you four were behind all this. You think we know nothing? That your *ustads* are ignorant? We know who sneaks around, making plans for *masthi*. All this mischief would not have happened without you four. I knew as *soon* as we got the call that I would find you four in the middle of it. Why?"

It was a question that needed no answer. Heart Attack One turned to address the rest of the students.

"This is what happens when you join these four. Keep this in mind. Remember this. These four are selfish. They don't care about you; they don't care about being good students, about helping you learn and memorize. You've seen them, right? In class? How you guys got pulled into their nonsense?"

No one said anything, and Heart Attack One continued.

"Look what they pulled you into. Look how they got you into trouble. Why did you trust these four? Look what happened. If they don't want to learn they don't want to learn. Don't worry, we understand and see *all* the nonsense they do. We know exactly everything they do, they plan. We keep watch. We will know, and if they don't want to learn, we will deal with them. But if you trust them, this will happen to you too. They don't care about you. Look, look! They just wanted to make a mess in the kitchen and needed your help, so they used you for this nonsense and look what they did to you. They used you. *Chaar bainchod!*"

As we continued our up-downs, Heart Attack One kicked us over one by one while the rest of the students continued theirs.

"You destroyed my kitchen," Sharmil Bhai said quietly. "I don't know how you will eat tomorrow." The destruction of the kitchen had rattled him. His precious space had been desecrated and we'd crossed a sacred boundary.

Heart Attacks Two and Three walked deeper into the room and began beating students through their up-downs seemingly at random. They would skip some students and strike others, choosing perhaps by reputation—who was more responsible and who less. They were angry that they'd had to wake up in the middle of the night for this. They pulled the youngest kids out of line and dragged them to a separate area, delivering blows along the way. The four of us were beaten at the back of our necks by Heart Attack Three, who paused to deliver a few extra blows to Maaz.

"Idiot! How can you fool? How can you mess around here still? You . . . should . . . be . . . studying!" Every pause was a smack. He whispered through gritted teeth so only those nearest to Maaz could hear.

The students who'd completed their up-downs watched while we struggled through our extras. My knees were aching, my lower back was screaming in pain, and each one took seconds that felt like hours to complete. I'd bend at the knee, go down, gasp and take forever to come back up. I'd pause, freeze halfway up, fight, claw, struggle, push and finally rise at a snail's pace. Maaz, Nawaaz and Farid were faring no better. We had no concern about losing count, though, as Heart Attack One had been eyeing us like a hawk. He knew exactly where we were.

"No, no mercy tonight," Heart Attack One said when he saw Farid pause. "You can die or collapse, but I don't care. All six hundred will be complete, and your classmates will watch you finish them so they know what happens to people like you."

By the time we finished we would have preferred death. We would have accepted and preferred any punishment that came in the grave, or in hell itself. We would have accepted anything else Heart Attack One had planned for us, and we would have embraced it, as long as it wasn't another up-down. We lay on the floor, legs outstretched, while Heart Attack One and Sharmil Bhai dismissed us. Sharmil Bhai went back into the kitchen to mourn, and Heart Attack One went up the stairs and disappeared. The four of us were left to drag our bodies up to our rooms and crawl into bed.

"We should have put a third desk in front of his fucking door," Nawaaz said.

"Yo, for a hot minute before you showed us the pizza, I legit thought you made bannock, for some reason," I said.

My three companions cracked up quietly. Even through the pain, Cynthia could reach us.

"Yo seen, I should've done that!" Farid said. "It would've been blessed."

"Nah fam, even Cynthia said that shit tasted like ass," Maaz said. "She had more luck than us though, not getting caught and all."

—

We read the next diary entry piled into Farid's bed the following morning, the four of us squeezed together under one blanket, nursing aches and bruises while a storm raged outside.

1/30/78
Dear Mark,
I really did think that this was all I wanted. That I'd just go to school and become a virtuous person in the service of God. I want you to know that things change and sometimes you'll want other things too. If you ever grow up and feel something else one day, that's okay. You grow, and you read things, and you meet people,

and maybe you won't feel the same way you did yesterday and that's okay.

The other day we got in trouble for making snow angels. Snow angels. I didn't think there was anything particularly religious about them—I mean, sure, "angels," but we're just kids having fun making things. When Father Frances caught us in the snow, she saw red. She dragged me and Cat into the basement and made us kneel in front of her to recite a hundred God of Graces. She was weird about it too. She stood way too close to us, then pulled our hair and yanked it up so we'd have to say it to a crucifix. But then she'd keep her hands in our hair and like, I dunno, be weird with it. We tried to talk about it after but it was hard. How can bad actions lead to good people? Can her punishment lead to virtue? Isn't there a better way? I'm still learning I guess, and I want you to know that it's okay if you're confused too. And if you're still learning and asking questions and stuff. If you find yourself out of place in a place, question, fight and at least look for a person who makes you feel like you're not out of place. And that's from your sister.

Cat could probably tell that I was pretty peeved about what Father Frances did to us (over snow angels, no less), because yesterday she made sure we had our revenge. We filled up these huge pails with water, cornstarch and some food colouring, then waited at the top of the dorms until Father Frances started climbing the stairs. We dumped both pails all over her and heard her scream for whoever had done it to come down immediately. I was scared shitless, but as soon as I heard that shrieky banshee try to command us, I burst into laughter and ran away with Cat. Serves that old batty bitch right.

—Cyn

That day was especially sombre. We were still processing what had happened the night before, and most of us had probably got no more than a half hour of sleep. We weren't even sure if we had the right to venture into the basement after Fajr to see if breakfast was still a thing at Al Haque. Students didn't dare speak to other students lest it be misconstrued as a continuation of the night's mischief, and the *ustads* didn't speak to students out of spite and anger. The few who had stayed in bed and were woefully ignorant of the new impasse ventured down to the basement as usual, and we followed them pretending we were ignorant as well. When we entered we were greeted with the normal placemat paper on the ground, but on top of it were plates and heaps of biscuits and jugs of steaming milk tea. We took our places and began digging in. We weren't sure if this was a punishment because it felt like a reward. Even cookies were better than what we were used to. We were too young to appreciate effort, duty and sacrifice. If we were meant to feel sorry for the kitchen escapade, then giving us cookies was the wrong way to go about it.

I snatched an interesting-looking one from Farid's hand and popped it into my mouth. "Do you think we should be worried about what Heart Attack One said?" I asked through a mouth full of cookie.

"What do you mean?"

"How he told everyone not to trust us. He said we were all out for ourselves."

"He says that because they're scared," Farid replied. "They're worried. We did so much damage, had so much fun, he had to throw a Hail Maryam to try to get the students to, like, distrust us."

Farid's explanation made some semblance of sense. He was

doing his part, dragging Al Haque and everything else like it to reckon with the world.

On our way upstairs that night, wondering how we'd break this wordless new rift between the students and the teachers, we saw Sharmil Bhai heading down from the second-floor landing. We avoided eye contact and tried to make ourselves invisible. One wrong never made another wrong guilt-free. The larger person is the one who suffers. And because we'd chosen not to suffer his beatings without breaking into the kitchen, we were in uncharted territory, unsure of what our lines were or what the script looked like that would fix the mess we were in. We didn't have long to worry, however, as that narrative was already in motion.

Hafiz Abdullah had been reading the Quran in the main prayer area when we'd all headed up to bed. He'd waited until even those who'd stayed up for Tahajjud had gone to sleep, and then he'd snuck downstairs to the basement and into the kitchen. He rolled up his sleeves and cleaned and scrubbed every last surface until it sparkled, rearranging and tidying everything for Sharmil Bhai in the morning. He got down on his hands and knees and wiped and swept until the kitchen was returned to its original state.

Naturally, Sharmil Bhai had no idea who was responsible, but he assumed that some of us were full of contrition and had cleaned the area without alerting him. The next morning he was moved, and word got back to the maulanas, who ended their silence strike on account of our purported actions. In reality, it was just the greatest one of us who'd saved us, and returned to us our breakfast of pale eggs and thin haleem.

CHAPTER 12

Those Old Internet Romances

Because exercise hours meant we could spread out and wander the grounds, we were able to escape to the roof consistently without being noticed. One afternoon, we got to the roof and noticed that Farid was missing. We weren't too alarmed though, because we knew he was most likely at the field phone booth, talking to the sex-chat girl, and had probably been in too much of a rush to get to her to tell us where he was going.

He'd had an especially taxing morning that day, culminating in a legendary beating from Maulana Hasan for daring to compare Wolverine's martial prowess to Khalid ibn Walid's in a rebuttal to a story of the latter's greatness.

It was like the more time that passed and the more his *aalim*-hood was becoming a reality, the more he was rebelling. The more that time moved forward, the more he protested it. The more people grew, the more he grew violently in another direction. After that night in the kitchen, he was dangerously close to expulsion or worse. I doubt he knew any of that, though, as the concept of laying low was an affront to his soul.

Maaz, Nawaaz and I were staring up at the sky, lying in snow angels we'd made on the roof, while sounds of the younger kids playing in the fields below reached our ears.

"Let's go find Farid," I said. "He's probably at the phone booth. We gotta try to talk some sense into him, at least try to make him easier to handle 'til we're a bit older and can actually leave. We can't have him die here."

Bored on the roof without him, we trekked across the soft white field towards the booth. By the time we got to Farid, he was just stepping out, and he had on a stupid glazed grin we just had to say something about. He still had no facial hair, and his round, smooth face and dopey brown eyes didn't match the look of a kid who knew as much as he did.

"*Astaghfirullah*, you know they're being paid to listen to you, right?" Maaz said.

"Yeah, I don't care. I know exactly what it is. If I can't have Del, imma have Krystal tell me all about what Del's missing out on."

I couldn't believe he still thought about the vegetable girl. Alana had long since been buried in another lifetime.

"What do you mean what she's missing out on, huh? What about what *you're* missing out on? You're missing out on valuable exercise," Nawaaz said. He grabbed Farid and put him in a head-lock. "What did she say you were missing out on? Huh?"

We were starved.

"Allow that fam. It's between me and Krystal!" Farid said, trying to shove Nawaaz off him. Nawaaz wouldn't let go however. He was too big and too strong, and he started dragging Farid across the snow.

"Lemme go! Please! I'll tell you how we can get a car. *Wallahi* fam, I'm not lying." He was coughing and squirming.

"Why do you keep saying that?" Nawaaz asked. "We already know how to get a car here. What's wrong with you?" He twisted his headlock tighter.

"Okay seen let's do it. Please!" Farid begged when he felt the pressure from Nawaaz.

Nawaaz released the headlock.

"We're waiting 'til we finish the journal aren't we? And can find Cynthia's number in the phone book from the principal's office?" I looked around at the group as I asked the questions.

"I mean, we're already here. We could just make the call for a car," Nawaaz said with lifted eyebrows.

"Say word you have the money," I said, turning my attention to Farid.

"Word!"

"Don't listen to this idiot, man," Maaz snapped. "How would we even hide it here? Who would drive?"

"Don't watch that. My dad taught me how to drive," Farid said hurriedly.

"Wait, really?" I asked. We didn't know Farid had received informal teaching from his dad on how to drive, this did change things somewhat.

Having a car would open up a whole new world. Not just to the final, permanent escape, but to small interludes that would carry us through the coming months and years. It was way too difficult to turn something like that down. Imagine being able to leave for a few hours to watch a movie or to eat something other than the same three curries.

I turned to Nawaaz. "Your boy Marcus, he's good for this typa shit?"

"Yeah, mans come through still."

"Seen then, how much you think we can get it for?" Maaz asked.

This was uncharted territory again. Our crimes were growing larger and larger as our souls grew smaller and more pious. Love for the world caused all these problems, of course, but what were you going to do? We weren't in the afterlife yet, and it was difficult to be cold, weary and anticipating an afterlife so young. How could I not devote myself to them and them to me? I don't know how to argue on behalf of the world other than to say we weren't dead then, wrestling in the snow, stealing food from each other's plates, salving heartbreaks, chasing beatings and protecting each other. And we wouldn't be dead later, wherever we were, in whatever state, wrestling whatever, stealing whatever, salving whatever, chasing whatever and protecting whatever. By the bones of Bill Barilko, we've been good.

Nawaaz went into the phone booth and dialled his friend while we waited outside. He emerged after a long conversation, when the light in the sky was beginning to darken.

"Yeah we can do it. But it's gonna cost us."

"How much?" Maaz asked.

"Seven bills."

"Ouch," Maaz said.

"Nah it's fine. I'm good for it," Farid said.

"No, I'm gonna throw in a bill too," Nawaaz said. "I want this car to be part mine, and it won't be fair if it's just you putting in money. We should all put in something."

Nawaaz looked at me and Maaz. We nodded in agreement. The car was ordered.

When we got back to the madrasa we separated after Asr, as we all had things to do. Farid was on laundry duty, Nawaaz was helping Sharmil Bhai with kitchen prep, and Maaz and I were vacuuming on the second floor.

"Yo, lemme know if you don't wanna talk about it, but just being at the phone booth, I was wondering, does the thing with Alana still bother you?" Maaz asked.

I was quiet for a minute.

"No, it doesn't bother me," I finally said. "It was probably always going to end with her eventually anyway. I just don't like how it was . . . forced to end. By Al Haque or my life here or whatever. But it's all over and buried now."

"True. I just wanted to check on you."

"Chill with that shit, I'm good. When we get outta here I'll be fine. Mans get bare girls."

"Okaaay," Maaz said, exaggerating his disbelief. "Whatever you say."

"What does that mean?" I said, turning off the vacuum in starts and stops so we could keep talking.

Maaz held up the cord behind me. "Fam you prob'ly be talking to girls about video games and shit, like 'Hi, do you want to play *Mario Kart* with me?' You don't get shit."

Maaz had no doubt overheard a few of the conversations Farid and I had had.

"What about you? You can't just show them a drawing and chop that shit. Like, 'Here, look at this tree I drew. Look how green I made it.'"

244

We both cracked up.

There was no one else like Maaz at Al Haque. His sideburns had turned into a faint beard, and when he smiled, he would throw his cheeks into it, making sure you knew you'd made him happy. I was touched that Maaz had thought to ask about Alana after such a long time. I wanted to make sure he felt the same way.

"Ey bro, it's not a one-way street you know?"

"What do you mean?" he asked.

"I doubt that Cat and Cynthia ever held shit back from each other. So I want you to know you can talk to me about anything. Even stuff that you're going through here bro."

"Yeah I know," he said.

"Nah for real. Like anything, anything. I don't care. I got your back, no matter what. I'm really lucky I found you and we got each other, you know what I mean? If nothing else, Al Haque helped us meet."

"Yeah for real."

"I don't care what you do. I got your back through everything. If there's some shit between you and Nawaaz—"

"I know," Maaz cut me off. "I know. I know you got me. I know you probably know about some of the weirder shit that goes on here. I know I can trust you. But there's some shit that's not even worth talking about. Some shit this place just forces onto us. Weird shit. I've said it before and I'll say it again: you and I are different. That's *why* I'm telling you. That's *why* I trust you. We stay together. We leave together. Farid, Nawaaz, whether they stay or leave, just like the rest of the students, they'll all forget. They're all the same. Eventually, they forget, bury all the weird shit and pretend it never happened. You and I don't forget. We stay together. We leave together."

I kept vacuuming. Maaz didn't need me to say anything to know that I agreed. I had tried to ask him about Nawaaz, but that was as close as I got and as close as I needed to get. I had all the answers I needed.

—

That night there was a shocking turn of events in Cynthia's diary. We read it together using a tiny penlight Nawaaz had extorted from some kid.

2/20/78
Dear Mark,
It finally happened. They kicked Cat out. I still can't believe it to be honest. Father Frances walked in on us. I'm not sure what else to say. If you thought I'd tell you about that stuff, you must be out of your mind. I wanted to tell you about my life—all the good stuff, and advice, and things I saw and all that. But I was hiding something I'm not so sure can be hidden, ever. I was trying to keep it a secret from myself too. And telling you now just makes it real. Catherine and I love each other.

It all started after we'd dumped the pails on Father Frances last month. When we ran away from her and out into the cold, away from everyone else, we just kissed. There, out of sight, I felt no cold when our lips touched. It just made so much sense when we did it that I wanted to cry. It's like puzzle pieces falling into place when we touch. It's more than friendship. The last month never felt like a month—it was a lifetime that was too good to be true. And now this place is intolerable without her. I look around and see nothing and feel nothing. Nothing interests me. She ruined me. All I see are bodies from Night of the Living Dead, walking around and being yes-girls to everything the clergy and teachers say. None of them think for themselves, question or do anything without guidance first. And if they do question or show a bit of spunk, they break down as soon as the teachers crack down on them. What kind of life is that? They got rid of her because she'd been raising hell for so much longer than I had, and they figured she was the bad influence on me and they could still "save" me, but what do they know? I'm ruined and I'd have it no other way.

—Cyn

"Jeezus Louise-uss, she was a Lebanese the whole time," Farid whisper-shouted.

No one laughed.

We had no idea what to do with the information. There weren't many entries left, and we were worried about what was going to happen.

"It's just a dumb diary," Maaz grumbled. "We're almost done with it . . ." But his words sounded hollow. We all know how much it meant to us.

"Yeah. We gotta go to bed anyway," I added, relieved by the deflation and eager to get away from this sinking feeling.

But the universe was aligning, and there was no escape from this. The same way you run into an old friend right after thinking about how you haven't seen them in a while, or you get a crit just when you need it to knock out Lance's Dragonite.

When we got to our room, Farid revealed something he'd seen while distributing linens to the dorms. "Bruh, that shit between Cynthia and Cat? It's real. It just reminded me. You need to know, just in case they kill me. Syed and Ikram were going at it in their room."

"What do you mean?" I said, turning over in my bed.

"I mean I walked in on them doing some homo shit," he said. "You need to know. Remember when we talked and you were so shocked that shit went down here? You need to know it happens."

"You sound more shocked than me to be honest."

"Well yeah! It just happened! And the fact that it happened at Sacred Heart too . . . I mean, it's still surprising to see it though in person. Every place I've been."

"Is that why you got kicked out of the last madrasa?"

"Nah, that was just over some regular shit. I would've stuck around there, but it was boring man. No one like you guys over there, and no chance of meeting someone like Del."

I rolled my eyes in the dark. Del was a one-off encounter, and Al Haque deserved no credit for making such an encounter possible.

"For real though, why do you think we're like this?" Farid continued. "Everyone's on the internet now, and we're out here with our fuckin' imaginations."

It was the early days of the fledgling Myspace romance, when we'd begun to reveal ourselves to one another, shed barriers and shells under the guise of anonymity. Left without the ability to reach out to someone across the world through a punk song, we did things we couldn't talk about under roofs in the middle of nowhere. Days and months were lost while people exchanged glances on a subway, passed notes in class and skipped heartbeats over text messages and flashing orange icons. Hands reached for hands, bodies held secrets and you carried codenames discreetly from school to home. You shared headphones, entwined fingers and shared a bumpy, dirty bus ride to a subway station. Your part-time backrooms and bedrooms were filled with this new world, the possibility that someone might actually understand you, whether it was someone you shared a class with that you could now speak to after-hours, or someone in some other class thousands of miles away you could now speak to after-*after*-hours. Who would understand us but us?

"Let's find Cynthia," I said.

Farid didn't reply.

"I mean, like, actually find her. Let's find her, find her. Not just talk about it. I wanna see if she's real. Like, did she ever make it out? Let's really get at that phone book in Mufti Abbas's office and find her. Let's at least break in and have a look, no matter what the journal says."

We discussed it at length with Maaz and Nawaaz the next day, but we were in a rut. Accessing the phone book would be the hardest thing we'd ever planned. Principal Abbas's office was right outside the prayer hall, in the main hallway leading to the stairs. Not only was it a high-traffic area, but we'd have to get in before Isha. Ever since our kitchen escapade, Sharmil Bhai had been extra vigilant in ensuring that no one snuck out of their rooms at night. We'd seen Jara take a beating a week earlier just for walking down the hall to use the bathroom. Sharmil Bhai would not be caught unawares again. We'd need to cause a large enough distraction to work on the door unencumbered, picking the lock without anyone passing by.

"I feel like involving Heart Attack One in this is the key somehow," I said, mostly to myself. The man's anger was unrivalled, and matched that of a beast more than a human. If we could bait him into unleashing that anger somewhere, or towards someone, we might be able to cause a scene large enough that no one would notice one or two of us sneaking away.

"How?" Nawaaz asked. We were hanging out in our stairwell foyer before bed.

"I think I get it," Maaz said. "Mans get so angry he can't control himself. If he's wildin' about some shit, no one will notice one or two of us in that hallway. But where and what exactly, right? Like we can't act like he's a kid we can just play with like that, still."

"Yeah that's my issue exactly," I muttered. I thought through what could make him angry and came up with a list of almost everything. Misdeeds, misbehaviours, mistakes, talking back, talking too much, talking too softly. He really believed the worst of us.

"Ey don't you have any ideas?" Maaz said, looking at Farid, who'd been staring off into space as we plotted in the stairwell.

"Hmm?"

"He's a Patel. You guys have to have some weakness, no? Patels gonna know Patels."

"That's the dumbest thing I've ever heard," Farid replied. "I'm not asking you for the key to Maulana Ingar's heart because you're both Siddiquis."

Maaz chuckled in response. It was something about the way he laughed that brought it home to me. He laughed not only because he realized what he'd said was ridiculous, but also because he'd avowed by a name, took ownership and recognized a name as part of an ilk and blood. I learned about a weakness in that moment. Anyone who swore by a name—an old-stock anything—had that same weakness.

"Wait," I said. "I think I know what we have to do."

They turned to me.

"That fight league he runs in the basement—he has this weird thing about names, I'm pretty sure. He calls on people by their last names right? You guys noticed that?"

They nodded in agreement.

"He asks people where they're from—especially you Gujis, right? Maybe we can like, piss him off. Insult a Patel and force him into doing something stupid."

"Hmm. We're going to need a bit more than that," Farid said. "Thing is, he'll beat on us if we do something like that, but we need the other maulanas to be there too, to see it. We need most of the madrasa there. School and students. Otherwise, people will still be in the hallways, or they might walk by and miss it."

"There's only one time during the day when everyone's in the same place," Nawaaz said.

"Technically five times," Maaz added.

"Wait lemme see if we can get some help from some of the younger kids on this," I said, remembering Abdi. "They're his students right? They might be able to help."

I wasn't sure if Abdi would be amenable, but it couldn't hurt to ask. Gone was the time when we wouldn't involve anyone else in our sins. There were greater blessings at play.

—

The next day at breakfast, we made sure to sit near Abdi and his friend, who both had their heads down in their meals. When Abdi's friend left to get more eggs, I slid over, stealing the kid's spot, and sat directly across from Abdi. He pretended not to notice me. When his friend came back with a plate of eggs, Nawaaz took it from him and grabbed the kid by the collar of his jubba.

"Go take a walk. We gotta talk to your friend." Nawaaz shoved the kid away and put the plate of eggs down in front of me and Abdi. The kid knew better than to protest.

I took a good look at Abdi. He could not have been more than eleven or twelve, and yet there was a maturity about him I had to respect. He wouldn't be pushed around. I remembered how he'd handled the frying pan and the oil hitting his skin with barely a reaction. He was dark, with thin brows and a long face, and if I had to guess, I'd say in a few years he'd be taller than all of us. There was no hint of the beginnings of a beard on him, and his white cap hid his short hair. Judging from his appetite, he was no stranger to eating, but he didn't have an ounce of fat on him.

"Listen, uh—" I began.

"Not interested," he said.

"Hear us out."

"Doesn't matter. Not interested."

"You're going to hear us out," I said with finality. Champion gladiator or not, he would hear us out. We were something else. The other students at Al Haque knew exactly what we were now. Not quite hopeless, but not yet saved. Heart Attack One had us on his radar and would clock how we'd huddle together after prayer, or how we'd make a younger kid laugh with a funny face.

"We're not gonna force you to do shit. But we're gonna say our piece. And if you're still not interested, that's fine. We'll walk away."

He didn't say anything.

252

"My boys and I, we just need a distraction. We know you probably run shit in your year, so we just wanted to say wassup. We're asking you cuz the distraction we need has to be big. Like real big. And it needs to happen in the prayer hall. We know there's not many who could probably whup your ass, but we want you to start a fight, basically. That's all. Just start a big fight in the *namaaz* area and make it last a long time."

"With who?" he asked.

"Heart Attack One."

Everyone was quiet. Kids munched around us. Maaz, Nawaaz and Farid leaned in to hear Abdi's response.

"When?"

We weren't expecting such a ready response. I wasn't sure what to say.

"Uh . . . aren't you going to ask us what's in it for you?"

"There's nothing I want, really. But then you told me I might be able to fight Maulana Furkan. I guess I want that."

Smart. He was using Heart Attack One's real name, à la Voldemort, reducing the fear. We didn't know it back then, but Voldemort, aka Heart Attack One, aka Maulana Furkan, and Abdi, aka the Boy Who Lived, had a long and checkered past.

We didn't see it then but Heart Attack One was racist. His racism was just a little different compared to what we were used to. Maaz, Nawaaz, Farid and I—and all of our peers, for that matter—were joined together by a common faith and a common enemy, and we didn't see the differences between us. Heart Attack One, on the other hand, saw all the little differences the good old boys in Timmins saw too. Bloodlines, tribes, sacrifices, ancient offerings and honourings. What this town was famous for or what this person's uncle used to do. What a magistrate was and how many nieces removed you were from him. These quotidian details coloured their background and stood in for personality and culture, giving them an identity they were afraid of changing. Why change when you're safe and comfortable, right? If you could be sure that the farmland you tilled owed its ostentatious plunder to the sacrifices your great-grandparents made, you could feel good about yourself. Your efforts in Midland, Jubilee and Tillsonburg felt chaste, blessed and bloodless. Of course you would be furious if anyone told you about the sacred burial grounds beneath your feet, or the business deal that was more akin to theft. So just imagine that bloodied, dirty thing without a name or land, a connection, a history, sitting in your class and behaving like some entitled liege with the right to laugh and speak to people whose parents had made all the sacrifices. Or worse, whose very existence suggested that there *could* be blood on someone else's—anyone's—hands. He should be kissing the other kids' feet, thanking them for having opened this country's gates to the likes of him. No one could ever possibly have it worse. *They* were the hard-working immigrants, saving their money, buying a house together for the price of a house. All the bullshit *they'd* gone through—his older brother and *that* generation had gone through—when there was no one here who was brown. This kid was smiling like it was his right to sit in a room with other Muslims. But Abdi was just a kid from Regent Park, sent away for a better life the same way his grandfather had sent his father away from Somalia. He didn't understand why he was beat harder than the other kids. He just felt it. Didn't know why he was pushed harder than the other kids. Just was. His chores were the most difficult. He had the worst luck with seating arrangements, sleeping arrangements and shitting arrangements. His *sabaq* was the longest, meant to induce failure. He was the whipping boy of whipping boys, humiliated at every opportunity by a man who wouldn't believe that people from certain countries were the same as him. All because Abdi wasn't deferential, dared to see himself as equal and met eyes with eyes. Double-duties of dishes were meant to break him but instead they made him double-stoic and double-strong, until pan sizzles couldn't even break skin. And so, Abdi was put through the wringer, made to fight against every Siddiqui, Malik, Nakhuda and other land-magistrate-officer-minister-chairman-*sahib* in an effort to show him his place.

And he would beat the shit out of each of them.

Animosity would grow on both sides, ad infinitum. Enter the gibbon-otter, the jackal-falcon, the cobra-owl and the tiger-moose.

CHAPTER 13

Abu Rukana/Reena Virk's Revenge

Our plan was multifaceted. Abdi would have a classmate complain to Heart Attack One about him, inducing another punishment. Abdi would then continue to humiliate the same boy both verbally and physically in front of Heart Attack One in the prayer hall, forcing the kid to do whatever Abdi said while Heart Attack One watched. The idea was that if the kid endured enough humiliation without fighting back, Heart Attack One would eventually intercede as the divine defender of the last name. It was a huge gamble, however. There was no guarantee that Heart Attack One would intervene. We were presupposing his anger as greater than his fear of Allah, because there was no precedent for punishing or beating a kid in a sacred prayer space, not to mention the fact that the other maulanas would be there. Though they were not oblivious to Heart Attack One's nature, and even agreed that you could beat children based on one or two sayings of the Prophet, they liked to believe they were above these uncouth displays of discipline, and avoided revelling in such corporal indulgence if at all possible.

For his part, Abdi was eager to put the plan into action. He'd suffered too long under Heart Attack One, and their cold war had to end. The ultimate homunculus of suffering versus the ultimate homunculus of pain. Still, I had no idea what Abdi was thinking, taking on Heart Attack One. There was no way he could beat an adult in a fight. Regardless of how strong he was for a kid, Heart Attack One was something else.

A few days later, Abdi gave us the heads-up that the plan was in action. He had a fresh black eye when he tapped us on the shoulder after Isha.

"Tomorrow night" was all he said. He pretended the black eye was normal. As a result, we pretended the black eye was normal as well.

The next night at Isha, we noticed Abdi and his accomplice praying suspiciously close to Heart Attack One. When Heart Attack One began additional independent prayers in front of Abdi, we could see the boy ordering his accomplice around in a humiliating manner. Pointing at Qurans on shelves, gesturing to fetch his socks from the other side of the room. Things the bad type of immigrant shouldn't be doing to the good type of immigrant. Heart Attack One was immersed in prayer however, so we couldn't be sure he was noticing this. The four of us were worried. If nothing happened soon, kids and teachers would begin to leave the prayer hall. There was nothing keeping them there after their prayers were complete. We'd already decided that the break-and-enter squad would be Farid and Nawaaz (whom I'd taught to pick locks). Maaz and I, being more persuasive, would hang back in the prayer hall to keep people from leaving, if possible.

Abdi kissed his teeth real loud, and it echoed through the

prayer hall. I turned to look at my companions with raised eyebrows, surprised that someone not named Farid would have the gall to show anything but solemnity in the sacred space. We were apparently not the only ones to have heard the teeth-kiss. We saw Heart Attack One look up at the two of them in front of him.

"Ey!" he said. "Ey" was not a word in any language. But that's how Heart Attack One spoke. In sounds understood by all of humankind.

The kid turned around and Heart Attack One gestured for him to come nearer. When he moved a bare inch, Heart Attack One yanked the kid in by the elbow and whispered harshly into his ear. The kid said something to Heart Attack One to make his eyes light up. It was like watching a Special Summon. Whatever Heart Attack One was, he turned into Red Eyes Wild Beard looking at Abdi, who looked right back at him with the same harsh gaze.

"You said this?" Heart Attack One asked, looking at Abdi.

"Said what?" he responded.

"This is a racism. What you say about Gujaratis?"

"Nothing. It's not racist. I just said, 'Gujis are really good at service,' that's all. How is that racist?" The feigned ignorance coupled with repeating the actual words set Heart Attack One off. He stormed to the back of the room and picked up his plywood. His Excalibur, his Longclaw, his Orcrist, his Master Sword and his Masamune, all rolled into one. He walked back towards Abdi.

"Come." He motioned for him to follow. If Abdi refused, he'd be dragged out of the prayer hall and beaten in the hallway. He'd have to go with Heart Attack One, and our plan would disintegrate before our eyes. It dawned on us then that we'd thrown Abdi into a horrible fate, all so we could find some woman who may not even still be alive. I tried to find his eyes beyond all the students and teachers who were now paying attention. For the briefest moment, Abdi's eyes and mine met. It was just a flash, and I doubt anyone caught it except for me. In me, I hope he saw regret and apology, instead of my desperate selfishness and mourning of the failed plan. In him, I saw strength. And if anyone could carry on a conversation with just a look, it was the students of Al Haque. So I hope he also saw my respect, and wherever he is today, I hope one monster didn't turn him into another monster, though I know it's likely this isn't likely.

"Can't take me without that stick eh?" Abdi said, slowly getting up, resigning himself to his fate.

"Egh?" Another sound understood by all.

"I know you're gonna beat me out there. It's fine. You need that stick to whup me," he said, walking towards Heart Attack One.

The maulana threw the stick into the darkness of the prayer hall and walked towards Abdi. That was the day I learned how fragile manhood is. One insult, one look, one offhand remark, a snide reply, a silence that was too long, a poor imitation, a slight disrespect—any of these could send a child off to war, off to Africa to build a well for black kids or off to march across a prayer hall to beat someone half their size and half their age. These fragile identities were all the more fragile when they belonged not to men but to beasts. Abdi walked towards Heart Attack One with the same passion, ready to die at his bully's hands. Kids and adults watched together in shock as they started running at each other barehanded.

"Stop this!" Heart Attack Four yelled, but no one paid any attention.

It was already too late. A clamour rose as we all stood to watch the fight. The other maulanas and Sharmil Bhai tried to break through and pull Heart Attack One out of the fray, but there were too many kids surrounding the combat. The maulanas started beating their way through the fracas, and the four of us almost forgot what we were there for.

I turned to Farid and Nawaaz. "Go. Now!"

They dispersed through the crowd, and I turned again to watch the match. Abdi was taking a beating. The back of his neck, his shoulders, his arms and his ribs were being punched in. Heart Attack One was doing his best to teach all the kids a lesson by using Abdi as an example. Abdi wasn't no punk bitch though. He dodged, ducked and twisted through many of the blows, lessening their impact. Months spent levelling up against kids his own age had prepared him for this boss fight. He head-butted Heart Attack One, pulled his beard down and ate a punch to the neck as a result. Heart Attack One's weight and size helped him as he flung Abdi into the crowd. The crowd pushed their champion back out. The maulanas were still trying to force their way through, but the students weren't letting them stop this fight early. We ate slaps to the back of the neck and barred the maulanas from interfering.

For Abdi, this was a fight for his life. Red eyes met red eyes. A fight to make the other person feel a single percentage point of the pain he'd been feeling, we'd all been feeling. Did they know? How much pain we were in? How much we were suffering? Did they have any idea how mad we were? How unfair this life felt? Heart Attack One would know. His face showed it when he suffered the impudence of a punch to the balls from Abdi. The man fell to his knees, hands on the carpet. His bloodshot eyes bulged, rancour filled the spittle he coughed out onto the red carpet. Hellfire would not be permitted to touch *any* part of a student's skin that an *ustad* had laid his hands on with discipline in mind. What, then, of the fate of Abdi, who'd had every inch of his skin covered by disciplinary hands but beat the shit out of a teacher and committed a violent, heinous crime? He jumped on Heart Attack One's hand, and we heard an unmistakable crack. Heart Attack One yelped and punched Abdi hard in the face with his other hand, standing up to destroy him. The other maulanas finally broke through the crowd and wrestled their colleague to the ground as he continued shouting and fighting. Even against grown men, he was hard to keep down. He kept trying to break free of the arms that were holding him, screaming and swearing about "disrespect" and "*kallu*" and "black bastard." We were yelling, hollering for the bloodied homie. They could kill us, expel us, damn our souls to hell, it didn't matter. Now y'all motherfuckers knew.

The fallout from the fight was real and immediate. Abdi was expelled. Heart Attack One had a broken hand and was absent for weeks. The rest of the maulanas took care of his class and absorbed some of his students while the beast licked his battle wounds. The noose grew tighter around us. We were quieter; they were quieter. They'd caught a glimpse of the real us and realized that the cleaned kitchen after the cooking debacle was perhaps a ruse. The timing was horrible as well. With the *Qirat* competition around the corner, the last thing the faculty wanted to deal with was the disciplinary fallout of a wild fight between a teacher and a student.

But Nawaaz and Farid's mission had been successful. They showed us the page they'd torn from the phone book that night with a list of Cynthia Lewises. We had our work cut out for us.

We took turns at the phone booth during exercise hours, calling up each Cynthia one after the other. Sometimes the numbers were out of service, sometimes the person on the other end thought she was being prank called. They were always the wrong Cynthia Lewis though. We tried a number of different strategies.

"Hi, is this the Cynthia Lewis who went to Al Haque . . . uh, I mean Sacred Heart Catholic School in Northumberland County in like the 1970s?"

"Hi, are you Catholic?"

"Is this the Cynthia Lewis who, *nawuzubillah*, was friends with Catherine?"

"I'm wondering if you used to go to a *kaafir* school in the 1970s?"

"Hello, your daughter come to my house today, and she kick my dog."

The car arrived as well. Nawaaz had been using the payphone to connect with his friend Marcus in Flemingdon, and Marcus had the car delivered to us by two older men who drove it all the way to the outskirts of Northumberland County and left it in a turn-off by a ravine. One afternoon, we hiked through the melting snow, following the county road past the phone booth and into a thicket of pines, and spotted the beat-up black Civic dumped between two trees. The perfect car to blend in, stay hidden and survive with. We were scared and excited all at once. We pushed it out of the ravine with Farid at the wheel and then took it for a short spin up and down the county road. Farid and Nawaaz took turns driving.

Maaz and I were a little anxious about it all. I was surprised we'd even pulled off acquiring a car, and now I wasn't sure how I felt about it. We were making decisions and coming up with plans as we went along. We were in nebulous territory. Of course, young *sahaba* had run off into the same as teenagers without shirts, with swords tied around their necks to join conquests and adventures, sand between their toes and empty stomachs hungry for love and glory. They spread what they spread for eternal splendour, and we spread what we spread for eternal damnation, teenagers in faded Phat Farm coats and Enyce jeans, able to see through the leaps and stretches equating horses to cars, sand to snow and good immigrants to those who drank Molson Canadian.

We drove up and down the same stretch of county road until we were bored. We found a place to hide the car off the main road, parking underneath a few pine trees close to the phone booth where the road took a turn.

—

In the final few days leading up to the *Qirat* competition, we were busy scrubbing Al Haque top to bottom, putting on our best face for the students who would come from Al-Rahmah and Darul Uloom. We had no doubt that the kids at other madrasas were just like us and couldn't care less whether the place smelled like lavender or cumin, but to suggest that to Sharmil Bhai would undoubtedly result in Al Haque's first official murder.

A few nights before the *Qirat* competition, the slight, bespectacled Maulana Ibrar—aka Heart Attack Four—delivered an epochal sermon after Isha. He'd been deeply troubled upon witnessing the historic duel in the main prayer hall between teacher and student, and had been thinking about what to do for quite some time. That "what to do," though, became what it always was: a sermon. But what else did he know? The sermon would be effective for some people. Five percent, or fifty percent, or ninety percent, it's hard to say how many changed because of it. But it was imploring, begging—from a position of power no less—and thus, effective. It began with a "My dear beloved youngsters" and ended with a "please." Less perdition and a lot more tears. Love goes a long way. It was in this way that Maulana Ibrar would continue his meteoric rise as a highly influential scholar, preaching and teaching at Al Haque and other renowned institutions until he was old and grey. He'd carry on handwritten correspondence with former students by candlelight in the age of computers, answering every question with a "Listen to your parents," "Listen to your husband," "Listen to your elders," "Be patient," "Don't go there" and every other version of "no" he could think of. Inspiring obedience through words, both written and spoken, and believing that this would work for everyone. Experiencing shock when it didn't, but subsequently trying nothing different. Because you can't change the words, because that would change the truth and the truth doesn't change. And because it doesn't change, neither did we. That night at Al Haque was no different. Sermons, slaps and sermons that slap only go so far.

CHAPTER 14

Oh, What a Time, What a Year

The next morning brought an end to Cynthia's diary. We were
on the roof when we read the final entry, our knotted stomachs
churning.

3/1/78

Dear Mark,

I want you to know that death isn't that scary. It's kind of scary,
but not completely scary. If you believe in another life—an eternal
life anyway—you shouldn't be too scared of it. But of course, life is
great. It makes sense to be scared. When the sun hits your face at
the right time of day, at the right time of year, you don't want to die.
When you taste Grandma's corn soup and it's so good you know it
will grow a missing limb back, you don't want to die. So of course,
dying is scary, but I want you to know that's also why we're alive.
We have to be ready to die for those things no? Otherwise why are
you alive, and what will you die for?

I want you to know that that's why I'm going to do what I'm going to do. I'm not that afraid to die. I'm not just going to sit here. I'm leaving. Give anyone who's watching me a bit of hope maybe when they find me missing tomorrow. And if no one's watching, then it's for myself. I just have to see her one last time. God, I can't even write this out straight I'm shaking so much. I'm scared. I don't even know where to look but I can't stay here one more night.

One thing is for sure though: if you ever find a light in your dark life, and you taste something so good you need to share it and try to save everyone, I understand. But if people find a light somewhere else, can you please just leave them alone? Please. The world is an enormous place; there are street corners where people pet strange cats under green branches without names and don't know your light. They're not hurting anyone. The sun rises and sets again and again while they grow and worship and die happy in the company of loved ones. We find guidance everywhere, and can be virtuous and in the service of God everywhere. I don't even know if you'll understand this Mark. They want us to never make sense. I hope I'm making sense to you, and you'll understand these things one day.

Don't be afraid of death. If you find something that makes you curious, chase it. If you find a light, chase it. I'm going to find Cat or die trying. I don't even know where to start, but it's going to be as far away from here as possible. Maybe I can find a gas station or a bus stop to take me to Quebec or something. Even if I freeze to death and they don't find my body until years later, this dying is worth it. All I can see is her smile, and I want to see it one last time. Just to touch her once more and smell her hair. Feel her and know that feeling was real.

—Cyn

"She left. She actually left," I whispered.

"Holy shit," Maaz echoed, looking around at each of us.

"I didn't think she'd really do it." Farid was shaking his head, looking up at the sky with a smile.

"That's crazy," Nawaaz said quietly.

I know we all remembered the pact we'd made, but we avoided bringing it up. We danced around the fact that it was our turn now. Faced with the immediacy and the reality of Cynthia's decision, we balked. We stared at the sky in silence, lost in excuses. Sure, we had the elements of a plan. A phone, a car, a person. But we lacked the conviction. Though not for much longer. You can't escape the world.

It was on one of these world-affirming mornings a few days later that we walked across the melting, muddied field and heard the voice of Cynthia Lewis for the first time. The right one. We were nearing the end of our list and weren't expecting much.

"Hullo, is this Cynthia Lewis?" Nawaaz asked. He had the deepest voice, and thus the highest likelihood of being taken seriously.

"Yes. How can I help you?"

"Ma'am, we are pleased to inform you that your alma mater, Sacred Heart, is offering you a trip to France to see the Notre Dame Cathedral. Congratulations!"

"Hah. No thanks."

We were quiet so we could all hear her response. Our eyes lit up. We'd found her! We scrambled up from the road where we were sitting and rushed into the phone booth, cramming up against Nawaaz, who looked more annoyed than pleased, his face pressed against the glass.

"Wait wait wait. Sorry! Is this . . . uh the Cynthia Lewis who went to Sacred Heart in, like, the 1970s?"

"Yeah. Why? I mean, I was there for barely a year. Not sure how I'd win something. How did you even get my number?"

"Oh, uh . . ." Nawaaz's voice trailed off. He looked at us, snapping his fingers, begging us for a quick response.

I grabbed the phone. "We found your diary!" I blurted. "Your journal thingie. We go there now. Not there, exactly. But what used to be there."

"What are you talking about?" she asked.

"You went to Sacred Heart in the 1970s right?"

"Yeah . . ."

"Well, we found a diary or something. We think it's yours."

"I don't know . . ."

"Well, we found it and read it and, like, wanted to return it. It might be yours. Did you have a friend named Catherine?"

There was a long pause.

"Who . . . who are you?"

"Oh, we're just ki—students. We're students here. At a madrasa. It's like a Catholic school convent or something, but for Muslims. And we found your book. And we want to return it. Do you . . . do you want it back?"

We all held our breath. There was so much riding on her response.

"Sure. But . . . how did you guys find that thing? I completely forgot about it." Her voice was friendly and beckoning.

"Oh, we were just going through stuff in the attic. It was in a box. I'm sorry we read it. It was just . . ." I was running out of words.

"Interesting," Maaz jumped in. "It was interesting. It was kinda familiar. The stuff you went through and the stuff we're going through."

"How so?" she asked.

"Well, we have teachers who don't . . . get us. Who are trying to teach us but are full of it. We have things we miss and aren't supposed to do. We're stuck, the same as you were. Our old friends are moving on and getting new friends and stuff, and we don't fit in there anymore, and we don't fit in here either. It feels like it was the same way you didn't fit in."

Fitting in and creating a place for yourself was a problem we hoped Cynthia could understand because she'd been through it. It was the same problem, just eras apart. In 1970, the children of fascists would kidnap two men and claim the protection of their language as paramount in their demands. The October Crisis used sovereignty as a mask to protect racism forever, allowing a province and a nation to kowtow to the demands of children, saying "Aww, shucks" and smiling slyly about a badass chapter in history when we too had something dangerous and sexy in the form of terrorists. It wasn't all just constitutional amendments and tax rates. In the ensuing decade, while Cynthia and Catherine courted progress at Sacred Heart, polls revealed widespread support for the group, rolling in governments that had French and fake France first in mind. Years later, with four kids fighting another losing war on the same front, laws were put into place to combat assimilation and ban burqas, English and anything religious (except Catholic religious), all in the name of sovereignty and making losers feel better about a war they lost in 1759. Of course, the provinces and nation continue to change despite this, as brown and black and

Asian bodies fuck English and French out of existence. If they can't assimilate, you'll assimilate.

Cynthia recognized the parallels.

"You guys will be okay," she said quietly.

"How do you know?" I asked.

It was our great anxiety. Our great worry. The grand unknown. The big question. Would we be okay? What did the future hold? Was this woman a seer?

"Because I'm okay, that's why. If you really want to make it out, you'll make it out. You'll find a way. If you're serious about getting out, you'll get out."

"Yeah but how do you know?" Maaz repeated.

"How serious are you about leaving? Is this just bored mischief, or do you really want something different for your life?"

We were quiet. We all had the same answer.

"Things'll be okay. Trust me," she said.

"Do you still want your journal back?" Farid asked.

"Sure, yeah! Take down my address and let's find a time or something. Oh, and I don't know why I'm saying this—and I probably shouldn't, to be honest—but if you guys ever need to call me, feel free. Seriously. I know how twisted up things can get."

We had no pen and paper on us, but it didn't matter. At that point, we were master memorizers, able to commit to heart things that were mentioned only once. Maaz memorized the first half of her address, Farid the second. Nawaaz memorized the area she was in, and together with the number we already had, we held all four pieces of the heart container.

When we got back to Al Haque that night we were a little nervous. The fruits of our excursion weighed heavily on us. We were looking over our shoulders, snapping at Jara and Syed and whoever else happened to ask us innocent questions. It was why we only half heard the rules to the *Qirat* competition that night after Maghrib.

Maulana Hasan announced that verses would be placed in envelopes, and the competing students would have to pick an envelope from the pile. Maulana Hasan would then open the selected envelope and recite the *ayat* inside. The student would continue the recitation from whichever surah the *ayat* was from. Marks would be deducted for poor recitation, stumbling, lack of fluency and mispronouncing words. We had the great disadvantage of not understanding everything we were saying because we were still in the process of learning rudimentary Arabic. It was important though. Allah had chosen to reveal his holy book in Arabic and not Swahili, abetting a language and a people in empowering languages and last names so that other languages and last names were considered second class. Are all languages created equal?

Our ears perked up when Maulana Hasan mentioned that we'd have a pizza party at the end of the competition, regardless of the results. *This* was a serendipitous surprise. It was a big deal. It didn't matter whether one of our classmates won or lost the competition, we'd all eat. Maulana Hasan said it was contingent on us behaving ourselves for the two days while the students from the other schools were here, but we knew better. As long as we didn't end up killing each other, we would get pizza. To say we were looking forward to it would be an understatement. Maulana Hasan and the other *ustads* knew exactly what would motivate us. We wouldn't have the West, but we *would* have a slice.

That night, we were hanging out in our foyer when Maaz suggested we go up to the roof. It was the middle of February, but we decided to bundle up and brave the cold. There was no snow on the roof, but the gravel poked through our socks like pins. We leaned against the edge, looking up at a starless sky.

"Yo, I wanna run a mission for the envelopes," Maaz said.

"Huh?" I asked.

"The envelopes. From the *Qirat* competition. They have to be locked or hidden somewhere right? Let's snatch that."

Nawaaz, Farid and I looked at each other.

"Why? The pizza's guaranteed," I said.

"Yeah but we could guarantee a win too. We could win this thing."

"You want to win?"

"Well, why not if I can, right?"

Ever since our kitchen escapade, most students except for Hafiz Abdullah had relaxed about the *Qirat* competition. Maaz was still memorizing and reviewing surahs, but he wasn't as dogmatic about it as Khalid or Hafiz Abdullah.

"Fam, why we gonna take the risk after everything in the kitchen, Abdi, our car and Cynthia and shit?" I asked. "Listen, if you really wanna do it, we'll do it. You know we got you. Just say you're really 'bout it and we're 'bout it too."

"I know, I know. You're right. It's just so juicy that they're probably just right there, somewhere. It cheeses me man."

"Do you even know where they're hidden?" Farid asked.

"Nah. I was hoping you or Nabil would have some schemes ready to cook up," Maaz said, looking down.

Farid and I shared a look. I turned to Maaz.

"Bro, do your best. You don't even care about this competition, right? Just do your best. Don't worry about winning or losing. We got you regardless. This life isn't even for us anymore. Just do what it takes so you don't get beat or whatever, but hey, hey—"

Maaz still had his head down.

"Look at me. Look at me," I said.

Maaz looked up, brown eyes meeting brown eyes. "We got you. If this life isn't for you, it isn't for you. Leave with us. But if you want to do *their* shit—if Maulana Hasan, Maulana Ibrar and all of them are helping you and getting through to you—that's cool too. We'll steal this shit for you, or you can just play it honest and do your best. Whatever you wanna do, we got you. But know you don't need anything you don't already have."

Maaz didn't say anything but he understood. Fear and anxiety turned a lot of people towards Allah, the way the search for peace did.

"Listen, let's go call Cynthia and actually make some plans, get some advice from her," I said, trying to put our plan into motion.

When we got to the field phone I asked her a question that had been eating away at me. "Hey, did you ever end up finding Cat?"

We were all dying to know, but we didn't want to ask out of fear of Cynthia's response. I'd been debating whether to ask for that reason, collecting the gall to open my heart to a break. All that time spent together, and leaving to reunite with the one person who understood you. Were happy endings real?

"Wow, Cat. Yeah, there's a name I haven't heard in a really long time," said Cynthia.

"What do you mean? Did you meet up with her?" Farid called from over my shoulder.

"No, sorry. It was the 1970s right? There was no way for me to track her down. Maybe if it had happened today, there would have been a chance, but ..." Her voice trailed off.

"So you left and it came to nothing?" Nawaaz asked. This sounded like a tragedy at the end of a long list of tragedies.

"Oh no. No no no. Guys, it didn't come to nothing. You need to know, it came to everything. I *needed* to leave that place. I was depressed and miserable. You guys read the damn diary, right? I mean, I know every teenager is probably going through it, but Sacred Heart was something else completely. Running away saved my life."

We were quiet for a minute.

"What did you do when you left?" Maaz asked, but I heard another question. What would we do when we left?

"Honestly, my parents got the message. I called them from a payphone. I mean, I didn't tell them about Cat or anything—they found out about me years later, and that's a whole other story. But, guys, they'll get the message," she said.

We looked at each other with doubt. We knew exactly how much filial love counted for in our world. But it seemed that Cynthia was reading our minds.

"No, I know what you're thinking," she said. "They're probably immigrants, right? From another country? What would they get? And how they're extremely religious and would sacrifice you to do what they thought was right? I was there, guys."

"Yeah, but your faith and our faith—"

"Sorry, let me just cut you off right there, Nabil. Nabil, right? I know what you're going to say. Christianity, Islam, things are different. But you're calling me right now because things *aren't* so different, are they? You connected with something that's supposedly so different because we share something."

We were quiet, digesting her words.

"Sacred Heart had a curfew, and I bet you guys do too. Sacred Heart had a daily sacrament, and I bet you guys have some kind of prayer every morning. We were poorly staffed, and even the teachers who loved us and tried to look out for us couldn't stop all the fights and bullshit. The way they dealt with kids skipping classes or sneaking out was cruel. Does this sound familiar?"

We were still silent. Cynthia didn't sound finished.

"Your parents will get the message. You want to know how I know? Because if they *won't* get the message, will you still do what you're thinking about doing? Who are you doing this for? Are you willing to die for this? And if not, what *are* you willing to die for?"

We were quiet.

"We just want to know, though: Does it work out in the end? Do things . . . end up okay?" Maaz asked, forever measuring outcomes.

There was a long silence.

"Yeah man, they do."

Have you ever heard a smile?

When I went to bed that night, I remember dreaming of pizza so vividly I could smell the cheese and peppers. The next day, we learned that the contest envelopes had gone missing.

—

We were sitting in our *hifz* class in the morning with Maulana Hasan when Maulana Ingar came into the room and whispered

275

something into his ear. They looked out at our class, and my eyes accidentally met Maulana Hasan's. I looked down quickly, unsure of what was happening. I heard two hand slaps against the bench in front of him as he summoned silence.

"The *Qirat* competition materials have gone missing. We know one of you in this class or someone in Maulana Ingar's class has taken them. This is extremely wrong. We really believed you were learning, growing and becoming good students here. The level of untrustworthiness among you all is disgusting. Disgusting! There is no difference at all between you and the children of *kafir* in the public schools. Because the verses sealed in the envelopes were sent to us from the competition, we're unable to print new verses to prepare. Whoever did this must step forward immediately."

For Maulana Hasan, the parts of the world that were not the West were better because, according to him, these types of things didn't happen there. But of course, he hadn't been in those parts of the world in quite a few years. And when he had been in those places—India, the Middle East, Africa—rules to *Qirat* competitions weren't disclosed to students because maulanas were experienced. Maulanas were experienced because there were only a few of them, tenured for decades in strong institutions where men understood human nature. But the unmeasured growth of an *ummah* had necessitated more learned scholars in the West. The allure of a strong salary and rewarding work in a new land had drawn some of these *aalims* here before they'd learned all the ruses a person could employ. And then they grew old there, believing another "there" was better. Years later, when Maulana Hasan's long beard was grey and his back was beginning to crook, he would quit the country in disappointment and spend long summer afternoons at the Masjid-al-Haram, trying to forget that miniskirts were a thing. His golden years would be spent in Makkah and Madinah, listening to the different styles of *Qirat* and leaning against a pristine marble pillar in the shade while young students beautifully crooned the word of Allah nearby. He'd surround himself with the heat and smells of the unfamiliar, convinced they were supposed to be familiar, eating whatever he pleased in a place where he wouldn't have to worry about halal or haram. The flocks of fat pigeons, tattooed Africans, Bengalis and Filipinos missing their passports, and daily construction-related deaths were ignored. These were the Holy Lands. Maulana Hasan would close his eyes to the world, to the failed *Qirat* competitions of the past, the injustices of the present, and wait to die.

Those who were not waiting though, knew that whoever had stolen the *Qirat* competition envelopes was simply nothing more than an idiot. Those materials were way too vital to mess around with. In class that morning, we all looked around, the bright- and dark-natured alike, wondering who the culprit might be.

When we resumed reciting, I turned to Farid.

"Do you know anything?" I whispered.

"Nah man. Stupid though. How can they have a *Qirat* competition without those envelopes? Can they even make new ones in time?"

There was a noticeable pall over the rest of the day as we went from class to class. After Asr we sat around in the main prayer hall theorizing about what would happen next.

"You think they're gonna cancel the competition? Or just kick our school out?" Nawaaz asked.

"Nah it's way too late for that," Maaz responded. He was biting his thumbnail, deep in thought. "They'll come up with something."

"Yeah but this isn't over. They won't let this go. This was, like, their love child or something," I said.

The teachers had been so excited about the competition that messing with it was an immediate death sentence. They wanted to find the culprit, and I couldn't imagine the lengths they'd go to do it.

After Maghrib, Maulana Ibrar sat at the front with Maulana Hasan and repeated what he had said that morning, but with an added threat.

"Two days from now, students from the other madrasas are due to arrive. We will be an embarrassing excuse for a madrasa if we are not prepared, if we have problems with students and if we cannot conduct this competition properly. You lot continue to behave yourselves in a way absent of any fear. You do not fear the wrath of Allah *subhanat'u'ala*. So be it. If you only fear us, then we'll have to act accordingly. There is no more pizza for any of you. You can forget about it."

There was a murmur throughout the crowd. We couldn't help it. When we stood for Isha an hour later, our minds and hearts were far from where they should have been. Through each of the four *rakats*, our minds raced through the same things. Would the culprit step forward, catch the beating and let us enjoy our pizza in peace? Would the culprit have the guts and heart to take one for the team? It was one thing when a crime affected only the culprit and the madrasa. But if the rest of us were pulled into it, would the transgressor have the heart to back out? Did he care about the rest of us enough? How selfish were we? It was a fear-versus-love scenario. Which feeling was stronger? Fear of the repercussions, the beating, the possible expulsion? Or love for your classmates, their happiness and seeing them smile and have a good time? What motivated you more?

Before dismissing us after Isha, Maulana Hasan stood to address us one last time.

"If you step forward, nothing will happen to you." We knew this to be a bold-faced lie, but he continued. "We don't want to punish everybody. But if no one steps forward, we'll have to go through everybody's rooms, call everybody's parents. No one is sleeping tonight."

There was silence. We weren't sure if we were dismissed.

"No one can leave. Whoever it is, you've had all day to think about what you did. But someone *has* to step forward and return these materials or tell us where they are. Whoever it is, it's embarrassing it took you all day and you're still not coming forward. The jig is up. You've had your fun. Step forward."

No one moved a muscle. The younger kids looked afraid. The older students looked at us with the same eyes the maulanas did. Disappointment and condemnation. Everyone waited for a criminal to reveal himself.

"Listen, we can be here all night. It's not a problem. No more pizza party is not a problem for us. You can eat Sharmil Bhai's food all year. He works hard, he cooks for us, he cleans for us. So much *neki* in what he is doing for all of us. But if you want outside *khana*, it's too bad. You can forget it. If no one steps forward, no one can even say the word 'pizza' at Al Haque ever again. Not just tonight. Forever."

It was too much to bear for Farid. He stood up. He was sitting right beside me, and when I looked up at him I prayed he wasn't about to do what he did.

"It was me. I did it," he said quietly. Everyone could hear him. He didn't need to speak up. No one breathed. No one said a word. The younger kids had their jaws open in amazement. The older kids had faces made of stone. Almost everyone knew it wasn't Farid. I'm not sure how the others knew, but they knew. We didn't need explanations or evidence. We didn't need to see anything. We'd learned to read looks and glances and strange gaits in low lights, and a person's hesitation was all we needed. A stare, a wink, the absence of one—all told us who was guilty and who wasn't. When Farid stood up, everyone knew that things didn't add up. It didn't make sense. He wasn't in the competition. And if he did it for Maaz, then why weren't we standing with him? There was no way Farid's homies would let him stand and take the blame alone. It wasn't Farid. They all knew. But the maulanas at the front didn't doubt him. They didn't question him. By this point in the year, they knew something else: here was a troublemaker. And if they were going to salvage the year—if they were going to save some part of it, save their careers, their faiths, our faiths, and correct our course—Farid needed to be made an example of. So they didn't ask why or how. Instead—

"Come with us. Come on."

Farid waded through the bodies and stepped forward, and everyone looked up with wide eyes as he passed them. This was their saviour, and also their great idiot. They looked upon Farid with anguish because he'd revealed exactly how much they cared about pizza. Why did they care about pizza so much? Why were they so heartbroken over a taste of the outside? Why did their hearts flutter and float at the prospect? Farid stripped them all bare, and the students he passed on his way to the front of the room tried to meet his eyes, hoping for a crumb from their saviour. Time and time again he'd rescued them with laughter, food, hare-brained schemes and violent spectacles and this was no different. He was eager to play the part, to help, to rip away a facade that was trying to say that blessings were enough. All the other students looked for an answer in eyes that wouldn't meet theirs. The rest was theirs to figure out or forget about. Bury your head in *Hayat-us-Sahabah* or *The Lives of Girls and Women*. Choose. Farid had done nothing less than what he was. Ting-chopper, OG, the Hero, the Chosen One. The shadows of all the bodies in the room created a range of mountains along the wall, black lumps and hills against the sanguinary pallor of light as one small mountain rose and made a tectonic shift towards the front. Maaz, Nawaaz and I watched our friend move farther and farther away from us, and out of reach and safety forever.

Farid

Yeah I'm not gonna lie—I was scared shitless. As soon as I stood up I almost regretted it. Almost. There's something about walking through a crowd in dead silence I suppose that'll do that to you. I'm not even entirely sure *why* I stood up. I just didn't want the pizza party cancelled I guess. I just knew that if no one was going to stand up, if no one was going to come forward, it would be the same old shit for the rest of the year. The other guys didn't deserve this. And plus, there's a small chance that after whatever beating I had to catch was over, they'd still let me have the last coupla cold slices. Slim chance, but at least *someone* would get to eat pizza, right? Someone had to. It was worth it. There's a reason why it fully heals you in *Turtles in Time*.

Maulana Ibrar held me by the elbow and led me out of the room, followed by Maulana Syed and Maulana Hasan and Maulana Ingar. Thank God Maulana Furkan was still nursing his broken hand. Abdi had done more for us than we'd originally thought. Three of the four Heart Attacks coming together for a team-up episode was not what I had in mind for tonight. So yeah, your boy was a little worried.

As we walked through the dark hallway to the mufti-sab's office I could feel my heart in my stomach. I wanted to puke a little but I knew it would do nothing to change my fate. Shit, why did I care? I cared though. I loved Nabil, Maaz and Nawaaz, and I loved living. Jesus, is Abbu gonna kill me? This is going to be the third place I'm expelled from. Ugh, I thought I was safe here. If he sends me back to Gujarat, I swear to God.

Maulana Ibrar unlocked the principal's office and threw me in, closing the door behind him after the other *ustads* had entered. The mufti-sab wouldn't arrive 'til the next day to preside over the competition, so whatever justice needed dispensing would have to happen here without him. I wonder if he'd co-sign whatever they were gonna do to me.

They looked down at me on the floor. I knew better than to look them in the eyes. I had no idea what I was in for, but I knew that even the slightest shred of defiance would be stupid. Maulana Syed leaned in to whisper something into Maulana Ibrar's ear and I tried keeping my eyes focused on the door. I didn't know much about Maulana Syed, other than that he taught another class the same age as us, along with Maulana Ingar, Maaz's uncle.

"Why are you like this?" Maulana Ibrar whispered. "No games. No nonsense. Just, why are you like this? If you don't want to focus, that's one thing. But why ruin the entire competition for everyone?"

I had no idea who'd taken the materials, but clearly it was someone who didn't realize how ridiculous the crime was. It had to have been someone connected to the competition. Unless I said something, the smooth-brain maulanas would eventually conclude I'd done it to save Maaz. I had to protect him.

"Oh uh, I didn't want the competition to happen," I said.

"Why not?" Maulana Ibrar asked.

"I want Al Haque to lose . . . because I had a vision." I didn't know what I was saying. Would they believe it? There was a small chance they would.

"What do you mean a vision?" Maulana Syed interrupted, leaning his thin face in to question me.

"Oh it was just a dream. I just wanted Al Haque to lose. To, like, punish everyone for misbehaving."

I knew I was doing 360-degree kickflips with my logic, but there was a chance they'd follow. They 100 percent believed in the power of dreams, but they would not believe in the bond that made me protect Maaz from them. There was a chance, right? Now why a kid would want to punish the teachers and Al Haque for hijinks he himself had started was beyond me, but there was a chance it wasn't beyond them. I was hoping they'd see through the bullshit though, and conclude I was just a selfish prick who wanted to watch the world burn. It was not my night though.

Maulana Syed walked over to the mufti-sab's desk and pulled out a black box from one of the bottom drawers, then put it on the desk. He opened the box, pulled out two white gloves and put them on, then removed what looked to be a small Quran.

Maulana Ibrar stepped forward and grabbed me by the elbow. I was scared. I had no idea what the fuck this was.

"Just to be sure, we need to test him," Maulana Syed said.

"There's a slim chance he has one," Maulana Ibrar said, but not in a contradictory tone.

"One what?" I asked. They ignored me.

Maulana Syed opened the Quran and started reading out loud and I recognized the chapter immediately. Surah Al-Jinn. They thought I was possessed. This was uncharted territory. I panicked. I broke free of Maulana Ibrar's grasp and tried to run for the door but Maulana Ingar hit the back of my neck with his hand and I fell to the ground. I felt someone grab my collar and drag me along the carpet, blows began raining down on my back and ribs. I curled up, trying to cover my face. I knew what I had to do.

In 1994, the *Street Fighter* movie came out. I thought it would be just another shitty action-movie adaptation of an amazing game. And it was, for the most part. When I caught most of it on TV one time years later, I was just excited to see the game I loved on-screen for the first time. But there was one scene that absolutely nailed it. Balrog and Honda are locked up by M. Bison's men, and they're sharing a prison cell together or something, and Zangief comes in to torture them. He ties Balrog and Honda up to chairs and starts lashing Honda with a black whip. Honda does not react at all; his eyes are closed, and he's quiet. Zangief switches weapons, lashes Honda harder, but still no reaction. Honda's arms are crossed against the back of the chair, and he looks blissful, no emotion, barely making a sound while he's getting beat. Balrog is shocked watching it all, like "How is this mans not reacting to getting the shit beat out of him?" Balrog then gets punched in the face and feels it. He gets hurt. When Zangief finally leaves, Balrog turns to Honda and asks, "Like what the fuck? How are you not screaming?" And Honda says, "My mind can be in one place and my body another." And that's when I knew. That whoever wrote that scene in the movie probably grew up at Al Haque. Someone else knew the trick too. So when they dragged me along the carpet, as my body continued to flail and defend itself, as I raised my knees and pulled against the fist at my collar, as my hands were pulled above my head and tied, I watched it all happen from my mind, above them all, seeing it happen to someone else's body. I left through the door, rushed out the front of the madrasa, escaped into the woods and ran through snow that couldn't chill me. I couldn't feel the way they were silencing that other me with fists and sticks across my back and face, to still my body's fight. I was too busy climbing over hills and sliding across frozen creeks barefoot, cannonballing into snowdrifts and flying like the wind past black trunks and branches. I ran into all kinds of animals—foxes, owls and wolves—but I knew they wouldn't hurt me. In the forest, nothing would hurt me. I was nice and alone, away from the pain and suffering. Free to hoot and howl at the moon with the wild. It was only if I looked really closely that I could see some kid's body laid on top of a desk, bloodied and bruised and defeated, finally still except for his chest, which heaved up and down in desperation. A white-gloved hand clasped the forehead of the poor dumb kid while men in white repeated verses from a golden book around him. Hands were all over his body like warts and sores, holding his ankles together, grabbing his hips to prevent his squirming, pressing down on his shoulders while his eyes roamed frantic and bloodshot around the room, open wide in search of escape. Not my problem. There was a nice cave here between two jagged-ass rocks where it was warm and nobody could find me. My mind in one place, my body another.

CHAPTER 15

Dawson City, Yukon

After Farid disappeared with Heart Attacks Two through Four, plus Maulana Hasan, Sharmil Bhai stood up to address everyone left in the room.

"Okay, go to bed. He will be dealt with very severely, so you understand there's no more *masthi* that will go on here. We'll talk to everybody again tomorrow."

We all got up and started leaving the room, people murmuring and making their way up to bed. There was no chance that waiting up in the foyer for Farid was a good idea tonight. No one would be able to sleep, and even the slightest peep would be heard. Before I got to my room, Maaz tapped me on the shoulder.

"He's gonna be all right. It will just be like that time Bilal snitched probably. Just a whupping," Maaz said.

I shook my head and walked away. Maaz knew better too. He was saying that more for himself than for me.

I didn't sleep much that night as the empty bed across the room made its presence known. There'd be no dreamer at the window before Fajr the next day.

Farid wasn't present at Fajr either. Most people pretended not to care, but the concern was probably evident on the faces of me, Maaz and Nawaaz. At breakfast, Jara and Alif gave us extra roti and daal, but we had no appetite. We kept looking towards the entrance whenever someone walked through, hoping it was our idiot. When our *hifz* class began without any sign of Farid, I knew something was seriously wrong. There was no chance of talking to Maaz or Nawaaz about it until Zuhr though. The class was too small, the noise would carry and they were seated too far away from me.

We finally found some time together on the stools performing ablutions before the next prayer.

"Something's wrong," I said. "No one's been punished or gone missing from class for this long."

"You think they sent him home? Expelled him or some shit?" Nawaaz asked.

"No, his stuff's still in our room," I said.

"We have to find him. He knows about our plan," Maaz said.

Something about the way he said that irked me.

"We all know about the plan. And it's barely a plan. We gotta find the fucker."

"Well where can he be?" Nawaaz said.

"He's probably locked in an office or some shit," I said, rubbing my chin, unsure if that was a possibility.

"You think they'd lock him in there all day?" Maaz said.

"If Sharmil Bhai walks into one of the offices with food, it might say something," Nawaaz suggested.

The idea gave us a brief respite, even if we weren't hanging out in the hallways the rest of the day. We wouldn't know or see anything, but we had nothing else.

The rest of the day passed with bated breath. We never saw Sharmil Bhai carrying food out of the dining room. That night, Maulana Ibrar told us that the *Qirat* competition would go ahead the next day. The students from the other two schools would arrive sometime after Fajr. He commended Maulana Hasan for reaching out to the competition and procuring another set of materials and said they were excited to begin. Maaz, Nawaaz and I only half heard the sermon. Our minds and hearts were elsewhere. I had no idea how Maaz was going to perform the next day. It didn't seem to bother him either, even though his father would be in the crowd, with Maulana Ingar and the pressure of a studious reputation on the line. We were whispering together at the back of the prayer hall just as Maulana Ibrar dismissed everyone for the night.

"*Wallahi*, something is off. Something is really, really off," Maaz said. "Each time you check your room, his clothes and things are there. They wouldn't expel him or send him home without his shit. That doesn't add up. And if his dad came through, we would've seen or heard a car roll up or seen a man take him away. We haven't seen or heard shit. No one's come or gone. He's still here somewhere."

"Okay, okay. Let's meet at the chill-spot after everyone's gone to bed. We'll have to be really quiet. The night before competition, you know they're gonna be alert and shit."

We met later in our foyer and devised a whispered plan.

"Okay there's a chance he's somewhere in the offices downstairs," I said. "They're the only rooms that are locked, so we'll have to figure out a way in. Or at least figure out if he's in one of them. Maybe we'll break into all of them, I dunno."

We were desperate. We made our way through the hall and down the main stairs, creeping quietly around the spots we knew would betray us with creaks. We made sure to breathe only the most necessary of breaths, as even those would be carried by snitching angels to the slumbering Sharmil Bhai. When we made it to the main hallway, we stayed clear of the prayer hall just in case anyone was feeling extra holy that night. In the dark hallway, there were four offices. We tried twisting the doorknobs on each, and to no one's surprise, they were all locked.

"Maybe there's a set of keys somewhere," Maaz said, looking around.

"Nah we won't find anything like that right now," Nawaaz said.

"Hold up. Everyone wait. Shhhh." I'd heard something. Not approaching footsteps but something else. We squatted down, straining our ears. It sounded like *Qirat* . . . or singing. I crept closer to the door nearest to me and heard nothing. I told Maaz to go to the next door and motioned for Nawaaz to go to the one after that. We held our ears against the doors, straining for a sound that could have been imagined.

"It's here. Over here!" Nawaaz said.

We rushed over to him and listened. There it was, unmistakable. Some kind of humming and singing. I pressed my head against the floor and whispered through the crack.

"Farid!"

Nothing.

"Farid! It's us you dumbass."

Still nothing. Instead, the noise died. We couldn't hear anything anymore. No more singing or humming. We whispered again, saying his name over and over, but there was no response.

We were afraid that if we said it any louder someone would hear us. We stood in front of the door.

"What do we do?" I asked.

"We have to get him out. I mean, if we walk away, and he's in there . . ." Maaz didn't complete his thought.

"That's our friend," Nawaaz said. "What if they're gonna get rid of him, and this is our last chance to see him? Remember what it did to Cynthia?"

I looked at them. Since day one, it had always been me and Farid who'd advocated on behalf of the journal. Maaz and Nawaaz had been terrified of the harami nature of the thing. It was me and Farid who'd wanted so badly to read it, eager for a taste of something else and something new, unaffected by the fear that held Maaz and Nawaaz. And yet here we were, Maaz and Nawaaz craving a little of the love of their friend, thanks in part to a girl from a bygone time.

"Can we walk away if there's a chance he's in there?" I asked.

Nawaaz responded with action.

"Fuck that. If there's a chance to see his dumb, butt-ugly face . . ." He held the doorknob and slammed his shoulder against the door. It budged slightly and shook. He slammed his weight against it one more time and it cracked open. Maaz and I rushed forward into more darkness.

We snapped on the light and saw a body huddled against a heater on the floor, wrists tied to it. There was caked brown blood on the white kurta and no movement, even at the sound of someone entering the room. We rushed over to our friend.

"Yo . . . yo." I shook his shoulders gently, trying to get him to respond. Dried blood covered everything. The carpet, his face.

There was an enormous gash above his eyebrow. His eyes were closed. I feared the worst. I was afraid of touching him—I didn't want to exacerbate his pain—but I couldn't help it. I needed to know my friend was alive.

Maaz and Nawaaz were on their knees beside me, looking over his body for signs of life. Farid's eyes opened and welled with tears. Before I could say anything, my own tears fell. They welled up unbidden, filled my eyes and dropped onto my friend's face. For *dunya*, for love, for life, for this life, for the lie I could feel and for the feeling I could touch. Ya Allah, there my friend lay. Covered in blood, half-dead and broken, hanging on to what was left of himself, tied up to a heater like an animal there in Northumberland County for a crime he did not commit. Ya Allah, where is your mercy? Where is your forgiveness? Where is your justice in this life? We are not *there* yet. Is there anything for us here? We are here, paying for lives we did not ask for, in places that were chosen for us.

"They . . . they tried to take the djinn out of me bro," he whispered so quietly. "They tried. *Wallahi*, they tried."

His tears fell and mixed with mine. Nawaaz had his face covered with his hands, but I heard him sniff and rub his eyes. Maaz kept rubbing his eyes too, to prevent the tears from falling, but it was a race we would not win. The dam broke again and again as our saviour helped to hide our pain, concealing our shakes and sounds, muffled in his clothes. I reached up at the rope tightly covering his wrists and yanked at it, but Farid gasped in pain.

"No . . . no. Just stop. Leave it. I'm leaving tomorrow. They'll let me go. My dad's coming to get me. It's over."

I held him close to me and felt how warm he was, even weakened and bloody. There was no resisting anymore. Our bodies were racked with the anguish of seeing him in his condition. The pain of almost losing him. Maaz and Nawaaz cried onto his shoulder and legs, pulling at him, silently weeping, for noise would bring the angels down on us all. I was sick of it. The way the angels conspired to bring about our reckoning. There I was, wishing I was anywhere but somewhere in the countryside without a place or person to turn to. Stuck in the mud, afraid of crying too loud, praying for a place that wasn't Al Haque, again. Where was *our* place? All I wanted was to run. To get away and flee from this place that wasn't ours. Cold be damned, merciless nature was better than merciless nurture. Just one moment in the night was preferable to our fate. One final moment, to feel Northumberland's wind caress our tear-stained cheeks while we looked up to search for stars in the night sky.

"Fuck this. Let's leave. Now," I said, rubbing the tears from my eyes. I knew if we didn't leave that night, we'd never leave. We'd make excuses and put it off. Tomorrow and tomorrow. There would always be the next step, the next part of the plan that needed doing. Until we'd forget about it altogether—not just the plan but the feeling too.

"Now," I whispered again, looking at them through tears and clenched teeth.

They looked back at me with blank expressions. No one objected, so I continued.

"This is wrong. Our parents won't give a shit. They sent us here for this. And we can't go to no cops. How would you even explain this shit to anyone here? Let's leave. *She* left. *We* leave. At least to go see Cynthia, one time. But we can't be here tonight. We can't leave him here like this."

"It's fine . . . really," Farid whispered. His head was in my lap and the rest of him lay on the carpet while his bound wrists hung in the air. "I'm gone tomorrow anyway—"

"No fuck that. Fuck that! Miss me with that bullshit. Our lives are gonna end anyway. Either here, or whatever place we don't get expelled from. But they can't do this shit to you. They gotta know. When they wake up for Fajr and see a busted-down door and realize you're missing, they're gonna know. They can't do that type of shit without repercussions. There are consequences. And all the other kids are gonna know too. We ain't no bitches. We're not just gonna let you die all alone in some room or some shit."

I looked around and saw resolve. I saw love. I saw all the shit I needed in life. I felt what Crono must have felt when Marle and the homies brought him back to life. There's no other way to explain it. I knew exactly what it must have felt like.

"Okay, stay here a second. I'll be right back," Nawaaz said. He left the room and we tried to help Farid sit up. When Nawaaz came back, he had a bundle of coats with him and he put them down on the desk. He pulled a knife out of his pocket and cut Farid's ropes off the heater.

"Let's go," he said when he was done.

We stood up. Farid was still on the ground.

"I don't think I can stand," he said looking up at us.

Maaz and I leaned down and lifted him up, carrying him between us. Even though he was the smallest of us, we felt his weight, walking him out of the office and into the main shoe area.

"You're too heavy. Maybe we should just leave you here eh?" I said, hoping to catch a glimpse of my friend.

His head was bowed, and his eyes were only half open. It worried me that he hadn't said something stupid since we'd found him. I sat him in a chair in the main foyer and helped to put his boots on while Maaz and Nawaaz quietly scrambled to push Nawaaz through the top window so he could unlock the front door from the outside. We heard a clang and the door was pulled open, revealing a soaking Nawaaz standing in a freezing downpour.

"Let's go, c'mon. Hurry up before we're caught," he said, trying to quicken the pace.

We slid into our boots and jackets after I helped Farid into his. Maaz and I carried him between us, out the door and into the night. The rain crashed down on us, chilling us to the bone while the coats did their best to keep us dry. Our pajama pants were soaked through, and we could feel our clammy legs trudge across the gravel and onto the field. It was an uncustomary March rainstorm, but it wouldn't keep us from our mission that night. We made our way across the patchy field, which was muddy in places, icy in others, and brown and blue in some amorphous pattern known only to God. We were walking towards the spot where we'd left the car. We tried to come up with some semblance of a plan over the noise of rain.

"Listen, we have to call her first," I said.

"What?" Maaz said, across Farid's body.

"We have to call her! Cynthia. We have to call her first. We know where she lives, but we should call her. Ask her if it's okay if we bring Farid. Or come to see her."

"What if she says no?" Maaz said over the crashing rain.

"Fuck it. We'll take him to a hospital. He might be fucked up. We don't have a choice."

Nawaaz led us deeper and deeper across the patchy field, urging us to keep up with him. We'd all taken our turns at the wheel, but Farid and Nawaaz were definitely the strongest drivers. I was worried about the weather, but it was the furthest worry from my mind compared to the one beside me. I'd have to remember to remind Nawaaz to drive slowly.

The mud kept splashing higher and higher, slowing us down and taking us forever to cross the field. Every squish and squeak felt like the land was trying to keep us locked and trapped, like some natural defence system employed by Al Haque. The rain kept falling, cold and heavy, huge drops like punches, forcing our faces down into the dirt, refusing to allow us to look at the night sky or take in a fresh breath. The deafening cacophony of rainfall, sheet after sheet of uncompromising precipitation, drowned out our footfalls. Al Haque disappeared from view, a place frozen in time behind us, while layers of rain warped the space ahead of us on an unknown horizon that we hoped would give us more.

When we got to the car we placed Farid in the backseat and Nawaaz started the engine. He tried to drive up the hill, but the mud made it difficult. Maaz and I got behind the car and shoved as hard as we could until it was on the road. Luckily, it wasn't too steep, but it did take everything out of us. When we collapsed inside the car we took a few minutes just to breathe and listen to the rainfall on the roof. I could see Maaz's cold breath float up, drops of water hanging on to his sideburns, refusing to fall. Nawaaz coughed and shook his head, water flying out of his beard and locks, spraying us all. We laughed. Nawaaz broke out into a small smile.

"*Acha*, someone jump in the front with me. I need help navigating this thing."

I looked at Maaz, and he jerked his head forward to tell me to jump into the front. I exited and sprinted around the car to sit shotgun.

"All right, lemme call Cynthia real quick," Maaz said from the backseat.

He rushed out and into the phone booth while we waited. I wasn't sure what Cynthia would say, and I was definitely worried she'd be annoyed by the problems of children in the middle of the night.

Maaz came back after a few minutes.

"She wants to see us. We can go over! She wants to meet us," he said, unable to hide his relief.

"What? What did you say to her?" Nawaaz asked, looking into the rear-view mirror.

"I just told her the truth. That Farid hasn't said anything dumb in a few hours."

Nawaaz turned the key in the ignition and started the car, slowly rolling down the road. "Yo what's the *du'a* for driving?" he said. "We need it tonight!"

"There's no *du'a* for driving. Just for travelling on a camel to a faraway land," I said, looking out the window into nothing but rain.

Nawaaz kissed his teeth. "Fam, I'm serious. Don't cheese me. Maaz say it."

"*Bismillah, Alhamdulillah Subhaanal-lathee sakhkhara lanaa haathaa wa maa kunnaa lahu muqrineen. Wa 'innaa 'ilaa Rabbinaa lamunqaliboon.* In the name of Allah. All praise be to Allah. That you may settle yourselves upon their backs and then remember the favour of your Lord when you have settled upon them and say, 'Exalted is He who has subjected this to us, as we could not have otherwise subdued it.' And indeed we, to our Lord, will one day surely return."

And then—

"Del honey, daddy's coming!"

We all laughed, our hearts pounding with hope now.

"Maaz, slap him!" Nawaaz said.

We kept moving down the road, picking up speed.

"Listen," Nawaaz said, turning to me but keeping his eyes on the road. "Whatever happens after tonight—whether we all get expelled, whether we go back or stay—you have to promise me one thing."

"Sure, of course."

"No, I'm serious. I'm for real. You gotta promise me."

"Yeah, yeah! Of course!"

"You have to take care of Maaz. You gotta watch out for him. If we're separated or some shit, stay with him. You know him. You know how smart he is, how he sees everything. Wherever he goes, people will need him. They'll listen to him."

I twisted my head around to look at Maaz in the back seat. He just shook his head and rolled his eyes. This was clearly a tired argument between them. The wipers on the car worked overtime, squeaking back and forth across the windshield as the rain pattered the roof, forcing us to speak louder. I turned back to Nawaaz, who kept on about it.

"For real. I'm not joking. You know how sharp he is. You've seen him. He's special. The way he looks at people, the way he knows what's going on! That's a cold motherfucker, but we need that here. *Here*, wherever we are, y'know? We need that. He can't be wasting himself alone in some bullshit life around white people.

Promise me bro. No matter what happens, you'll help me take care of him."

"Yeah. Yeah, of course man." I wasn't entirely sure what Nawaaz was talking about but I wasn't entirely ignorant either. Maaz had always been the sharpest one. What he lacked in piety, he made up for in sheer promise. It wasn't luck that we'd found each other. Each of us had things the others among us needed. But I knew everyone in the world needed what Maaz could give them.

"Del honey, just a few more minutes! I'mma comin'!"

A high-pitched squeal rang out that could somehow be heard over the hammering of water on the roof of our speeding car. We all laughed. I remember laughing.

CHAPTER 16

Cynthia Lewis

TWO DEAD IN FATAL JOYRIDE, QUESTIONS RAISED OVER CAR OWNERSHIP

PICKERING—Questions have been raised in a fatal joyride that claimed the lives of two teenagers early on a tragic Tuesday morning in Northumberland County. Two 14-year-old Toronto boys have been charged after a car they were driving crashed and left two of their schoolmates dead.

The boys, who cannot be named under law, made a brief court appearance to attend their bail hearing, where the court heard the initial details of the night in question.

The accident took place just after 1:30 a.m. on Tuesday, when a car travelling at high speeds veered out of control, striking a guardrail southbound on Taunton Road, before hitting a ditch and crashing onto farmland, where it was found overturned on private property. All four boys were pinned inside the vehicle, with two surviving. Investigators believe that the uncustomary March rainstorm was a contributing factor in the crash, hampering visibility and affecting the surface of the road.

The two boys, who sustained only minor injuries before being released from hospital, sat expressionless throughout the proceedings, where they were charged with criminal negligence causing death.

Authorities are still trying to piece together details around the joyride, including why and how the teenagers were able to secure a car and leave the school. The court is also trying to determine ownership of the vehicle, while the two surviving boys claim that the vehicle belonged to their deceased friend.

The surviving teenagers appeared unhurt at the bail hearing, sitting together with their heads bowed. One occasionally bounced his foot or covered his eyes with a hand, where a hospital bracelet could still be spotted. The court also inquired into the immigration status of both youths, who were confirmed to be Canadian citizens.

The quiet private school, located on Bletchley Road North, was subjected to an uncustomary questioning yesterday at its front gates.

Al Haque Jamiatul Uloom Ontario has just under a hundred students enrolled in their full-time religious studies, where students aim to memorize the Koran and be religious leaders.

Sharmil Naik, who works as an administrator and caretaker at the school, made himself available for media questioning and commented on the situation.

"The students are not talking about it. They're very sad, of course. But I think they're just quietly doing their best," he said.

Mr. Naik also mentioned that they had no idea that the youths had access to a car.

"The kids don't know anything either, most of the kids are good kids here, but sometimes we have some others we can't keep an eye on all the time. Unfortunately I think it was like that," Mr. Naik added.

The school was asked about how the reeling students were handling the news and what was being done to handle their grief, and Mr. Naik mentioned "praying with the students."

Funerals have been held for the two deceased, and the school mentioned in a released statement that the families were grieving and did not wish to speak to media at the present moment.

When asked if the school could confirm there were no other students with access to a car, Mr. Naik said he could not.

Following the bail hearing, the teenagers were remanded to their parents' custody, where they'll remain under house arrest until a trial date has been set.

A student at the school also commented on the incident. The boy, 14, preferred to remain nameless, but said he had "no idea they had access to a car," but that he "wasn't surprised by it."

When asked to clarify on the lack of surprise, the student stated that the "strict nature" of the school meant the kids had to "find their own ways to escape," mentioning that they couldn't even make a phone call without written consent from their parents.

He was then asked if students had ever snuck out before, but his response was interrupted by Mr. Naik and another teacher who'd come outside to end the questioning.

The other teacher who came outside to end the questioning said that newer policies such as stricter curfews were now in place to prevent incidents like that from occurring again.

"We're doing everything we can, the absolute maximum. We're trying to protect them, even from themselves," said Farouq Ibrar, 44.

"Incidents like this are not common," he added. "Nothing like this happens here. This is a place of quiet, calm, peace and learning."

Epilogue

When I woke up at the hospital my parents were there and I wanted to be dead. I didn't know where Maaz, Nawaaz and Farid were, but I assumed they were also somewhere in the hospital. The doctors, the police officers, my parents—none of them would tell me what happened. I just remember blacking out and coming to in a hospital gown with a relatively unscathed body. Did the others look just as dumb and helpless as me? Were they unscathed too?

Even at court, after all the questions from cops, lawyers, counsellors, I thought they were just keeping me away from them. When I finally figured out what had happened, I felt nothing. I was empty. Of course we were expelled. My parents were sombre, skirting my misdeeds, grateful I was alive. I was grateful I didn't have to speak. How could I explain anything? It all seems like a dream now. Hafiz Abdullah, Abdi, Alif. Dreams from another life. Like it all happened to someone else.

How could I speak about it? The silence continues. When I open my mouth, my lips move but no sound comes out. Or if one does, it's all gibberish. How can anyone do anything about something they don't understand? I avoided juvie, and Al Haque avoided any reckoning because the alternative would've meant that the West had to understand our community and the circumstances that catapulted four boys into a rainstorm in the middle of the night. Did you think the investigation would be more thorough? If you did, we don't live in the same country. The ordeal exhausted me. I had nothing left in me. I just knew I was back in public school, the life that I'd desired so selfishly, that I'd dreamed of and idealized. I broke, gave in, was thankful for order and direction. My parents admitted the defeat of at least one of their dreams, content to see me safe and sound and silent. I sleepwalked through the babble of crowded hallways, saw the face of a girl I'd pined for in another lifetime and recognized the distance between us as too great. I kept loose connections, and stayed away from most people. Even the people like me were a little too dangerous to talk to. Remember, I told myself, don't tell anybody anything. As soon as you do, you'll start missing everyone.

I hope Nawaaz and Farid can forgive me. I'm just so worried and disgusted that if they could see me, they'd be appalled by how much I've changed. That they might be ashamed of or disappointed in me, with nothing connecting me to who I used to be. I'm ashamed I take this life for granted, after what they sacrificed for me and Maaz. Sure, I may not be a maulana now, but a 99.99 percent success rate is still exactly what it is. Working overnight IT shifts in a giant office downtown and riding empty subway cars to and from work was probably not the life we'd envisioned for ourselves back then, but I'm drained, sapped by the sacrifice and what it cost. I'm sorry. I really hope those two can forgive me. They're the only ones who need to.

But I'm not sorry about the choice we made. We made a decision and suffered for it. Our hearts were full in those days, and what we felt led us to the land of no regrets. To this day, I haven't felt a single version of happiness or sadness or anger or anything that was as robust as I felt back then. This land wouldn't have us; that land wouldn't have us. And rather than bemoaning some version of the past that was lost to time the way our parents did, we died carving out a slice of something we could call our own. So it was, as shades and memories that we committed to pass boldly into that other world, in the full glory of some passion, rather than fade and wither dismally with age.

Today, Hafiz Abdullah is a mufti. Khalid is a maulana. Jara is a maulana. Abdi is a maulana. Alif is a maulana. Jalil and Maruf are maulanas. You get the picture. The afterlife taxes at the modest rate of 100 percent. I'm only reminded of them in strange circumstances. Days with weird weather, uncustomary snow squalls or heavy rainfalls too early or late in the year. Or when I spot white umbrellas on the streetcar or remember long conversations with my father.

He would tell me that all the bullshit pleasure and suffering in this life, and all its passions, weren't worth committing to. Everything you could love you should love a little less. Hold something back in this trickster's paradise of pure smoke and mirrors. Shadows and lies, and all its pleasures and pains that were something so brief and weak they couldn't be measured against the Big Concern.

But this world is not a lie. I am alive, writing words right now, and my dreams and desires matter. That's not a lie. Even if there's no room for any of that. I just hope that one day, we can stretch our faith and our country and our communities just a tiny bit, to be able to fit me, Farid, Nawaaz and Maaz into all your grand plans and accept us for who we are.

A few years ago, before he passed away, my father and I were speaking about one thing or another and I mentioned some minor problem I was having at work. To which he said, "This world is a lie. Everything you see is fake." The conversation continued and turned to the topic of travels. My father said that sometimes, he would find himself alone inside a mosque in a faraway country and would be struck by an incredible bout of loneliness. He'd sit and cry and yearn for his children, who had grown and flown the coop. "I get so lonely thinking about you guys. You've all left me."

To which I said, jokingly, "This world is a lie."

My father looked at me for a long time without saying a word. His head was tilted slightly, and he had a playful smile on his lips that said he knew something I didn't. His eyes twinkled as he studied my face, while I waited for his response.

"Do you believe in the afterlife?" he asked.

"Yes," I said.

"What are you doing to prepare for the afterlife?"

I was stumped. I didn't know how to tell him. Would he get it? Would anyone from that generation get it? How much we'd all overpaid?

You work twice as hard in school because you missed a year at another kind of school due to a dream your parents once had. You play catch up, overpay, get a tiny bit back in return. Maybe a scholarship, maybe a job. You hear the same things in your little second-gen circle—people licking wounds that don't heal, nursing bruises that haven't disappeared in years. Kids going to piano classes to learn an instrument no one plays because it's what refined people do, parents unable to stop sucking Europe's dick. You mourn and grieve for people who die in silence silently, picking up more from your parents than you bargained for, overpaying for grief in the way you bark at your children for silly things. That's not all. Other people miss their grandmother's pierogis when she dies, but they find them every once in a while in a church or in someone else's home in the city. Where else will you find *shutki tarkhari* made out of ilish and PEI potatoes? Your parents die and you lose that food forever. So now you're sad forever. You try to fix that sadness through any means possible, throwing yourself into activities new and old. You talk, you go places, you bury your father and you see his *janaza* being performed by another second-gener you kind of recognize. One who once dreamed of drawing. He overpaid too. You can hear it in his sermon. Like he knows something only he, I and the other second-geners know. That this is the land of little.

ACKNOWLEDGEMENTS

When I got serious about trying to get published, I thought I could do it all alone. I thought all you needed was hard work, dedication, perseverance, etc. And while all that is necessary, I quickly learned you needed so much more. And none of it is possible alone. Still, I really have only a few people to thank.

The first group of people are all the people in my life, past and present, who saw me and didn't see anyone special, or didn't believe in me. People who wrote me off or just didn't see the vision, didn't bother keeping in touch or following up, or were too busy or blind. Anyone who didn't think much of me, didn't think I'd get anywhere. Thank you for giving me the necessary spite to succeed.

The second group of people are all the people in my life, past and present, who saw me and saw someone special, and believed in me. People who encouraged me, saw something in me, helped me and otherwise showed me love. People who listened, kept in touch, got me back on my feet and had the time. Anyone who knew I'd get here. Thank you for giving me the necessary motivation to earn your love.

A few people need to be named. My family, for all their love or guidance. A special shout-out to my older brother for all his love and kindness about my vocation. I'm sorry I'm weird and difficult. All my friends that I've made a family out of, too many to name here (though I'll try). Where would we be if we didn't waste our nights in the full glory of some passion? Andrew, AK, Phil, Brad, Jason, Samia, Alex, Kenny, Naima, Michelle, Wilfrid, May, Faisal, and many others.

My agent, Stephen Barr. Who saw the vision and saw this story for what it was, and who knew immediately what we could do together. It was so vindicating to finally connect with someone who had that much faith in me. I'm so looking forward to the future. Brother, we're going to destroy the world together. (And by destroy, I just mean write and publish many books.)

To John Glynn, my editor in the US, who connected with me, this story, and knew this for what it was exactly from day one. Thank you for believing in me, for taking a risk and for helping me bring this into the world. It means so much more than I can say that you chose my story for Hanover Square.

To Janice Zawerbny, my tireless editor in Canada. Thank you so much for believing in me and helping me turn this story into the best possible version of it that it can be. I'm so lucky I had another chance to work with you. Thank you for coaching me through my debut and ensuring we knocked this out of the park. Thank you for never pulling your punches and helping me grow as a writer.

Special shout-out to Janice Weaver. Thank you so much for fixing so much, English hard.

Another special shout-out to Naben Ruthnum, for supporting me with kind words when it meant an incredible amount. Having a professional writer vouch for me or support me means a lot because I don't know anybody and nobody knows me really. I respect the hell out of you.

To Jennifer Lambert and HarperCollins, thank you so much for taking a chance on me and helping me bring this story into the world. I'm so grateful and lucky and appreciative for the entire exemplary team backing me the entire way. I count my blessings every day because of all of you in my corner.

To Aeman Ansari. Man, if they only knew what you did for me, and everything you went through. All your downplaying about how you were just doing your job the entire time won't cut it. We are connected forever. I know how you championed me, advocated for me and went to war for me. I know how much this meant to you; you always knew how much this story meant to the world. And I know what it cost you. I promise to earn it.

To books, for ruining me.

Finally, to my partner and best friend, Laura. Thank you for trying to understand me every day, and helping me to make my dreams come true. Thank you for believing in me every day, for inspiring me to good and for being the best person I know.